Published in the UK in 2023 by Trixie Books

Copyright © Michelle Keill 2023

Michelle Keill has asserted her right under the Copyright, Designs and Patents Act, 1988, to be identified as the author of this work.

All rights reserved. No part of this book may be reproduced, stored in a retrieved system or transmitted, in any form or by any means, electronic, mechanical, scanning, photocopying, recording or otherwise, without the prior permission of the author and publisher.

This is a work of fiction. Names, characters, businesses, places, events, locales, and incidents are either the product of the author's imagination or used in a completely fictitious manner. Any mention of or resemblance to actual persons, living or dead, or actual events is purely coincidental or contextual within the story.

ISBN (Paperback) - 978-1-9997285-8-8
ISBN (eBook) - 978-1-9997285-9-5

Cover design and typeset by SpiffingCovers

# The Gargoyle

Michelle Keill

*For Paris*

# 1

I was sixteen years old when the nuns threw me out of the orphanage. They had tried to help me – if the unique treatment I received there could be described as 'help' – but, according to them, I was 'beyond redemption', and they had no choice but to expel me from their care.

'We have done our best,' Sister Thérèse said, 'but now we have to let you go. For all our sakes.'

They packed the few items of clothing I owned into a bag, along with a Bible, and enough food to get me through the day. I suspected they thought it would be better if I did not last much longer than that.

'Nothing will become of you, Inès,' Sister Thérèse told me. '*Nothing.* I pray you find salvation. I pray salvation finds *you*.'

She tossed the bag out onto the street, shoved me after it, and slammed the door.

The orphanage was the only home I had ever known, and now it was gone. But standing in the shadow of the Sacré-Coeur with my meagre possessions stuffed into a bag with broken handles, I did not feel afraid. There was a place I could go – a place where I would find solace. I cradled the bag in my arms and headed south, towards Notre-Dame.

I walked all the way there. It took over an hour, but I was accustomed to travelling long distances on foot, for the nuns had insisted we spurn public transport lest it 'encourage indolence'. When I arrived at the cathedral, I sat down in the nearest pew and thought about praying for guidance, but the words wouldn't come and no one would hear them anyway. I took out the Bible and placed it on the seat next to me. Then I got up and walked away, leaving the Good Book, and my old, miserable life, behind.

The inside of the cathedral had never captivated me – not in the way it did others, and certainly not in the way the nuns had thought it should. The exterior, though, was another matter.

I would spend hours admiring the stone facade and its portals and intricate carvings. The rose windows drew me into their kaleidoscopes of colours and patterns, and the gallery of chimeras and gargoyles that ringed the two towers seemed to beckon me, urging me to go up, up …

Although the nuns took us to Mass at Notre-Dame every Sunday, they forbade us from visiting the towers. Being up so high, they claimed, would lure us away from God and towards sin. Their warnings only increased the allure, and although the punishment was severe, every chance I had, I'd sneak away to make the long ascent to share the gargoyles' breathtaking view. It was the only place where I'd felt at peace, the only balm that soothed the chaos inside my mind. It still was.

The nuns were wrong. If God were to be found anywhere, it was there, at the summit – the heart – of the city's soul.

The entrance to the towers was through a doorway on the side of the cathedral. There was always a long queue of people waiting outside the gates, and I was unsurprised to find that today it stretched almost the whole length of the street. The queue moved slowly but steadily, and more than an hour ticked by before I got to the front. I didn't mind; being there was comforting. I had no home now, but I had Notre-Dame. And I knew it would welcome me.

I passed through the gates and up the short flight of steps that led to a modest souvenir shop, where tourists quietly browsed a tasteful range of postcards, rosaries and miniature models of the cathedral. I did not stop to examine what was on offer – the merchandise rarely changed, and I had seen it many times before. Behind the counter was a sallow-faced man with small, pebble-like eyes. His face showed no emotion as I asked for a ticket, and he did not blink as I patted my pockets for the money I had pilfered from the collection box the previous Sunday. I counted out the coins with care and placed them in his palm. In exchange, the man handed me a ticket that bore upon it a photograph of one of Notre-Dame's famous gargoyles. The one that, soon, I would come to think of as my protector.

The climb up the north tower was not for the faint-hearted. There were close to four hundred steps, coiled into a spiral so tight it was notorious for sparking bouts of paralysing claustrophobia, even in those who'd never suffered from it before. Warnings hung on the gates outside about the mental and physical robustness required to make the journey: warnings that were seldom taken seriously until visitors were confronted with the reality of what the towers demanded. I had seen people quake at the sight of the steep staircase that appeared to wind endlessly upwards. And once you placed your foot on that first step, turning back was not an option. The staircase in the north tower was reserved for the ascent, and another, in the south tower, was for those returning to ground level, with access only permitted from the top.

The steps were narrow, as though fashioned for tiny feet, and it was essential to position yourself precisely so as not to trip. Only the odd slash of daylight filtered through the stone, and the handrail was flimsy and offered minimal security. There was no room for error, and no space in which to pause to catch your breath. If one person slipped and fell, all those behind would topple like dominoes.

The sizeable gaggle of people heading upwards meant progress was particularly sluggish that day, but eventually I reached the final step and emerged from the gloom onto the viewing deck.

The overcast sky and the hint of rain made Paris appear contemplative, expectant. The river had a greenish hue, and the cars criss-crossing the bridges were tiny coloured dots. The Eiffel Tower, as resplendent from afar as it was up close, seemed to wink knowingly at me, and a pleasant breeze caressed my face, making a promise of summer – of better days to come. People jostled around me, talking and laughing, trying to get the best angle for their photographs, but I heard nothing, felt nothing, except the sigh of the wind and the sensation of untrammelled calm that never failed to find me up there.

I stood on the corner by the north tower, close to one of the gargoyles. Only when the dome of the Sacré-Coeur caught my eye on the horizon and I saw how far I had come did I allow myself to ponder the future.

'What *will* become of me?'

It was a surprise to hear myself say the question out loud, but no one was paying attention.

Or so I thought.

I took my eyes from the Paris skyline, which sparkled with all the wonders the city offered its faithful citizens, and turned to consider the gargoyle's peculiar face. At first glance it looked the same as always, with its elbows resting on the parapet, its chin cupped in its palms, a sliver of tongue protruding cheekily from between its lips. But there was something different about it, something I could feel rather than see – something that ran deeper than appearances. The gargoyle seemed alive, animated, as if it were in the middle of telling a story – as if it were giving a performance to the whole of Paris.

A *performance* … The word chimed in my head like an old church bell. I looked at the gargoyle, and in that instant I knew what I would do. What I would *become*.

Salvation had found me.

# 2

The first time I laid eyes on Christophe Leriche had been completely by chance. I was still at the orphanage, oblivious to the fact that my days there were numbered. The nuns were marching us across the city so we could carry out an 'act of humble benevolence' at a shelter owned by the Church, where we were to learn humility by feeding the destitute, washing their clothes and tending to their ailments.

'Count yourselves lucky,' Sister Thérèse said as we plodded in single file down the hill behind her, youngest to oldest. 'By the grace of God, you have a roof over your heads. You have food, you have warmth. You have kindness, and mercy.'

*Some of us do*, I thought. *And some of us know the definition of 'mercy' can be subjective, and surprisingly malleable.*

I was fifteen years old. It was an ordinary day, with the usual interminable quality to it that I had long stopped noticing. As the oldest child in the nuns' care, I was at the end of the procession, my gaze riveted on the pavement, as we'd been taught, so as to avoid the 'snare of temptation'. But when we came to a halt at a busy intersection, I felt a tingling at the back of my neck, as if a fingertip had gently caressed my skin. The sensation made me glance up, and there he was, staring at me from a poster pasted on the wall by the bus stop.

The poster was for a play he was headlining at the Odéon. The title meant nothing to me – little of popular culture did. The nuns had decreed that films and television were 'evil', and would corrupt our minds. Magazines were banned, and if any were smuggled into the orphanage, they were quickly discovered and immediately confiscated. In spite of this robust censorship, I was aware that a world existed in which stories were told, in which you could watch people pretend to be something they were not, and where you, too, could spend your life pretending. So while I might not have known who he was, I knew *what* he was, and what he did. And as I met his eyes – cool blue, gazing right into the camera, right at *me* – something inside me cracked open. A need, a yearning that emanated from the core of my being, was hatched.

The nuns and everything else forgotten, I moved towards the poster, my heart thumping, as if it were beating for the first time.

'Inès, come away from there! Come away from there at *once*!'

There would be consequences for my flagrant transgression, but I didn't care. Even as Sister Thérèse dragged me away, I knew I would take whatever punishment awaited me. And I knew he would be worth it.

*Christophe Leriche.* From then on, his name was on the

tip of my tongue; his face was in my mind as I knelt down to pray. He became my God, my religion, and I luxuriated in my blasphemy. That chance sighting had given me a taste of liberty – of forbidden fruit – and I wanted more. I wanted everything I had been denied.

I wanted him.

I found ways to seek him out. I volunteered to do more charity work, solely for the opportunity it provided to scour the city for posters, to sneak glances at the newspapers people carried and to peer at the racks of magazines in the kiosks. Every so often, I'd be rewarded with a glimpse of him emblazoned on a front cover: Christophe Leriche in a smart blue suit; in loose black trousers and a grey T-shirt; in a white shirt he appeared to be slowly unbuttoning; in a thick sweater, the collar pulled up to his chin as if warding off a draught.

I stole magazines in which he was featured and secreted them in places the nuns would never think to look. I devoured articles about him, hiding in a storage cupboard to read them by candlelight and soak in the hyperbole. Journalists listed his plaudits and lavished him with fawning praise. 'Quite simply,' one of them wrote, 'Leriche is the most gifted dancer and actor of his generation.' A review of his latest play boldly proclaimed, 'Christophe is a marvel,' and I agreed, even though I had never seen him perform.

I memorised the interviews he gave, absorbing quotes about his likes, his dislikes, his methods, his *craft*. I amassed as much knowledge as I could, but it was not enough. The details I had learnt about him were the things he had chosen to reveal. I had to get closer; I had to know *him*.

My inglorious exit from the orphanage had plunged me into a precarious, hand-to-mouth existence of tedious jobs, meagre food rations and squalid accommodation. However, there was an upside. For the first time in my life, I was free. Free to pursue my dream of becoming a performer, and free to follow Christophe's every move.

After blagging my way into the theatre, I managed to see him on-stage. I was nervous as I waited for the curtain to rise, for there was the possibility that I had made him into something he was not – that I would see him in person and be disappointed. But those fears were not borne out.

In person, Christophe was even more magnificent than he was on the pages of the magazines. He was enchanting, he was magnetic; he enthralled the audience from the moment he uttered his first line to the second he took his final bow. The sheer power of his presence, the blend of raw vulnerability and unwavering strength that he conveyed, inspired me to pursue my dream with everything I had. I would persevere. I would accept the thankless, forgettable parts in the shows hardly anyone came to watch, and shoulder the relentless rejections and stinging criticisms in the hope that, one day, my luck would change and fate would smile on me. My time, I was sure, would come. And when it did, I would be ready.

Close to a decade had passed. To my dismay, Christophe had withdrawn from the spotlight, and the trail I was following had gone cold. It had been almost three years since his last performance, and he was rarely seen in public. Speculation was rife. There was talk that he had relocated to New York to join a prestigious repertory, and rumours abounded of plans to transfer his formidable stage talents to the screen and transition to film roles. Some believed he was working on a memoir, one that promised to tell all about his dizzying rise to prominence and reveal the truth behind his enigmatic persona. Inevitably, there were stories that he was gravely ill, even dying, but considering his relatively young age, these were not taken seriously.

But one afternoon, without any preamble, Christophe emerged from his reclusion. At a packed press conference, he appeared in front of the cameras (looking, to my relief, in perfect health) and announced that he was to found and run his own residential performing arts academy. The initial intake would be small – *select*, was how Christophe put it. Admission would be open to all – prospective students would be judged on talent rather than experience – and Christophe himself would not only be overseeing the auditions but was to be the academy's sole teacher.

The clamour for places was immediate. When the news broke, I'd been rehearsing for a play in a cramped room off the Boulevard Voltaire, the latest in a long and depressing line of bit parts that allowed me to scrape by and just about call myself an actor. One of the cast members – the lead actor, who was late, as usual – rushed in, breathless and flushed.

'Christophe Leriche … Academy … Auditions!'

She was barely coherent, but her excitement had the rest of the cast grabbing their phones and scrolling furiously, relaying details from every source they could find. Focus shifted from the present, and our preparations for opening night, to the future, and how securing a spot at the new Leriche Academy would change our lives.

'Can you imagine, Inès?' the lead actor asked me. 'Can you picture it?'

I could. More clearly than I had ever pictured anything. And until I got my turn in front of Christophe Leriche, I would picture nothing else.

The day of the auditions was oppressively warm and humid – the hottest of the year so far. As Paris sweltered, hundreds of hopefuls stood in line for hours, desperate for a chance to impress Christophe Leriche. The man, the legend.

My love.

The queue edged agonisingly slowly towards the academy's entrance on Rue d'Enfer. Anticipation was at fever pitch; there was little conversation or small talk. People trembled with nerves as they gripped their audition pieces with clammy hands, muttering their lines to themselves. Some were crying, some vomited on the pavement and several fainted, succumbing to the heat and the tension. A few seemed to decide they couldn't handle the pressure and the endless wait, and as I watched them leave the queue, my competition decreasing by a small fraction, I wondered what it would be like to get that close to Christophe only to give up.

Notre-Dame was a few streets away, its towers bearing down on me. I looked up at them, and the swirl of apprehension in my stomach vanished. I stopped worrying about odds, and luck, and my age and limited experience. This was the moment my life had been leading towards: this was my purpose. I *had* to get into Christophe's academy. It was do or die, and I wanted to live. For him, and only him, I wanted to live.

None of the tribulations I'd endured so far were harder than walking into the tiny studio and feeling the blaze of Christophe's scrutiny.

The air smelled of sweat, of failure, of hopes that had been seized and then crushed. The marks on the floorboards were a testament to the hundreds who had gone before me, eager to dazzle him, to convince him they were *special*, that they had what he was looking for.

And now, it was my turn.

'Name?'

His voice. Smooth and honeyed. Turning me to liquid. For so long, he'd been a face behind glass, an image printed on glossy paper, a shape I had strained to see from the back of a theatre. And now he was only a metre or so away, flanked by two strangers whose feet I could see tapping impatiently on either side of his.

I swallowed the lump in my throat. 'Inès Corday.'

'And what will you be showing me today, Inès Corday?'

A thumb drummed on the desk. *His* thumb. His body, his eyes, his voice. My one chance to make an impression.

'Who I am,' I told him. 'I am going to show you who I am.'

Christophe's brows lifted. The people on either side of him exchanged a glance and made a note. Christophe's steely gaze remained focused on me. He sat back in his chair and put his chin on his knuckles, his forefinger pressed against the sharp plane of his cheekbone.

'Show me then,' he said. 'Show me who you are.'

It's not easy to discern when something has gone well, particularly something you crave too much to allow for any real objectivity. But when I finished the piece I'd chosen — a monologue from Christophe's most famous role — I knew. He looked at me, and I looked back at him, and I *knew*.

'I will be in touch with my decision,' he said, waving a hand to dismiss me and turning to confer with the others.

The letter arrived a week later. I delivered my acceptance in person on the same day, so there could be no mishaps, and no doubts about the seriousness of my intentions.

I walked back to the latest hovel in which I was living and began counting down the days until my new life would start.

My new life, with him.

# 3

Several months later, to great fanfare, the Leriche Academy welcomed its first batch of students.

There were thirteen of us in all. Not by design; performers can be superstitious creatures, and under less exceptional circumstances, the idea of comprising such an ominous number would be anathema to a group of artists. But Christophe promised that for us, thirteen would be lucky.

'Class sizes will never be this small again,' he explained. 'As the academy grows and becomes the most renowned performing arts school in Paris, which I know it can, and it will, I'll be able to take on more students, and more teachers. So make the most of it. In the years to come, people will envy the close attention you're going to receive.' He paused, and considered each of us in turn. 'You will forever be the original class of the Leriche Academy. Are you ready to carry that honour?'

'Yes,' came the reply, from Diana, from Liliane, Françoise, Veronica, Nathalie, Cécile, Maëlle, Déborah, Élodie, Hélène, Aurélie, and from mousey Roxane.

And, somewhere amid the babble of voices, from me.

At twenty-six, I was the oldest student at the Leriche Academy. But age was not the only thing that set me apart from them. The others – each of them blonde, and each as interchangeable as the last – had chosen their paths, or had their paths chosen for them, years before I'd had my epiphany at Notre-Dame. They had been groomed for a stage career as soon as they could walk, whereas my route to take my place among them was far more circuitous and much less calculated than theirs.

While I'd been praying the rosary and helping to feed the homeless, the blondes had been studying under some of the world's best teachers. As I was toiling in low-paid, monotonous jobs by day and acting for free by night, they were graduating from eminent colleges and waltzing into roles that paid them money for which they had no desperate need. Doors that had remained locked for me had burst open for them, and they behaved as though they were entitled to every stroke of good fortune they had received.

A pecking order was established immediately, one based entirely, so it seemed to me, on whose voice was the loudest and whose ego was the largest.

Quickest to stake a claim on the academy's throne was Diana, a moon-faced bore from London who shamelessly listed her credentials as she introduced herself and, with a toss of her frizzy hair, informed her new classmates that she had been wearing ballet shoes since she was six weeks old.

'I was *born* to be here,' she said, clutching the lapels of her baggy cardigan and gazing into space, as though imagining herself already on-stage. 'It's my *destiny*.'

This display of arrogance was equalled by Veronica, the American, who listened to Diana's monologue with her arms crossed and an eyebrow arched cynically. When Diana had returned to her chair to sit beside a baffled and slightly cowed Hélène, Veronica got up and launched into an extensive rundown of her 'résumé'.

'I've done a couple of movies,' she said, her chewing gum snapping between her molars. 'Just small parts so far, but it's still, you know, *Hollywood*, right?'

Several of the more impressionable blondes – Aurélie, Maëlle and Élodie – murmured their assent.

'And I've done a *ton* of commercials,' Veronica went on, lost in her patter. 'I did one for a super-famous deodorant brand. You've probably seen it.'

I didn't believe her – it was already apparent to me that the blondes were compulsive liars and prone to embellishment – but Françoise let out a squeal of recognition and rummaged in her satchel and produced a magazine. On page seven, alongside an article proffering advice on menstrual cramps and troublesome blemishes, was Veronica, her arms aloft as she stood in the middle of a field, her large teeth on full display as she beamed, seemingly at the wonder of her odour-free armpits.

'Let me see that …' Liliane grabbed the magazine and studied the picture, twirling a lock of her silky hair around her fingertip. The others watched her, spellbound.

Unlike Diana and Veronica, Liliane had not veered towards tedious boasting or attempted to dominate the group. She didn't need to. Liliane was distractingly beautiful, with delicate, symmetrical features that begged the eye to linger upon them. As she skimmed the advert, Déborah and Cécile, who had already become inseparable, gazed reverently at her. Hélène, who thus far had revealed little about herself other than to express her gratitude to God for her place at the academy, was transfixed as Liliane extended a thin but muscular arm and passed the magazine back to Françoise.

'Well done,' Liliane said to Veronica, with no hint of envy or sarcasm in her tone. But, I supposed, someone as stunning as Liliane had no cause to be snide or jealous. Her beauty allowed her to be generous, and she had to do nothing to earn the admiration of the others.

Liliane stood up and gave us a few basic facts about herself: she was twenty-two (this surprised me; she looked much younger), hailed from a village in Provence no one had heard of, and her primary skill was dancing. We'd not yet had any classes together and had seen nothing to verify this assertion, but the blondes nodded in agreement, accepting her word as truth.

Sitting slightly apart from the group, a gap of about a metre between her and Nathalie, was Roxane. Except for a few furtive glances at Liliane, Roxane had kept her eyes fixed on her shoes. When it was her turn to introduce herself, she did so in whisper, prompting Diana to cup a hand behind her ear and say, 'For goodness' sake, speak up!', which earned her a stern glare from Nathalie.

Roxane ran her palms along her dress, tugging the hem further past her knees. 'I … I'm Roxane,' she said, and clamped her mouth shut.

After some gentle coaxing from Hélène, Roxane added that she had just turned seventeen – making her the academy's youngest student – and that she was from Marseilles.

'I miss home,' she said with a sniff.

'But you've only been here a few hours,' Diana said.

'Home is where the heart is,' Veronica said, flinging an arm around Roxane's quivering shoulders. 'And your heart is here now. Your future starts today, this second. With us. With Christophe freakin' Leriche!'

There was a whoop from Maëlle, and the others were quick to chime in with cheers and chatter about how marvellous Christophe was. I wanted to scream. What did they know about Christophe? What did they know about *anything*?

I was the last to stand up and say a few words. I tried to make the best of my limited experience, but as soon as I started speaking they began to fidget and talk among themselves. Déborah rolled her eyes and Cécile mimed a yawn, while Nathalie and Françoise were still staring at Liliane. Even Hélène, who had been so supportive during Roxane's pitiable first impression, appeared to be dozing. I should have expected it. To them, I was a nobody: ancient, uncultured, with no 'credentials' and no pedigree. They had a determination to pursue fame and glory that they couldn't conceive I might share, because in their eyes I was not the sort of person who had a right to want those things, and I was not the sort of person who belonged at the academy. I could imagine what they'd say if they knew it wasn't an inflated sense of destiny and entitlement that had led me there but an idea inspired by a gargoyle.

I'd harboured no illusions that I would make friends at the academy, but being excluded was still painful, and a constant reminder of how my past made me different from most people. Without Théo to confide in, it would have been intolerable. It was fortunate – I was fortunate – that he was there to save me from them, and from my loneliness.

Aside from Christophe, Théo was the only non-student to reside in the on-site living quarters. He and I had met at the auditions – he'd had to earn his spot as the academy's pianist, and had been handpicked by Christophe from dozens of other candidates. On first sight, we recognised in each other a kindred spirit, and had formed an immediate, and somewhat complex, alliance. Despite Christophe's praise of his talents, Théo had little regard for him, and was, he insisted, only at the academy for the free board and the regular income.

'But perhaps now,' he'd told me as we embarked

upon what was to be the first of many long walks around the city together, 'I am here for someone else.'

He had reached for my hand, and without thinking, I'd taken it.

There was no ambiguity about who I loved – Christophe was the only subject on which Théo and I vehemently disagreed – but he was sure I would change my mind.

'Someday, the scales will fall from your eyes,' he'd said as we convened in my room after dark one night, an act that Christophe probably would have forbidden, had the possibility of it arising occurred to him. 'One day, you will realise Christophe Leriche is just a man. Just an ordinary man.'

But as I lay next to Théo, curled in his embrace, I could not envisage a world in which that would ever happen. Where Christophe was concerned, my vision was clear.

There was no settling-in period, and no time allotted for orientation – not even for Diana and Veronica, who'd both come from overseas and were unused to France and the vagaries of Paris. Christophe thrust us into a strict routine, and his exacting standards had to be adhered to without exception or excuse. The timetable was demanding, and although the blondes were accustomed to the rigours of life at performance schools, to each other they admitted that this was unlike anything they'd ever experienced. By contrast, I might have been new to the punishing schedule, but I was no stranger to hard work. I enjoyed the throb in my limbs as I crawled into bed each night; I was grateful for the blisters on my feet from dancing, and the scratch in my throat from learning to project my voice. Learning from *him*: the maestro, the best. Each day, I got to see him, to listen to him, to watch his hands as he demonstrated moves and corrected us, guiding us through the words and music. Having unfettered access to him was exhilarating. Intoxicating.

Part of Christophe's vision was for us to bond as a group – to forge close friendships and become firm allies.

'So much of performing is about trust,' he told us as we sat cross-legged around him on the studio floor during our first class. 'Trust in yourself, in your abilities. But above all, trust in each other. Without trust, then you – *we*, each of us – have nothing. The collective dream is more important than your individual ambitions. We have to encourage each other, support each other. Otherwise, we won't achieve anything. Do you understand that?'

As one, they bobbed their heads and answered yes, but I'd seen enough to know they didn't mean it. Their lives were built on a foundation of self-interest, and the notion of 'the collective' was alien to them. They would have betrayed each other in a heartbeat if there was something to be gained from it.

One aspect of my new routine mirrored that of my life at the orphanage: like the nuns, Christophe insisted that we attend Mass at Notre-Dame every Sunday. This provoked some grumbling, particularly from Veronica, but Christophe was adamant.

'The cathedral is integral to this neighbourhood,' he told us. 'And so are we. We need to be involved. We need to be *seen*.'

The blondes were confused by this edict, but to me, Christophe's intentions made perfect sense. He wanted his patrons to see him with us, his inaugural class of students, and to note that he had *arrived*.

Each week, we would put on our smartest clothes and follow him through the gates of the academy to make the short walk to the cathedral. We'd file into the nave and spread across a pew close to the altar, but not close enough as to appear too eager.

'Never show your hand,' he would tell us. 'Maintaining an air of mystery is paramount to success.'

As was making the right connections.

The services were a surprisingly fruitful way for Christophe to forge links with the rarefied echelons of Paris society, and that his face and name were already known to most of them gave him an obvious advantage when it came to soliciting support for his new venture. He would scan the congregation, clearly seeking out someone who might prove useful, and who might be persuaded to make a substantial donation to his cause.

As Mass drew to a close on our third Sunday at the academy, Christophe's gaze settled on a tall woman with a freckled complexion and lustrous red hair. He stopped her as she sashayed past our pew towards the doors, smiling modestly as he introduced himself. From the way her eyes widened, it was apparent that she was well aware of who he was.

'I saw you on-stage,' she said. 'Three times. You were quite something.'

'Thank you,' he replied with a small bow. 'That's very kind.'

'I thought you'd retired, or become a hermit,' she said, flicking a lock of hair from her forehead. '*Everyone* thought you'd retired. Don't you have a private island you can disappear to? Or some secret country retreat where you can grow vegetables and forget the world?'

He chuckled. 'I *have* retired. What do I have left to achieve?'

'There is always another role, surely.'

'True. But I realised the one I want, more than any other, is this one. To guide, to mentor, to pass on what I have learnt. To leave a legacy.' He touched a hand to his chest. 'Paris has been so generous to me, and the lure of giving something back was too much to resist.'

A delicate smile played on her lips. 'So the famous Christophe Leriche is now a *teacher*.'

'Yes. I am.' There was no mistaking his pride in his new incarnation. 'And I hope that you will visit my academy.' He extended an arm and gestured at us. 'Let me present my students – my talented *artistes*.'

On cue, we rose to our feet. The blondes stood ramrod straight, their shoulders rolled back. Françoise sucked in her stomach, making her abdomen appear concave. Élodie pursed her lips into a pout; Déborah dipped her chin coyly. They relished the woman's scrutiny. Attention – of any kind, it seemed – was what they lived for.

Théo leant in closer to me, his lips brushing my neck. 'You know he won't introduce her to us,' he said. 'There won't be time.'

There was never time. Théo and I were always at the end of the line, always last, always forgotten – the dregs of the academy. Sitting at a slight distance from me was Roxane, who looked more miserable with each passing day. We'd all heard her crying in her room at night, and the blondes ridiculed her for it. But as desperate for solidarity as Roxane was, she could not bear to speak to me, or even sit close to me.

At the front of the line, in the prime spot beside Christophe, was the idiotic Liliane. Christophe claimed we were all equals, but she was the queen bee. And much to my chagrin, she was also Christophe's favourite.

Bile rose in my throat as he told the woman how fabulous Liliane was, and how 'exciting' her talents were. Naturally, Liliane basked in his compliments, turning her head from side to side as though inviting the woman to concur with Christophe's assessment. I couldn't blame her. If Christophe gushed about me in those glowing tones, and if I were even half as stunning as Liliane, I would be just as insufferable.

Christophe went from Liliane to the equally loathsome Diana, who shook the woman's hand and began rattling off the list of productions she'd starred in, which by now I suspected she could do in her sleep. From what I'd observed so far, Diana's skills were mediocre at best, but Christophe believed she had a unique flair for acting, and that he 'saw something in her'. I had tried my hardest to fathom what that 'something' was, but remained stumped.

I studied Christophe as he moved deftly from Diana to Veronica, and then to Nathalie, so light on his feet, so poised, so handsome.

'What I wouldn't give to be that close to him,' I said, watching Nathalie giggle as she sidled up to him.

'Luckily for you, it will never happen,' Théo said. 'And, even luckier for you, you have me instead.'

Théo's hand came to rest on the small of my back, but I hardly felt it. I was thinking of Christophe – I was *always* thinking of Christophe. What else was there? He was only a few feet away, and yet he remained as unobtainable as when he was on-stage and I was a faceless member of the audience.

I nudged his hand away. We were simpatico, Théo and I, both of us at the mercy of desires that would never come to pass.

Just as Christophe was about to reach me, the woman checked her watch and said she had an appointment to attend.

'Sorry,' she said. 'But it was nice to meet you.' She nodded at the blondes. 'All of you. I wish you every success.'

'It was our pleasure,' Christophe said. 'And perhaps you would like to visit the academy soon?'

But the woman was already walking away.

'There goes that, then,' Théo whispered.

'Don't be so sure,' I told him.

We left Notre-Dame as we had entered it, trailing after Christophe in the same order as before, Théo and me lagging behind.

'Look at him,' I said, admiring Christophe's powerful shoulders and the precise line of hair at the back of his neck – trimmed, without fail, every other Friday at an exclusive salon in the second arrondissement. 'He is a god.'

Théo snorted. 'Didn't the nuns warn you about false idols, Inès?'

I wished I hadn't told Théo about those years. I wished I hadn't told Théo anything about myself at all.

As we were about to turn onto Rue d'Enfer, Christophe came to a sudden halt. He glanced back as his name was called, and we, his shadows, did likewise.

'Wait!' The red-haired woman hurried towards him, her heels clicking on the cobblestones. 'Mr Leriche!'

'Yes?' he said as she reached him, an enquiring lilt to his voice.

'On reflection,' she said, slightly out of breath, 'I

would like to see this school of yours – this "academy".' She opened her bag and slid a business card from a platinum holder and offered it to him. 'Perhaps you could give me a tour sometime.'

Christophe must have felt triumphant, but he showed no trace of smugness as he took the card and scanned it.

'It would be an honour'—he consulted the card again—'Madame Deschamps.' He spoke her name as though it were unremarkable, not that of one of the wealthiest families in Paris.

'Please,' she said, offering a coquettish half-smile as she tucked a strand of hair behind her ear. 'Call me Justine.'

Théo took his cigarettes from his jacket pocket. 'I bet he fucks her by the end of the week.'

'Don't be so vulgar,' I said. 'And anyway, you have nothing with which to place a bet.'

He draped an arm around me. 'If I'm wrong, you can do whatever you like to me. *Anything.*'

Mindful of the others, I pushed him away. 'That's hardly an incentive, Théo.'

He put a cigarette between his lips and fumbled in his pocket for his lighter. 'Don't forget that I know you, Inès. I know what you like. What you *crave.*'

I snatched the lighter from him and flipped the lid open. Théo bent his head to bring the tip of the cigarette to the flame.

'What I crave,' I said, 'is him.'

'And you understand as well as I do that your craving will never be fulfilled.' He nodded at the others, who were scuttling towards the academy gates. 'Are you coming?'

'No,' I said. 'I have an errand to run.'

I needed that peace; I needed the tranquillity that only one place on earth could provide.

I plucked the cigarette from Théo's fingers. It tasted familiar – of him, of our secrets, and the bitter tang of our unrequited longings.

Théo stared at my mouth as I exhaled. 'What errand? Where are you going?'

I pressed my lips to his ear. 'Up. Up as high as heaven.'

I turned back to Notre-Dame. Théo called after me.

'Be careful you don't fall,' he said. 'It's a long way down from there. A very long way down.'

# 4

When I returned to the cathedral, the scene was totally transformed.

The streets around Notre-Dame, bustling and vibrant only a short while ago, were now deserted. The cafés, restaurants and shops were empty. There were no cars on the roads, and no pedestrians hurrying along the pavement. There was nobody in sight at all. It was as if the whole quartier had been abandoned.

'Hello?' I called, turning in a circle to survey the desolation. 'Anyone?'

The only response, the only sound, was the echo of my own voice.

The gates at the entrance to the towers were wide open. Beyond them, the door that led inside was ajar.

*You should turn back*, I thought, but the idea seemed to vanish from my mind, as if a hand had reached inside me and ripped it out. Before I could deliberate any further, I was walking through the doorway and mounting the steps to the souvenir shop. And there, I discovered that the place was not entirely empty.

A man I hadn't seen before was standing behind the till, his palms resting on the counter. He was slender and swarthy, with hooded eyes and jet-black hair. He was smiling broadly, apparently unperturbed by the unusual lack of visitors.

He made no comment as I entered his line of vision.

'Where is everyone?' I asked. 'Has something happened?'

He looked at me, unblinking. 'Everyone is where they should be.'

'Can I …' I paused. Meeting his eyes was like staring into an abyss. I cleared my throat and tried again. 'Can I go up?'

'You can *always* go up,' he replied. 'And you've come at just the right time. The conditions are perfect.'

He lifted a hand. Beneath his palm was a ticket with the gargoyle's face on it.

'For you,' he said. 'Although, strictly speaking, you don't need it.'

'What does that mean? What do—'

The man nudged the ticket across the counter. 'Take it. Then you will receive the answers you require.' He pointed to the staircase. 'Go!'

As I took the ticket a faint buzzing sound filled my ears. The man's smile vanished, and it was a relief to turn away from him and begin the gruelling journey upwards.

It was the first time I had climbed the staircase with no one else around me. Although it was a novelty to be able to move at my own pace, unimpeded by others, it was disconcerting to be alone in that dark, medieval place.

The spiral seemed to coil more tightly than usual; the gradient was more punishing – steeper somehow – and my legs were shaking when I reached the last step. At the top, the isolation was even more profound, and only deepened when I peered over the edge of the parapet and saw Paris bereft and eerily vacant. The street lamps were lit, their soft glow illuminating the barren pavements and bridges. The silence was jarring, but also enticing, one that, I felt sure, no one else had ever experienced.

The gargoyle was in its usual spot by the north tower, its tongue poking mischievously from its mouth. I sidled towards it, thinking of how much history had unfolded under its stubby nose.

'What is going on?' I whispered. 'What secrets do you know? What do you see?'

A brisk squall carried my words away. The sky became murky, and there was a crack of thunder that made the ground ripple beneath my feet.

The gargoyle's head turned and its lips curled into an impish smile.

'I see *everything*,' it said.

Lightning flashed. The scrape of stone shattered the silence as the gargoyle shifted from its customary position and stretched its arms above its head. The sight of it moving was abhorrent. I wanted to scream, to run, but my throat had closed up and my legs refused to budge.

Its mouth, which was too broadly proportioned for its

face, opened in a languorous yawn. The wings on its back spread wide, as if it were about to take flight, and then closed again. Its limbs were spindly, and it stood tall but bow-legged on webbed feet, regarding me with interest. As I stared at it in horror, trying to convince myself that my eyes were deceiving me, the gargoyle spoke again.

'I see every tragedy in Paris.' Its voice was low and guttural, and vaguely familiar. 'And there are rather a lot of them. Truth is'—its chest rose and fell as it sighed—'I'm becoming rather bored watching the same scenes over and over again. The plot never changes, only the actors. No matter how many times the film begins, the ending is always the same. Wouldn't that bore you?'

I knew that voice. I had heard it before, I was sure of it.

*This is wrong*, I thought. *I should leave – leave, and never return.*

'Yes,' the gargoyle said. 'You probably *should* leave. But you don't want to, do you?'

I opened my mouth to deny it, but I realised the gargoyle was right. As terrified as I was, I wanted to hear what the gargoyle had to say. More than that – I *needed* to hear it, and that need overrode the flare of my senses warning me that listening to it would be dangerous.

'Well?' the gargoyle said. 'Wouldn't you get bored of watching the same film on a loop?'

'No,' I said. 'Not if the actors were good.'

The gargoyle chuckled. 'I suppose you would say that.'

'What are you?' I asked. '*Who* are you?'

'I am no one,' it said. 'Just a gargoyle.'

But that voice was so familiar … I *knew* that voice.

'I can change my voice,' the gargoyle said. 'If you'd like. What would you prefer?'

'I would prefer that you didn't speak at all.'

'Ah, come on now. We both know that isn't true. And it was *you* who spoke to me first.'

'You didn't have to answer.'

'I must *always* answer,' it said. 'I have to say, I'm surprised it took you this long to strike up a conversation. After so many years of acquaintance, we have a lot to discuss.'

I screwed my eyes shut, hoping the gargoyle would be gone when I opened them – hoping it was all just a vivid nightmare. But no, there it was, its empty eye sockets fixed on me. Two cavernous pools of infinite darkness.

'I think we can consider ourselves old friends by now,' the gargoyle continued, poking a tapered fingertip into a divot in the weathered stone. 'Wouldn't you agree? And when I said that I see every tragedy in Paris, I was including yours. *Particularly* yours. The orphanage, those cruel nuns … You really ought to have told someone what they did to you. It's not too late for that. For justice. For redemption.'

My scalp tingled. 'You don't know anything. How could you?'

'I told you,' the gargoyle said. 'I see everything. And

I see *you*. I've watched you blossom and grow. You are the most beautiful woman in the whole of Paris ... You know that, yes?'

'Don't be ridiculous.'

Its laughter gave me goosebumps. 'How easily you dismiss a compliment. I saw you embark upon the path you're following now. I saw you audition for Christophe Leriche ... You were wonderful, so *impassioned*, quivering with love and lust. How well you did to beat so many other hopefuls ... how *providential* that you are now a pupil of your idol, your inspiration. And, of course, your great love.'

The gargoyle leant in towards me.

'I see how you are with him,' it said. 'I see your bitterness, your envy, your lies, your sordid games with Théo ... Oh, there's no need to look so aghast. I'm not judging you. I never would. I understand your fondness for him. He is a remarkable young man. So *loyal*. And he has perfect hands, and such dexterous fingers. But you know that better than anyone, don't you, Inès?'

'How ...' The tingle in my scalp spread down the length of my spine. 'How do you know all this? How do you know my name?'

Around us, the other gargoyles and chimeras that adorned the perimeter of the towers were frozen, inanimate. I wondered why this particular one was moving, why it was talking – why it was talking to *me*.

A thought occurred to me. I felt stupid articulating it

but could not refrain from doing so. 'Are you *God*?'

The gargoyle's features contorted into a sneer. 'I am not "God",' it said, its voice thick with scorn. 'And you have long ceased to believe in *him* anyway. Which is just as well, for he doesn't believe in you. Where was he when you needed him, when you were suffering, when you cried out for him from that cold, dark place underground? He was not the one who came to comfort you, was he?'

'You can't know those things. You can't know *anything*.'

'And yet,' the gargoyle said, 'I do.'

The breeze came again. I pulled my coat tighter around me.

'Is this how you pass the time?' I said. 'By taunting people?'

'Only certain people. People with potential. People I can assist.'

'You? What could *you* possibly assist me with?'

The gargoyle fell silent, and I thought that might be the end of our improbable conversation. But then its head tilted towards the steeple, as if it had simply paused to contemplate its response.

'I see the way you look at Christophe,' it said. 'Such unwavering devotion. You loved Christophe the legend, the star, and then, when you got to know Christophe the man – or what you think you know of him – it only intensified your feelings. When you experienced his talent up close, you became lost forever.' The gargoyle flicked its tongue across its lips. 'I know you fantasise about him. I know that when you play your games with Théo it is Christophe of whom you think. You rarely think of anything other than Christophe. It's fair to say that you are obsessed with him. Unrequited love is a peculiar but delicious blend of ecstasy and pain, isn't it?'

There was another peal of thunder – louder this time – that seemed to come from below rather than above. It reverberated in my ears, almost knocking me off my feet. The gargoyle smiled as it watched me try to steady myself, as though it had conjured the thunder itself.

'Do you enjoy showing off?' I said.

'I don't need to resort to such indignities,' the gargoyle said. 'Not like your friends at the academy. The "blondes", as you insist on calling them.'

'They're not my friends.'

'Unlike your *friends*,' the gargoyle continued, ignoring my correction, 'you don't yearn for the adoration of the whole world. You yearn only for him. For his love, his devotion.'

It wasn't a question this time, but I answered anyway. 'Yes.'

'Did you say something?' The gargoyle cupped a hand behind its ear. 'I didn't quite hear you.'

'*Yes.*'

The frigid stone seeped through the soles of my shoes, spreading into my bones. The gargoyle nodded.

'And how do you intend to make him yours?' it said. 'What is your plan?'

'Why should I tell *you*?'

'Because, as I said, I can help you.' It loped back to the parapet, and as I observed its uneven gait I thought, *It cannot be moving, and this cannot be happening.*

The gargoyle flapped its wings. 'I can assure you it *is* happening, Inès. Now, tell me, how will you make him yours?'

'Through my talent,' I said. 'I will make him see that I am as good as the blondes.'

'You are indeed. Even better than they are. You have a tenacity those girls will never possess, no matter how much they rehearse, or how many lessons they take. You understand how real life works. You know what it is to be destitute. You know hunger – *true* hunger. You know pain, you know hardship, and cruelty. The other girls will never know what you do, and will never be any match for your talent. Which makes it even more of a travesty that Christophe will never choose you over them.'

My heart plunged to the pit of my stomach. 'You can't know that. You can't see the future.'

'Can't I?' The gargoyle lifted a hand and curled its fingers to examine its nails. 'From up here I can see things in a way you could never conceive. I see the different routes laid out before you, and the crossroads at which you currently stand. And I assure you that if you continue following the path you're on now, Christophe will never love you. Not while those others are in the way. Not unless you are prepared to take extra measures.'

'What extra measures?'

The gargoyle's horns twitched. 'Sometimes tall flowers must be cut down to allow the others to bloom.'

The sky turned black. The wind whipped around me, icy and sharp. A few spots of rain spattered my cheeks.

'What are you suggesting?' I said.

'It's not a suggestion. Consider it sage advice from someone who has your best interests at heart. From someone who knows how it ends.'

I gathered the courage to study the gargoyle, to hold its empty gaze. It stared back at me, and somewhere in the distance, a bell started ringing.

'You are mad,' I said.

The gargoyle smiled. 'Perhaps as mad as you.'

'Who *are* you?'

'I am no one,' it replied. 'Just a gargoyle.'

# 5

Back on the ground, it was as though nothing untoward had occurred. People were now everywhere, filling restaurants and cafés and browsing the shops opposite the entrance to the towers. The roads were clogged with cars and bikes, the air punctuated with the usual blaring horns and screeching sirens.

I stood on the corner next to the cathedral and tried to make sense of what I'd just experienced. The gargoyle had been alive. Alive, and moving. Talking. *Knowing.*

A memory pierced my mind: hunger, thirst – terrible, unending thirst – and Sister Thérèse's voice drifting towards me from far away.

*You are weak, Inès. Your mind is warped. You must never let your imagination take over. You must never believe the lies you hear in the darkness.*

But the gargoyle *had* spoken to me. It knew my thoughts, my desires, my past and my present – and, so it claimed, my future.

The gargoyle knew *me*.

I returned to my room to find Théo lounging on my bed, reading, a pillow propped up behind him. As I closed the door, his eyes shifted from the page and narrowed.

'Where have you been all this time?' he said.

'Nowhere. Nothing. No one.' *Just a gargoyle.*

My hands shook as I fumbled with the buttons on my coat. It was disturbing how everything was exactly as I'd left it but was also radically altered.

Théo continued staring at me. 'Why do you look as though you've had a fright?'

'I don't,' I said. 'Do I?' I shrugged off my coat and sat down on the chair in front of the mirror. My face was ghostly white and my lips pale. I put my hands to my cheeks and turned to Théo. 'Did anyone see you come in here?'

'Yes,' he said, in the droll tone that usually presaged a bout of sarcasm. 'Everyone saw me. I banged on their doors and announced that I was going to your room. Roxane sobbed and shouted, "Théo! Théo! Don't go to that miserable Inès! Spend the night with me instead and take my virginity!" She was much more dramatic than she ever is in class. I was so embarrassed for her that I was tempted to grant her wish. But, in the end, I decided it was kinder to leave her crying.'

I had to laugh. Théo was an exceptional mimic, and Roxane was easy prey. Her timid nature and perpetual homesickness provided limitless fodder for the blondes' jokes, but Théo could never be as cruel as them.

'You wouldn't say that,' I said. 'Not to poor, innocent Roxane.'

He rolled onto his side and tucked a hand under his head. 'You don't know what I'm capable of.'

I picked up my brush and teased the knots from my hair. 'Is Roxane really still a virgin?'

'Of course,' Théo said. Somehow, he knew those sorts of things – things he shouldn't. 'I think, like you, she is waiting for Christophe to realise he's in love with her. Oh, don't look like that,' he added as I scowled at him. 'You know Roxane has a crush on *someone*.'

That much, I did know. Gossip about Roxane's mysterious infatuation was rife, but there were always scurrilous stories circulating about some twaddle or other.

'No need to fret, though,' Théo said. 'Roxane has no chance with Christophe either. From what I hear, it sounds as if he has decided to make Liliane his protégée.'

I bridled at the mention of her name. 'She doesn't deserve it.'

'Clearly Christophe thinks otherwise,' Théo said.

My chest tightened, as if there were something trapped inside it. Something straining to be unleashed.

*Christophe will never love you. Not while those others are in the way.*

I glanced over my shoulder, half expecting to see the gargoyle standing by the bed next to Théo, or hovering outside the tiny window, its wings flapping as it peered at us.

Théo sat up. 'What are you looking at?'

'Nothing,' I said, and ran the brush through my hair

again. 'How do you "hear" all this bilge anyway? The blondes don't confide in you. And I can hardly imagine you and Christophe sharing secrets over a glass of wine.'

'And isn't it lucky for you that we don't?' he answered with a wry smile. 'Think of the tales I could tell him about you.' He snatched a scrap of paper from the bedside table – a flyer advertising some play or other – and stuffed it inside his book to mark the page. 'The advantage of being insignificant is that people talk as though you're not there. They'll say anything in front of me … when they've started their period, whether they have an itch in a peculiar place … I even know that Nathalie's right breast is bigger than her left.'

'I'm sure it isn't,' I said. 'The blondes are perfect in every way.'

Théo frowned. 'Why do you insist on calling them that? And they're not perfect, they're human. And, actually …' He got up from the bed and stood behind me, stooping to rest his chin on my shoulder. 'I think you're the most beautiful woman in the whole of Paris.'

A chill rippled through the room. I looked in the mirror and saw the man from the souvenir shop grinning at me, his hooded eyes gleaming.

I shuddered, and Théo rubbed the goosebumps on my arms.

'Cold?' he said.

'No, I …' I looked in the mirror again. The only face staring back at me was my own. I twisted away from it.

'Do you have any cigarettes?'

'Nope. I was so bored without you that I smoked them all. Where *did* you go, anyway? I missed you.'

'Did anyone else miss me?'

'By "anyone" I assume you mean Christophe.' Théo rolled his eyes. 'He was in his room for most of the afternoon, probably working on his stupid script.'

'It's not stupid,' I said. 'The showcase is going to be fantastic.'

'Whatever.' Théo yawned and lifted his arms to stretch. 'The others, the "blondes" … *They* missed you.'

I snorted. 'Yeah, right.'

'It's true. I heard them talking as they left. They were trying to find you. Liliane was worried something might have happened to you.'

'As if *she* would be worried about that.'

The scene was easy to envisage: the girls tearing around getting ready for one of what Diana called their 'Sunday excursions', their smirks as Liliane aired her 'concerns'. No doubt they were crossing their fingers and hoping some disaster *had* befallen me. My departure would be a relief to them all.

'I wonder what Christophe would do if something did happen to me?' I said.

Théo exhaled. 'Why do you do this? Why do you torment yourself by loving someone who has no feelings for you?'

'Love *is* torment, Théo.'

'I know that,' he said with undisguised scorn. 'Better than anyone.' He went to the window and rubbed at the glass with his fist, squinting through the grime. 'I hate this view. I hate this academy, this city ... I hate it all.'

I rose from the chair, pressing my chest against his back and snaking my arms around him.

'Let's leave,' Théo said. 'We could go tonight. What's stopping us?'

'There's nothing stopping you.'

He turned to face me. 'You know I wouldn't go without you. And you'd hate it if I left you. If we stay, this place will crush us, Inès. And do you really think it'll ever be a success?'

'Christophe will *make* it a success,' I said. 'He has the contacts, the skill, the prestige ... I believe in him.'

'And I believe in *you*. There are so many other schools where you could shine – *truly* shine – and so many other tutors who are more deserving of your admiration. We could just go, start somewhere else. Somewhere we both have a chance. We don't owe him anything.'

'I owe him *everything*,' I said. 'I'm a novice. I don't have the training or the experience that the blondes do. And, compared to them, I am *old*. Only Christophe would've taken a chance on me. Only he would've taken the risk.' I placed my hands on Théo's waist, pulling him closer to me. 'And how would we survive without him? How would we exist? We would be back on the streets, hustling and struggling, but here ... here, we get to do what we love. We can be who we really are.'

'And who is that, exactly?' Théo said. 'Who – *what* – is he moulding us into? I'm not sure I want to be the work of Christophe's hands.'

I searched Théo's face, thinking for a second that I had found something in his expression, and then stepped back as the chill ran through me again.

'What is it?' he said. 'Something did happen today, didn't it? Tell me.'

I wanted to tell him, but the notion of relaying the story of the gargoyle filled me with unease, and not just because of how implausible it would sound. There was something else, too, an underlying dread I couldn't place.

'Nothing happened,' I said, returning to the mirror and studying my reflection.

Who was the gargoyle to say that Christophe would never love me? Surely it couldn't see everything it claimed to; surely it couldn't truly know my future? I would prove it wrong; I would show the gargoyle – whatever it was – that I was on the correct path.

I picked up a lipstick and tugged off the cap. Théo lay on the bed with his cheek on his palm and watched me layering it onto my lips.

'What are you doing?' he asked.

'If Christophe can't see that I'm the one,' I said, 'then I must *make* him see. I'll go to him and explain that I'm his star. That I'm his *everything*.'

'What, now?' Théo said, his brow creased in surprise.

I pressed my lips together to even out the colour. Red,

it had to be red. 'Théo, have you never heard of seizing the moment?'

'From you, never,' he replied. 'Why tonight? What's prompted this?'

I swivelled on the chair to look at him. 'I can't wait any longer. I want him. I *need* him. It's torture being so near and yet so far away from him. I can't take it. I *can't*. I have to make him realise that he is perfect for me, and I am for him.'

'Christophe Leriche is an arrogant pig,' Théo said. 'He will break your heart into tiny pieces without a second's thought. He's not worthy of you. You deserve someone who can see how wonderful you are, someone who doesn't need to "realise" it.' He shook his head. 'Why does it have to be him? Why?'

'Because it always has been,' I said. 'Him, and only him. I told you that. I was honest with you, right from the start.'

'But not with yourself.' He sat up and dragged a hand through his hair. 'I suppose I'll be here when you come back. Waiting for you.'

'*If* I come back.' I took one last look at myself and stood up. 'Christophe might decide to whisk me off to dinner to celebrate.'

Théo laughed. 'I think the air at the top of Notre-Dame must have had some strange particles in it today. I think you inhaled too many of them and now you've gone mad.'

'Perhaps as mad as you,' I said, and blew him a kiss as I closed the door behind me.

# 6

Our rooms – the 'luxurious living quarters', as they were described on the website – were in a decrepit building in the grounds of the academy, which had been hastily converted into a ramshackle hall of residence, known to us as 'the dormitory'. Each room led off a long corridor illuminated by a series of bare lightbulbs that dangled from the centre of the low ceiling. The floorboards were warped and perpetually cold, although we had been promised that a refurbishment was 'imminent'.

At one end of the corridor, nearest the staircase leading up from the courtyard, was my room – the smallest and the dingiest. At the other end was Christophe's.

As I stalked towards his door, my heart thundering in my chest, I could hear sounds coming from inside the girls' rooms: Diana's drone as she made her nightly telephone call to her mother; the strains of Françoise's favourite Beethoven sonata; the thud of Veronica's feet as she practised her pliés; and Roxane's whimpers as she wept in the dark.

From behind Déborah's door there were peals of laughter, the voice egging her on unmistakably Cécile's. Hélène's room was silent, which was not surprising, for she often took to her bed as early as possible in order, so she said, 'to commune with a higher power'.

'Hélène is communing with *something* every night,' Théo had quipped. 'But it is not a higher power. Hélène hides in her room to fantasise about Christophe. She's in love with him. They all are.'

Théo was mistaken. Hélène couldn't love Christophe – none of the blondes could. Loving Christophe was not a passing fad that would be outgrown, and it was not a girlish crush on a teacher. Loving him – *truly* loving him – eclipsed everything else. It meant loving the entirety of him, not just his public persona, and accepting that the things that drew you towards him – his charisma, his talent, his knowledge and insight, the assured way he spoke, the intensity of his gaze – were also the things you despised about him, because they drew others towards him too.

What the blondes loved was his illustrious credentials, and the cachet of being at his feted academy, handpicked by him. They loved what his tutelage had the potential to do for them, the advantage it provided, but only I loved him for who he was. They would've done anything to realise their ambitions, but only I would've done anything for Christophe.

I hovered outside his door and imagined him behind it: working on the script we were all desperate to read, engrossed in one of the novels he'd recommended to us, or lying on his bed, thinking of me, as I so often lay on mine, thinking of him. What was beyond his door was a mystery, but I hoped that after tonight, I wouldn't have to wonder about it any more. The mystery would be solved, and my longing would end.

I took a deep breath, wiped my palms along the front of my dress, and knocked.

Almost at once, a voice came from inside, muffled by the thick wood. 'Just a second!'

The door creaked open, and those cool blue eyes, the ones I had first seen on that poster all those years ago, were shining on me like spotlights, and I was falling, falling …

'Inès?' Christophe peered around me, checking the corridor as if he were expecting someone else.

I thought my legs might buckle at the sound of my name tumbling off his tongue.

'Well.' He folded his arms. 'This is certainly a surprise.'

'Is it a bad time?' I said, feeling a sting of panic at the idea that he might be about to send me away. 'Are you going out?'

It was clear that he was getting ready to go somewhere. He wore an elegant black suit that was obviously expensive, and the crisp white shirt beneath his jacket appeared brand new. The top two buttons were undone, exposing a triangle of his chest. I tried not to stare at it.

He glanced at his watch. 'I will be shortly.'

'This won't take long,' I blurted. This had to be my moment. I had to tell him what he meant to me. 'Could

I …?' I gestured hesitantly to his room.

Christophe mulled it over briefly, then stepped aside. 'Just for a second.'

His room was enormous – easily several times the size of mine. The décor was modern and stark, but the cushions on the chairs provided splashes of colour, and a few personal touches offered some clues about him: half-melted candles on the windowsill, an old record player on the sideboard, a framed poster of his most celebrated play hanging above the sofa, the books crammed on the shelf. There was a large rectangular rug in the centre and a desk in the corner, upon which were several reams of paper and an old typewriter, and I pictured him hunched over it long into the night, working on the script we were due to perform for the academy's showcase. At the far end of the room was a door that was slightly ajar, and a cloud of steam and the aroma of something citrusy and sensual hung in the air.

Christophe lifted a sheaf of loose papers from the wingback chair by the desk. 'Please, sit,' he said.

I sank into the velvety fabric, doing my utmost not to look at the bed opposite. It was huge, made up with starched white sheets edged with gold stitching. Beside it was a fitted wardrobe with mirrored panels, and Christophe went across to it and slid one of the doors open. After a moment's deliberation, he selected a black tie from the extensive collection on the rail.

'I hate these things,' he said as he began knotting it.

'I have never understood why it is that the only way for a man to be considered smart is for him to fasten a noose around his neck.'

'Whether it is a noose depends on the occasion,' I said. 'If it is a business meeting then, yes, the tie is a noose. A noose on which you will either hang or escape until the next time. But if it is pleasure, then perhaps the tie signifies constraint – a bind on your passion.'

Christophe pivoted from the mirror in a slow, exaggerated movement, like he often did when he was demonstrating a step to us, and stared at me in surprise. I was surprised too. I hadn't meant to say all of that – *any* of that. But I was no longer in control of myself.

His gaze roamed from my head to my feet. 'Well, well …' He turned back to the mirror. 'A very enlightening analysis. So, which do you think this is?' He lowered his hands, his tie now knotted perfectly, so that I could assess him. 'Business or pleasure?'

I hesitated, as if I were giving it careful consideration. 'Business. Definitely business.' I *hoped* it was business.

Christophe nodded. 'You are right. It's a business meeting. With a very tiresome, but very wealthy, individual.'

'The red-haired woman?' I remembered her name – Justine Deschamps – but thought it prudent not to disclose the extent to which she had permeated my consciousness.

He reached for the bottle of cologne on the dresser. 'I haven't made contact with her yet. But I will. The timing must be right.'

'Of course. Best not to appear desperate. To maintain an air of mystery.'

He smiled as he tipped the bottle and splashed the liquid onto his palms, inclining his head from one side to the other as he rubbed the cologne onto his neck. It smelled rich and woody, and I inhaled as stealthily as I could, so as to absorb as much of it as possible.

'You know ...' He put down the bottle in the exact same spot. 'You are very astute, Inès. I sensed it the instant you walked into the audition. It was one of the reasons I offered you a place.'

'One of the reasons?'

He adjusted his tie again, apparently dissatisfied with the calibre of the knot. 'You're not like the others, are you?'

'No.' Every bone in my body, every sinew, screamed out to him. How could he not hear it?

His eyes glittered as he came to sit in the chair opposite me. The scent of his cologne enveloped me, so that I was swathed in him.

'What can I do for you, Inès?' he asked.

'Um, well, it's ...' I faltered, my bravado wilting in the heat of his presence. 'It's just that ...' I sat up straighter. 'I've been thinking about the showcase. You're always saying we need to make a big impact, to give Paris something different, something fresh. Something it has never seen before.'

He put his finger to his temple. 'Yes. And?'

'I think …' I took a breath and rolled the dice. 'I think I can do that for you. For us.' I shifted to the edge of the chair. 'I can help you launch your academy into the ranks of the most esteemed performing arts schools in the city.'

The corner of his mouth twitched. 'Oh really? And how, exactly, will you do that?'

'Give me the part,' I said. 'Make *me* the lead in our first showcase. I can make it a success. I know I can.'

The room plunged into silence. I pictured the blondes listening outside the door, smothering their laughter.

Christophe ran his gaze over me again. 'You? The lead?'

'You said yourself that I am not like the others.'

'That is true. But now you sound like them. They are forever knocking on my door begging me to choose them.'

I sprang out of the chair and paced the room. 'But their motives are selfish. They want the glory for themselves, for their own advancement. Whereas I am thinking of you. Of the *collective*. I can be the jewel in the crown. I can be the star. I can do it all – I can dance, I can sing, I can act … I am the best here. No one wants it like I do.' *Wants* you *like I do*, I almost said, but caught myself just in time.

'I will give everything I have for the academy,' I said, 'and for you. You know that I … that I …'

*That I love you, I love you. I have always loved you. You, and only you. You, you, you, you, you …*

But I couldn't say it. I was too afraid. Afraid of how

much I loved him, and of the scepticism I could see etched on his face. Afraid that being rejected by him would be the one indignity from which I could not recover.

I slumped back into the chair, depleted and embarrassed, and wished I had never let the gargoyle persuade me that this was a good idea.

Christophe considered me, his knuckles pressed to his lips. After a long moment he took his hand from his mouth and said, quietly, 'I agree.'

Hope returned, restoring my energy. 'You do?'

He nodded. 'I wouldn't be much of a teacher if I couldn't recognise that you are by far the best student here. You are the only one who understands what it means to perform. You are the only one who *feels* the words, the steps, the music. You are capable of losing yourself on-stage, whereas the others …' Christophe paused, glancing over at the typewriter as though it might produce the word he was searching for. 'They'll never *become* a role the way that you do. They're too conscious of their egos to completely transform into someone else. Some*thing* else. They will require a lot of moulding, but with you, I hardly need to offer any direction. The others could be stars, yes, but you are an *artiste*. Why else do you think I offered you a full scholarship? You were born with a gift, Inès. I knew that the second I saw you.'

The blood rushed in my ears. My pulse thumped; I pressed the soles of my shoes harder against the floorboards to prove to myself that I wasn't dreaming.

'Unfortunately,' he continued, and my heart seemed to stop, 'being gifted is not enough. These days, people are not particularly roused by talent. What the public wants is to be in the presence of that which they can never possess, to aspire to what they can never become. *That's* what they will clamour to see, and that is what I must offer them in my first showcase.'

My cheeks burned with shame. I had brought this misery, this defeat, upon myself. All Christophe had done was point out the truth.

'I can change,' I said. 'It wouldn't be hard, when you think about it. A few alterations here and there … I'll dye my hair. I'll smile more. I'll stop reading books and take up magazines instead.' I was babbling, but I could not stop. 'I'll fill my head with frivolous things – celebrities and make-up and fashion. Whatever it takes to become like them, I'll do it. I will.'

I rose, teetering slightly. 'I'll start tonight. I think the pharmacy is still open. I'll go there now. I will be blonde before midnight.'

Christophe frowned. 'What? Blonde? You don't need to do that.'

'Oh, I do,' I said. 'I do. Being blonde is everything. Being *perfect*. I can be—I could be—I can—'

He held up a palm. 'Stop, please. It is not as simple as making "alterations".' He grimaced, as though the idea were offensive to him. 'I'm talking about catering to what is in vogue. Like everything else, performance has trends, and at the moment the fashion is for light entertainment. The world is too serious, too precarious. People want comfort, something that helps them to escape their lives. And if I am to get my academy established, I have to give them what sells.'

'But what about art?'

'Who says that isn't art? If I can make money now by feeding the public the sugary treats they crave, then I will be able to move on to richer, more satisfying work.'

'And you don't feel that you'd be compromising your artistic integrity?'

'No,' Christophe said sharply, like this was a point he'd defended before. 'Either I do it this way now, or I don't succeed at all. Faced with those options, I can live with making a few compromises. Couldn't you?'

'No. I don't think I could.'

'You say that because you have the luxury of not having to make that choice.'

'I don't have the luxury of making any choices at all.'

I moved towards the door. Christophe stepped in front of me and held my arms.

'Inès, look at me.' The heat from his palms spread through my dress and onto my skin, and it took all my will not to melt into him. 'Look at me.'

I trembled as I met his eyes.

'You might not be the lead,' he said, 'but people will still see you. It will be you who lingers in their minds. It might not be your face on the posters this time, but one day it will be. Soon. I promise you that. The light of a true star cannot be outshone.'

'Like yours,' I said.

He shook his head. 'My star has faded, Inès. But yours is on the ascendancy.'

Christophe took his hands away and my skin burned and hummed; dark places inside of me longed to feel the light – *his* light – shining on them.

'I'll soon be unveiling my script,' he said. 'There will be a great deal for you to learn.'

'I'll do whatever it takes,' I said.

'You know something?' Christophe said. 'I think you and I could have a future together. Maybe one day, when we have more time, we could—'

A tap on the door bludgeoned our precious, tender moment.

'We could what?' I said, unable to hide my desperation. 'We could *what*?'

But Christophe's attention, if indeed I had ever wholly captured it, was lost as the handle turned and the door opened.

It shouldn't have been a shock to see Liliane's blonde head poke round the door, and I should have guessed that she would be the one to thwart me. But still my heart sank to see her there.

She, too, was attired as if she were going somewhere special. Her sequinned dress clung to her body, a deep slit on one side offering a tantalising glimpse of her long, toned legs. Her hair was styled into loose waves, and there was a dusting of rouge along her cheekbones and a touch of mascara on her lashes, though the make-up was hardly necessary. She was radiant: more beautiful than ever.

When Liliane saw me she did a double take, her eyes widening.

'Inès!' She barged into the room with the confidence and presumption of someone who had done so many times before, and lunged at me with her arms outstretched.

'I am *so* pleased to see you,' she said. Her perfume was sickly sweet, making me instantly nauseous. 'Are you coming out with us?'

*Us?* Rage blocked my throat. I couldn't answer.

'Inès and I were just discussing the showcase,' Christophe said. His tone was different now. He was curt, business-like, as if the drawbridge he had briefly lowered had been yanked up. 'She has some interesting ideas. But, no, sadly she won't be joining us.'

Liliane pouted at him. 'She *should* come. She'd be much better at these things than me.' She unclasped her bag, took out a compact, and proceeded to scrutinise her reflection. I wondered what it was like to look in the mirror and see no flaws, nothing that needed to be changed, or improved.

'You're going out *together*?' I said.

'I find it useful to bring a student along to these meetings,' Christophe said. 'It helps potential investors conceptualise what I'm trying to achieve. And helps them understand how the Leriche Academy operates.'

'*She* helps?'

Liliane laughed. 'That's what I keep telling him. I'm useless. All I do is sit there like a mannequin. You'd have much more interesting things to say than me, I'm sure.' She stared into her compact again. I hoped the glass would crack, although seven years of bad luck would not be nearly enough.

Christophe reached across and held the door open. 'Thank you for sharing your ideas, Inès,' he said. 'I'm sure I can rely on you to be discreet about what we've discussed.'

I could only nod glumly.

'See you in the morning,' he said. 'Bright and early, as usual.'

I looked at them – Liliane fiddling with her hair, Christophe scanning his phone – and wondered how I could've been gullible enough to think I could ever capture Christophe's heart in a world where women like Liliane existed.

# 7

True to his word, when I got back to my room, Théo was sprawled on my bed, a book open on his lap, his hair tousled from the pillow.

'Back so soon?' he said. 'That dinner Christophe "whisked you away" for was very quick.'

I pushed the door shut and threw him a withering look. 'Is that why you waited for me? So you can gloat?'

'I waited because I care.' He snapped his book closed. 'So, come on, tell me all about it. Did he fall to his knees and profess his undying love for you? Or did you see him for what he is and tell him to get lost?'

'Neither,' I said, kicking off my shoes. 'We talked.'

'And? What wisdom did the egocentric idiot impart this time?'

'He told me I'm his best student.'

'Well, that's stating the obvious. I assume this means he's giving you the lead, then?'

I sat down next to him and poked at a hole in the sheets. 'Not quite.'

Théo tutted. 'He's such a coward.'

'He needs to build the academy's reputation,' I said, more defensively than I intended. 'He has to have a lead who will attract maximum attention. Grab the headlines.'

'That makes no sense. Surely having the best student as the lead would grab the headlines. He's just making excuses.'

'He's *not*. He knows the industry, and I support him. I *trust* him. And I will do whatever it takes to help make the academy a success.'

'Whatever it takes?' Théo sighed. 'Don't sacrifice yourself for him, Inès. Think of *your* ambitions, *your* dreams. You're wasted here with that spineless man.'

'He's not spineless,' I said. 'He's trying to establish something magical. Something enduring. He thinks that having one of the blondes as the lead is the surest way to achieve that.'

Théo stared at me. 'And you believe that nonsense? What happened to Christophe the risk-taker?'

'He knows what he's talking about. It's about giving the audience what they want and I …' I broke from his gaze. 'I don't have the right look.'

'What?' He sat up. 'Of *course* you do. And what do looks have to do with it, anyway?'

'Open your eyes, Théo. Appearance is *everything*. The crowds won't come to see someone like me on-stage. They want beauty, they want perfection. They want someone untainted, uncomplicated. I am not those things. Being perfect, beautiful … It's the one part I cannot play.'

'Yes, you can. The things you think about yourself are not true.' He took my hands. 'You should leave this place. It's not good for you.'

'This place is all I have.'

Théo threaded his fingers through mine. 'Not *quite* all.'

We sat in silence, the lapse in our conversation saying more than we ever could.

'So, who is it?' Théo asked. 'Who has he chosen?'

'He didn't say. And what does it matter? One is the same as another.'

'It should be *you*.'

I nestled against him. 'It will be, one day. Christophe said he and I could have a future together. That must count for something.'

'I want to tell you it does,' Théo said. 'Truly, I do. But Christophe is not the man you think he is. And do you want to be in his thrall forever? Do you really want your future to be entwined with his?'

The answer was as clear, and as raw, as it had ever been.

We stayed up – him reading, me ruminating – until Théo's eyelids began to droop and I could no longer tolerate the whir of my thoughts. He drifted easily into sleep, but I lay awake for hours, staring into the darkness.

Just after two, a car pulled up outside. Moments later, I heard them coming up the stairs. Liliane giggled as they walked down the corridor, her stilettos making arrhythmic clacks on the stone floor.

I lifted Théo's head from my chest and nudged it onto the pillow. He stirred and mumbled something, but his eyes remained closed. To see him sleeping, you would assume he was at peace, but if he slept alone, in his own room, he would have terrible dreams in which demons came for him, and he'd wake rigid with fright, too afraid to close his eyes again. As long as we were together, Théo insisted, he could sleep. As long as he was with me, the demons couldn't touch him.

Carefully, I eased back the covers and crept to the door, opening it only an inch or two. Every bulb in the corridor was on, the light they emitted muted by a layer of dust. Christophe and Liliane were standing outside his door. His tie was undone, his jacket folded over his arm. Liliane's hair was mussed and her make-up had lost its glow, but she was still flawless. She could never be anything less.

Christophe gazed at her. 'You are perfect,' he said. 'Completely perfect.'

My toes curled. If I had him, if Christophe looked at *me* that way, I would be perfect too.

Liliane leant up and threw her arms around his neck.

'Thank you,' she said. 'Thank you. For everything.'

Unable to witness any more, I closed the door on them and slid back under the covers. I hugged Théo's waist and battled the images entering my mind: Liliane and Christophe entangled in the sheets on his huge bed, Théo being torn apart by a demon. And me, plummeting from a great height.

Sleep came only when I allowed the words that had been circling me all day to take root in my mind.

Tall flowers must be cut down.

They must be cut down.

They must be.

Cut.

Down.

# 8

As the dawn light poked into the room, I clambered out of bed and woke Théo.

'Cover for me,' I said.

He sat up, groggy with sleep, and rubbed his eyes. 'Cover you for what?' He stretched across to check the clock and groaned. 'It's so early. Where are you going at this obscene hour?'

'For a walk.' My dress from the previous night was in a heap on the floor. I slipped it over my head and buttoned it hurriedly.

'A walk ...' Théo watched me, his expression dubious. 'Why the urgency? What about class?'

'I'll be back in time for that,' I told him, but I had no idea if I would. I knew only that I had to go *now*, that I had to talk to the one person who would understand my plight.

'What should I say if Christophe asks me where you are?' Théo said.

I reached under the bed and found a lone shoe. I stood up and glanced around for the other. 'Tell him I have a fever.'

'Do you?'

'Of sorts.'

'It's not like you to miss class.'

'Being like me has got me nowhere.'

Théo threw off the covers and swung his legs over the edge of the mattress. 'I don't like this, Inès. Stay here. Talk to me.'

'I can't. And he'll certainly notice if *you're* not in class.' I spotted my missing shoe by the dresser and sat on the chair to put it on, careful to avoid catching a glimpse of myself in the mirror.

'He doesn't need me,' Théo said with a recalcitrant shrug.

'Don't be silly. How will the blondes dance without music?' I lifted my coat from the hook on the door and took my keys from the pocket. 'Make sure no one sees you leave.'

'That won't be hard. No one sees me as it is. Inès?'

I turned, my fingers curled around the handle. 'What?'

'I have a bad feeling,' Théo said. 'A feeling you are about to do something very foolish. Something that will destroy you. Destroy *us*.'

'Not foolish,' I said. 'Necessary.'

'Can you tell the difference?'

'Goodbye, Théo,' I said, and left his question hanging.

The air was still, the city shrouded in an unearthly quiet. At that time of the morning the pavements should have been crowded with people hurrying to work, to school, but there was nobody around. The quays and bridges would normally have been busy with traffic, but there were no cars anywhere. There was no sign of life as far as my eyes could see, and no sound. Paris was an empty city filled with foreboding.

I walked the short distance to Notre-Dame, thinking how the absence of people made the streets feel less serene, not more, and steeled myself for the unnerving sensation of facing the gargoyle's stony gaze and hearing its uncanny voice. Part of me hoped that it wouldn't say anything, so I wouldn't have to find out what those 'extra measures' were. But deep down, I knew this was the only way. Without the gargoyle's guidance I would forever remain on the sidelines, forced to witness Christophe looking at Liliane the way he should have been looking at me.

The towers didn't open until ten, but the gates at the entrance were unlocked, and I was so relieved that I hurried through them without questioning why. As soon as I was inside the cathedral boundary, the gates clanged shut behind me. The noise startled me, and I panicked and tried to wrench them open, but they would not budge.

With no choice other than to press on, I slipped through the doorway and climbed the steps to the souvenir shop. The echo of my footsteps made me feel like an intruder, though I sensed that my presence was expected by someone. Or something.

'Hello? Hello, is anyone …'

The words died on my lips as I saw the man with the hooded eyes at the counter. He smiled cunningly and beckoned to me.

'Come,' he said. 'You will like it up there today. You will see everything.'

'Why is it so empty?' I asked. 'Where have all the people gone?'

His pupils appeared to change in the murky light, becoming darker, then paler, narrowing to slits. 'Who's to say they've gone anywhere?'

'What do you mean?'

'You know what I mean,' the man said. 'You know *exactly*. Here …'

He reached an arm out to me. Held between his thumb and forefinger was a ticket with a picture of the gargoyle on it.

'For you,' he said. His eyes seemed to glow red as I took it from him. 'Although *you* don't need a ticket, of course. You are almost part of the place now. Part of *us*.'

'Who?' I said. 'What do—'

The man's face became slack. He bowed his head and pointed to the spiral staircase.

'Up,' he said. 'You must go *up*.'

The stairwell was cold, almost glacial. As I climbed the steps, I was certain something was following behind me. Something so awful, so despicable, that if I glanced back at it, I would go insane. But that knowledge did not quieten the voice in my head urging me to turn and look at it – just once, just to see its face. The higher I went, the louder the voice became. Only when I placed my foot on the final step did the voice die away.

After the freezing stairwell, the crisp morning air was a relief. The sun was shining, offering a stark contrast to the gloom inside the tower. I thought the gargoyle might be waiting for me, but it was in its usual, iconic pose, still and unmoving. My breath ragged from the steep ascent, I moved towards it.

The gargoyle's head whipped round.

'Greetings,' the gargoyle said, its peculiar mouth stretching into a devilish smile that revealed a row of pointed teeth. I didn't want to think about what it might need them for.

'What's the matter?' it said. 'Cat got your tongue? Or something else, perhaps …?'

'No, I just …' I thought of the locked gates. There was no way out.

The gargoyle turned from the parapet and came to stand in front of me. I backed away, but it soon closed the gap between us, its movements surprisingly nimble.

'Come on now,' it said as I stared at it in revulsion. 'I know you're not *scared*. Not of me. And there's *always* a way out. After all, that's why you've come, isn't it? For the answer to all your problems. Except …' I tried not to flinch as it came even closer, its nose almost touching mine. 'Except you already know the answer, don't you?'

'I wouldn't be here if I did.'

'That's what they all say,' the gargoyle replied with a chuckle. 'They like to blame me. To pretend it's *my* fault. I suppose you're going to do the same, to tell me I'm responsible for what happened last night, and for how dejected you feel now. Liliane looked rather lovely in that sequinned dress, didn't she?'

'I went to him because of *you*. Because of what you said.'

'Oh yes, how they love to pin it all on me.' The gargoyle crossed its reedy arms. 'I seem to recall I was the one who pointed out that you would never win his heart using your own wiles. It was *your* choice to test that for yourself. Your little experiment has only confirmed what you already suspected.'

'I preferred it when I simply suspected. Now I *know*.'

'Unrequited love is easier to bear when there is no hope. But to realise there *could* be hope if it weren't for certain barriers, well, that makes the burden even heavier.' It extended a leg and admired its toes. 'Have you ever considered that the rejection you're feeling now is precisely how your "friend" feels constantly? *Théo.* You should bring him here one day. Introduce him to me.'

The thought of it made my guts churn. 'I would never do that. *Ever.*'

'Perhaps you should. He is afraid of heights, is he not? He is afraid of so many things … especially of you.'

'Me?'

The gargoyle nodded sagely. 'We always fear those whom we love the most. They're the only ones who can truly hurt us. Do you not fear Christophe? Were you not lying awake last night worrying that he might fall for Liliane?'

'He won't,' I said. 'You know he has never married? There has never seemed to be anyone special in his life.'

'Of *course* I know. Christophe Leriche is the archetypal bachelor. Perhaps because his ego won't permit him to love anyone other than himself.'

'No, because he hasn't met the right person.'

'And you think that person is you.'

I said nothing. The gargoyle waggled one ear, and then the other, as it studied me.

'Why him?' it said. 'Why not save your love for someone kinder? Someone less selfish. Less conceited.'

'He's not like that,' I said. 'And you can't choose who you love. It descends upon you, out of nowhere. Like a sudden rainstorm.'

The gargoyle tapped its teeth. 'Or a curse.'

On the corner of the parapet was a chimera carved into the shape of a dragon. The gargoyle sneered at it and extended an arm to give it a sharp prod, as though mocking the chimera's inanimateness.

'What do you know about love anyway?' I said. 'What *could* you know? As you said yourself, you're just a gargoyle.'

'That I am.' Its head swivelled to scan the panorama. 'But being up here, keeping vigil over this beautiful, deceptive city, has taught me everything there is to know about love. Things that, were I to share them, would make you want to throw yourself from this tower.'

'I doubt that.'

'As well you may. For now. But the fact that you've returned shows you are willing to do things for love that others would balk at. So cast aside your doubt.'

The sun slipped behind a cloud, and a desolate chill seemed to seep from somewhere below the earth.

'What you said … about tall flowers.'

'What about it?' the gargoyle said.

The sky was now dark, as though night had fallen.

'What are those "extra measures"?' I asked.

'You already know. You don't need me to explain it.'

My chest constricted; when I swallowed, my saliva was like razor blades. 'But how …' I was certain we were alone, but still I lowered my voice. 'How would I do it? Assuming I was going to, that is.'

'Yes, assuming you were,' it said with a smirk. 'You could do it however you wanted to. However you felt was appropriate.'

'What if I got caught? The police would come for me.'

'They won't. No one will suspect you. I will make sure of that.'

'How?'

'I can't say. You have to trust me.'

'Why should I?'

'Because I am a friend,' it said. 'An ally. I want you to get what you deserve. And I have your best interests at heart.'

'You don't even have a heart.'

It laughed. 'My heart is stone, as all hearts should be. If yours was too, then you would not be in the predicament you're in now. But I'm offering you a solution. A simple, easy way to fix this.'

'Simple? *Easy?*' I shook my head. 'Just the idea of it makes me feel sick.'

'Do not underestimate your abilities,' the gargoyle said. 'Those nuns told you lies. You are not weak – far from it. Think of all the difficulties you have overcome, all the adversities you have faced, all the horrors you have survived. You can do anything, Inès. *Anything.* And imagine what it would be like to get what you want. Imagine being with him. Can you imagine it? Have you truly visualised it? Try it now, just for me. Go on, Inès, imagine. Imagine …'

I closed my eyes.

'What do you see?' the gargoyle whispered. 'Tell me what it's like. Tell me everything.'

'I see …'

*Christophe's eyes staring into mine. His hands on my skin. My cheek resting against the soft hair on his chest. His mouth on my ear. His voice in my head.*

'What do you hear?' the gargoyle said. 'What is he saying to you?'

*I love you, I love you, over and over again. I love you, Inès, only you. I have always loved you, you and only you. I love you, I love you, bouncing off the buildings, winding through the tunnels of the Métro, cresting on the waves of the Seine. I love you, I love you, I love you. You, you, just you, only you, forever you …*

'What is it like?' the gargoyle said. 'How does it feel?'

*I have his complete attention; he cherishes my every word. I am the most important thing in the world to him. He would do anything for me. Without me, he would wither and die. His love makes me soar; his love makes me better than I could ever be alone. With him, I am complete. Because of him, I am perfect. Because of him, I am falling, falling …*

I opened my eyes. The clouds were gone. The sky was bright and clear. Everything was clear.

'Tell me how,' I said. 'Tell me which one.'

The gargoyle licked its lips. 'Those decisions are yours to make. But whomever you choose, and whichever method you choose, the story will unravel as it should. I will be watching over you.'

'Why?' I said, summoning the strength to stare into its eye sockets and finding no life there, no warmth, no emotion. A dark expanse of *nothing*.

'Why are you helping me?' I asked.

'Because you spoke to me,' the gargoyle said. 'Because you believe in me. Because you saw me, and I saw you. And because when I look at you, I see myself. We are exactly alike, Inès. As you will see.'

The gargoyle's feet grated against the stone as it

settled back into place, lowering its chin onto its palms. 'Come to me again. When the time is right.'

'How will I know when that is?'

The gargoyle did not reply. Its features, battered and weathered from countless Paris storms, were set in its familiar expression. Silent and lifeless, as if it had never uttered a single word.

# 9

Life at the academy was tightly regimented. The choices open to us were confined to what Christophe's curriculum allowed: for every question we had, an answer was provided. But now I was faced with making the most consequential decision of my life, and for this there was no framework to follow, and no one to whom I could turn for counsel. The wealth of possibilities was daunting, but I was determined to choose wisely from all the options open to me. Twelve of them, to be precise.

Every opportunity that arose to study each of the blondes, I seized. I appraised Déborah and Cécile as they warmed up at the barre, and although it was intriguing to imagine what would happen if their clique was broken in two, I saw nothing to persuade me that it was worth taking such drastic action to find out.

I wasted a precious few hours spying on Aurélie and Élodie as they practised together, but they were so staid, so bland, that I concluded that little would be gained if one of them were to suddenly suffer a misfortune.

I eavesdropped on Françoise, Nathalie, Maëlle and Diana as they sat in the changing room after class. The four of them didn't notice me sitting at the end of the bench, tucking my shoes into my bag. They were too busy talking over each other.

Naturally, Diana's voice was the loudest.

'He's going to pick me for the lead,' she declared. 'He *has* to. It makes sense.'

'Why you?' Maëlle said.

'Because I am right for it.'

'Based on what?' Nathalie said.

'Based on what her mother tells her,' Françoise said with a yawn.

'No,' Diana said, patting her hair. 'Based on *evidence*. It has to be me. The rest of you cannot comprehend Christophe's artistic vision like I can.'

If I were judging solely on arrogance, then Diana would've been the one. Her constant boasting, the self-satisfied way she smiled whenever Christophe praised her technique, set my teeth on edge. But despite the hatred that burned inside me whenever I was near her, I knew it wasn't Diana.

Veronica's turn came when we were in the studio, all of us sitting close together on the wooden chairs. It was a momentous day: Christophe had just given us copies of the script he'd been working on for the showcase – the first he'd ever written. He stood in the centre of the circle we had formed around him, his voice as smooth as ever as he talked us through the essence of the story, but because I knew him so well, I could sense that he was anxious to gauge our reactions. So far, everyone had been respectful, showing deference to the grand occasion. Everyone except Veronica.

I watched her as she pored over the pages, a marker pen in her hand, poised and ready. Her large blue eyes were ringed with heavy liner, her hair scraped back into the tight bun she wore for class. I'd never encountered anyone who was always immaculately turned out. Even on Sundays, when we had no classes, Veronica would parade around as if she were about to go on-stage – unlike the others, who made the most of the chance to be sloppy with their appearances.

'Looking your best makes you feel your best,' she'd explain, even though no one had asked. 'And when you feel your best, you *are* the best.'

It was one of her annoying sayings, of which she had a mind-numbing supply. And that was the main problem with Veronica: she did not know when to shut up.

'Mr Leriche?'

It was the sixth time she had raised her hand to interrupt since Christophe had begun talking us through his script – the hallowed words that would determine the course of our futures. He halted in mid-flow, his irritation plain, and looked up from the page.

'What *now?*' he said.

'Okay, so I love the script, I really do.' Veronica gestured to the copy on her lap, which was already creased and covered with her looping scrawl. 'But I don't get it.'

Christophe's arms tensed, revealing the definition in his biceps. 'What is it you are unable to "get", Veronica?'

His blunt retort caused Nathalie and Françoise to exchange a worried glance.

Veronica shrugged. 'Well, like, is it a musical, or a play, or … what? What genre are we working in here?'

He bristled, putting his hands on his hips. 'It is *every* genre. I wrote it so you could demonstrate all of the talents you apparently have. Hence the term "showcase". Does that help you to "get it"?'

Roxane gasped. Maëlle bowed her head, and Cécile and Élodie followed suit. Déborah squinted at one of the posters Aurélie had tacked to the wall, as if it were suddenly fascinating to her. Only Veronica seemed impervious to Christophe's irritation.

'Ah, right,' she said, nodding at him. 'Okay.'

Christophe exhaled and picked up where he had left off. He had spoken only a dozen words when Veronica interrupted again.

'Sorry,' she said, 'but I have another question.'

'Really.' Christophe turned to consult the clock behind him.

'Yeah. I was thinking that if there were some *guys* for us to work with …'

'Guys.' His voice dripped with disdain.

'Okay, *men*.' Veronica shifted on the chair, warming to her theme. 'If there were some *men* here then we could cast the roles properly.'

The other blondes were now looking at Christophe, curiosity apparently overriding their nervousness. Until then, the issue of *men* had been a subject no one had dared to broach.

'No men,' Christophe said.

'Why not?' she said.

His expression hardened. 'Because none of the men who auditioned for me were good enough. This academy is for the most promising performers, and the most promising *only*.'

Christophe shook his head as Veronica's lips parted again. 'There are other schools, Mademoiselle Sellers. If you wish to join one of those instead, feel free.'

Veronica seemed to contemplate a response but then, after a sharp nudge from Nathalie, finally closed her mouth.

Based on that exchange, Veronica should've been the one. And yet, as much as I wanted her to be, as much as she irked me like a mosquito bite I couldn't scratch, I knew in my bones that she wasn't.

It was the same with Roxane and Hélène. I gave them equally careful consideration, observing them as closely as I had the others – which was a chore as they were both so dreary. Hélène spent most of her free time praying, and as for Roxane, when she wasn't crying or moping around the academy grounds, she was writing letters on pink notepaper. She'd gaze into the distance and tap her pen against her mouth – sometimes the wrong end of it, so that her lips became dotted with blue stains. When she finished she'd fold the letters carefully and slide them into an envelope – also pink – and hide them in her bag.

As boring as Hélène and Roxane were, they weren't the ones either.

I had tried to make the selection process fair, to be as neutral an arbitrator as I could, but there was only ever one real contender for the crown, and only one head large enough to wear it.

I was crossing the courtyard after practice when Liliane called out to me. Since that night in Christophe's room, she'd taken to giving me sly looks whenever she caught my eye, as though we were complicit in something, and under normal circumstances I would've ignored her unusual interest in me and kept walking, but these circumstances were anything but normal, and Liliane's name was still on my list of blondes to consider. This, I thought, could be a useful opportunity to help me decide which of those names was to be etched out, and which was to remain.

I stopped, and Liliane came bounding over.

'Hey, Inès.' She smiled, showing off her luscious lips with their Cupid's bow. I had seen the effects of that smile on many occasions. It could win over strangers, it could exonerate her; it could make Roxane forgive her latest spiteful remark – a true testament to its power, given that Liliane was often the meanest and most vindictive blonde of them all. No doubt she expected her smile to work on me, too.

'Can I walk with you?' she said.

Without waiting for an answer, she linked her arm through mine. The blondes did not need permission. Why should they, when the world acceded to their every whim?

We passed the section of the building that housed the academy's meagre library, a boxy, musty-smelling room that was intended to be used for study and quiet reflection but instead had become a place for idle gossiping. Next to it was a second dance studio, which wasn't yet operational, and the main theatre, which was modest in size and mostly out of bounds. Directly above that was the dormitory. I gazed up at my window, wondering if Théo was waiting for me.

'I've been meaning to talk to you,' Liliane said. 'But you're so elusive these days. Where do you go? You never spend time with us any more.'

Her attempt at humour made me seethe. The 'joke' was that I had never spent time with them, and they had made it crystal clear that they didn't want me to.

'It's all right,' she said. 'I understand why you're keeping a low profile. It's because of that business with Diana, isn't it?'

A high-pitched whine started up in my ears, and white dots floated across my vision.

'What business?' I said. 'What are you talking about?'

'I know, I know … You'd never say a word against

her.' Liliane prodded my ribs playfully. 'I understand.'

'I don't,' I said. 'What do you mean?'

'It's okay.' She drew her finger across her mouth. 'We don't have to talk about it. But listen, Inès, about the other night … with Christophe.'

The breeze picked up as we came to the entrance to the dormitory building, giving me a waft of Liliane's scent – a mixture of grapefruit and bubblegum. The cloying smell of it, and my confusion at the drivel she was spouting, made me feel bilious.

'We don't have to talk about that, either,' I said.

'No, please.' She pawed my arm. 'I'm sorry if you were upset about not coming with us. I asked Christophe to invite you. I *begged* him. God knows you are so much better at talking to his boring donors than I am.'

'And?' I hated myself for giving her the satisfaction of asking, but I had to. 'What did he say?'

Liliane prodded the cobblestones with her toe. 'I offered to stay behind, but Christophe said he'd already told them I'd be there, and he didn't want to disappoint anyone. Not that you'd be a disappointment … Oh no, sorry … Inès, wait!'

I didn't need to hear any more. I tugged the door open, planning to return to my room and stay there for the rest of the evening, but she darted in front of me and pushed it closed.

'Inès, please.' She touched my shoulder. 'I need your help.'

That was a first. But the blondes were not to be trusted, and I was not a naïve fool like Roxane. I was, however, intrigued.

'Help with what?' I said.

A lock of hair fell across her eyes. She did not sweep it aside, as though she were waiting for a camera to capture the moment.

'You remember that café we went to?' she said. 'Where you persuaded that lovely woman to pay for our meal?'

She had to have lost her mind. Liliane and I had never been to a café together – or anywhere, for that matter – but I needed to hear the rest of the story, so I let her gibberish continue.

'I went there alone a few weeks ago,' she said. 'And I … I met someone.' Her lips spread into a smile I hadn't seen before – one not intended to charm or manipulate, but a genuine smile of unrestrained joy.

'Oh my God, Inès, he's *amazing*. His name is Jacques, and he makes my heart skip. He's a dentist.'

'A dentist?'

Liliane nodded. 'He's older, but *very* witty, and *so* charming.' She wrapped her arms around her waist, hugging herself. 'I think I'm in love with him. But I'm not sure. How do you tell?'

'If you're in any doubt,' I said, 'then it's not love.'

'Maybe I'm in denial. Maybe I can't accept that I'm in love with him. Maybe I'm afraid. I've read that people often deny their feelings because of fear. Because they're scared to let go.'

I laughed. 'Where on earth did you read that rubbish? One of Françoise's magazines?'

'One of *yours*, actually,' she said. 'And it's not like I can ask the others. It would be a disaster if they found out.'

'They don't know?'

'Ha! No. They'd go straight to Christophe, and he'd stop me seeing Jacques. You know how strict he is about us not having outside distractions.'

I longed to slap her stupid face. Of *course* I knew. I knew him better than she did – better than *anyone*.

'You won't tell the others, will you?' she said. 'Especially not Diana.'

'Why on earth would I tell *her*?'

Liliane gave me the same grateful look she'd given Christophe, only I didn't fall for it. The blondes were self-serving creatures: she was only confiding in me because she wanted something.

'I'm meeting him tonight,' she said. 'Why don't you come?'

So that was it. She wanted me to be her lapdog.

'No.' I shook my head. 'Absolutely not.'

'Please,' she said. 'It would mean a lot to me. I need your opinion.'

'Why?'

'Because you know about this stuff. And you're

discreet. You never brag, unlike Cécile and Déborah, who haven't done half the things they claim to. They don't know the first thing about love, or about *anything*. You're the only one I can trust. Please, say you'll come.' I recoiled as she reached for my hand and gripped it. 'I'm meeting him at a hotel. We can dress up in our best clothes. It'll be so much fun. *Please.*' She tugged at my sleeve. 'Please come, Inès.'

It was then that it came to me: *this* was the clarity I'd been seeking. This was fate – or something else – solving my dilemma.

'All right,' I said. 'Why not?'

Liliane punched the air. 'Yes! We'll sneak out when it's dark. I can't wait! And, also … I need to thank you.'

'What for?'

'You *know* what for. For not telling anyone about the other night – about me going out with Christophe. I would hate for the others to think …' Her eyes met mine, and I saw in them the belief that we were sharing a secret – that I was her *friend*.

'You would hate for them to think what?' I said. 'What is it?'

She paused, chewing the inside of her mouth, then broke into a broad grin. 'Christophe's going to give me the lead role.' She clasped her hands to her chest. '*Me!*'

'He told you that?' I said. Uttering each word was like hurling a brick through a sheet of glass.

'He did!' Liliane bounced on the spot. 'When we

were out that night. He said I have what it takes to be his star. He said people will flock to see me on-stage.'

'Is that so?' Some other self was speaking for me now. The real me, the real Inès, had departed from my body, and someone else had taken her place.

Liliane's voice became a whisper. 'He says it's me, Inès. He says *I'm* the one.'

I looked at her, taking in her aquamarine eyes, her porcelain skin and high cheekbones, her silky blonde hair.

I took her hand.

'Yes,' I said. 'You are.'

# 10

Liliane stood outside the academy gates, shivering under a street lamp. She was wearing the sequinned dress again, paired with the same clutch bag, and a black faux-fur coat that was at least two sizes too big. Her lips were painted a gaudy red, her lashes caked with mascara. Perhaps she had thought the ensemble would lend her an air of sophistication, but to my eye it gave her the air of a young girl playing at being a grown-up.

It occurred to me that I could go back to my room and leave her to meet her suitor alone, and she need never know the fate she'd narrowly escaped. *No one* need know. But events were already in motion, and despite the twinge of doubt, I could not stop myself from advancing towards her.

Her head turned when she heard my heels tapping on the cobblestones.

'Inès!' Her face flushed with relief. 'I was starting to think you weren't coming.'

'Lost track of time,' I said.

Or rather, Théo had made me late.

He'd done his best to detain me, demanding to know where I was going, and who I was going to meet. I refused to say – for his own good as much as mine – and at one point he'd even taken my keys and dangled them from the window.

'Stay here,' he'd said. 'I am begging you. *Begging* you. I have the bad feeling again. And I know this'—he'd gestured at my outfit—'has something to do with *him*. Nothing good ever comes of obsession, Inès.'

'We'll see about that,' I'd said, and snatched the keys from him.

Liliane pulled at the lapels of her voluminous coat. 'It might be good if we're late,' she said. 'Men like to be kept waiting. Well, I think they do …'

She looked at me for confirmation, as if I were an authority on the subject. I decided to go along with it. I'd play the role of the friend she apparently thought I was.

'Definitely,' I said. 'It keeps them keen. I like your dress. It's wonderful on you.'

And it was. The dress clung to her as though it had been tailor-made, emphasising her waist and inviting a palm to rest in its tempting curve.

Liliane, though, seemed unconvinced. She glanced down at herself, a faint frown creasing her brow. 'You think so? I'm not sure if it's too much. Do you think Jacques will like it?'

'I think your boyfriend will love it.'

She nibbled her lower lip. 'Can you still call them your boyfriend if they're old?'

'I suspect he'd like it if you did. How old is he, anyway?'

'Oh, I don't know.' She waved a hand, and I noticed she'd even painted her nails for the occasion. 'Forty, fifty … It doesn't make much difference once they're past a certain age.'

'What about Christophe? Do you find him "old"?'

She wrinkled her nose. 'Let's not talk about Christophe. For one night, I want to forget all about him.'

She might be able to, but I did not have that luxury. Christophe was everywhere I went; he was everything I saw. And if there came a day when I wanted to forget him, when I *could* forget him, then there would be no point to my existence.

Liliane prattled on incessantly as we walked to the Métro, and I soon realised that little was required of me other than to corroborate her vapid theories about life and love, and to ease her anxieties about her impending tryst. It was laughable that she had chosen me to boost her confidence – that her confidence would *need* boosting – but this was my chance, and I could not afford to waste it.

We boarded the train at Hôtel de Ville and huddled near the doors. There were no free seats, so we stood with our heads close together, our voices low, as if we were plotting something, or sharing intimate confessions. The people around us could have easily mistaken us for friends, or maybe even more than that.

'You look amazing,' Liliane said, tugging my jacket open. 'I *love* your clothes. Where did you buy them?'

After Liliane's fortuitous invitation, I had paid a visit

to the blondes' favourite store, where I found just the right outfit: cropped black trousers, cut from the finest fabric, and a sheer black blouse with ruffled sleeves. It was unlike anything I owned – anything I *could* own – and was therefore perfect for a night like this.

'How much is it?' I'd asked the salesperson.

The clothes were priced far in excess of what I could afford, but I left the store with them anyway. The theft was audacious, even by my standards, but the alarms were silent as I sauntered through the main exit with the clothes stuffed under my jacket. The security guards did not so much as glance at me as I passed them, despite the fact that, as I discovered later, one of the trouser legs was poking out from my sleeve, and nobody came after me as I hurried down the street as fast as I could without running. The lack of repercussions had dared me to believe that if I could get away with that, then perhaps I could get away with worse. Much, *much* worse.

Naturally, I told Liliane none of this, and let her assume that I had bought the clothes.

'You always look so chic,' she said. 'We're all so envious of you – Diana especially. You know how hard she tries to copy your style.'

Liliane laughed, and I did too, because the idea of the blondes wanting to emulate me was preposterous.

'What about you?' I said. 'Who bought you that gorgeous dress? Was it Christophe? He has a good eye for fashion.'

'Yeah, right,' she said. 'You've seen what *he* wears.'

'He dresses impeccably. We're so lucky to have him as our teacher.'

The train lurched into the tunnel and she gripped the rail to steady herself. 'He pushes us too hard. He's obsessed with perfection.'

'Everyone's obsessed with something. And who doesn't want to be perfect?'

Liliane sighed. 'Perfection is exhausting.'

So easy for her to say. *Try being flawed, damaged … broken beyond repair. See how exhausting that is.*

'Christophe has been so supportive of my dreams,' she said, becoming uncharacteristically pensive. 'He says I'm going to be famous. He's promised me that, soon, everyone will know who I am.'

Liliane seemed to drift away, staring across the carriage as if she were visualising her name in lights and her gorgeous face on posters all over the city.

'I've never told anyone this before,' she said, 'but sometimes I think …' Her gaze shifted to a sweet wrapper stuck to the floor of the train. 'Sometimes, when I think about being famous, about being *known*, I can't imagine anything worse. What I want most in the world – what I've always wanted – terrifies me. Not because I might never get it, but because of what might happen if I do.' She looked at me. 'Does that sound weird?'

'No,' I said without hesitation. 'And I know exactly how you feel.'

She beamed in gratitude. 'You're a good friend, Inès. I couldn't manage without you.'

'I'm sure you could.' On any given day, Liliane and I barely spoke.

'But I wouldn't want to,' she said, her dazzling smile drawing the attention of the passengers clustered near us. 'Anyway, what about you?'

'What about me?'

'Have you got a boyfriend? Françoise is convinced you spend your nights with some hunk. She swears he's tall, even taller than you, with thick black hair and deep brown eyes.'

'She makes him sound real,' I said.

'Perhaps he is.' She winked. 'So? Is there someone?'

I thought of Théo.

'No,' I said. 'There is no one.'

Just a gargoyle.

By the time we exited the Métro onto Avenue d'Iéna, I knew most of what there was to learn about Liliane Lacroix.

She had regaled me with stories of her childhood: her doting parents, the idyllic upbringing in a house she described as being perpetually filled with sunlight, and the yearning to be a performer that struck her when she was an infant dancing to old records in her grandmother's bedroom. While she gabbled, I was wondering how I'd do it, and what it would be like. Whether I had the nerve, the fortitude, to go through with it.

We crossed the wide, tree-lined street, and although Liliane had been vague about which hotel we were going to, I'd assumed it would be somewhere bland and generic, and that we would keep walking until we got to a less salubrious area of the city. So when Liliane pointed at the gated building opposite, my jaw dropped.

'That's it,' she said, coming to a halt. 'That's the place.'

'There? He's meeting you *there*?'

The hotel was one of the most luxurious in Paris, the kind that regularly made the top five in the 'world's best' lists, the kind in which regular people – like Jacques – could not afford to stay. But men like him did imprudent things for women like Liliane, and the price could never be too high for so great a potential reward.

'He's booked a suite,' she said. 'For the whole night! It's so exciting.'

It was utterly daunting. As we walked up to the entrance that managed to be both grand and understated, I expected somebody to spring from behind a pillar and inform me that I was not welcome there. But the doorman doffed his top hat and held the door open for us with a gloved hand, and Liliane thanked him and breezed inside as though she belonged there. I followed, feeling as conspicuous as an infected boil on the end of a nose.

'Wow,' she whispered, as if we were in a church. 'This is incredible.'

Without question, it was. The lobby was vast, with polished mosaicked tiles that looked too pristine to tread upon. Everything shone: the chandeliers, the gold fittings, the wrought-iron banister that curled up the marble staircase. Even the staff seemed incandescent, with not a single strand of hair out of place.

Liliane was awed by our surroundings, but apparently not intimidated. She made a beeline for the sleek reception desk and asked the concierge where we could find the bar.

'Just there, to your left,' he replied, appraising us coolly.

Liliane laced her fingers through mine and ushered me in the direction the man had indicated. Our heels made loud gunfire taps on the tiles as we crossed the lobby, attracting the gaze of the people waiting by the doors, monogrammed luggage at their feet.

'This is so fantastic,' Liliane said. 'I'm going to absorb every detail. I'll never forget a single thing about tonight. Tonight, I am free!'

The bar area was just as lavish as the lobby. The Empire décor was complemented by huge leather armchairs, and the candles on the tables flickered in smoked-glass holders. The bar itself was a few metres in length, the flecks in the marble sparkling under the lights. Three of the four stools positioned along it were unoccupied, but the one at the end was taken by a man in a grey suit. He had his back to us, his phone pressed to his ear.

Liliane's nails dug into my arm. 'That's him!' she

hissed. 'There!' She snatched at my wrist and yanked me behind a bushy plant that dwarfed us both. 'How's my hair? Do I look okay?' She opened her bag and took out her compact. 'Oh God, my hair is awful.'

I peered around the foliage. The man had his elbows on the bar, spinning a coaster beneath his finger as he talked on his phone.

'How did you meet him, exactly?' I asked.

Her eyes glittered as she launched into the story. 'It was after class,' she said. 'I went to a café, and he came through the door just as I was leaving. He looked at me and I looked at him and I thought he was *so* handsome. And he is, don't you think?'

'He's … nice.'

He was average. He had short black hair which appeared to have been freshly cut, and his build was typical of a middle-aged man who had more pressing concerns than honing his physique. I suspected he was married. They usually were.

'Aren't you going to go and say hello?' I said. 'He might think you've changed your mind.'

She bit her lip. 'What if he's changed *his* mind?'

I cupped her shoulders. 'Impossible. I'm sure he thinks he's the luckiest man in Paris.'

Liliane tilted her head to rest her cheek against my hand. 'I'm so glad you're here. So, *so* glad.'

'Go to him,' I said. 'I'll wait here. And don't be afraid.'

She pulled me into a constricting but fortunately

brief hug. 'I'm not. Not now you're here.'

Liliane tipped her chin up and sashayed towards Jacques. His head turned as though he had caught her scent, and his eyes grew wide, like he had forgotten just how stunning she was. He ended his call and kissed her – lightly at first, and then deeply, as if they were the only people in the bar. He didn't stop touching her – her waist, her neck, his palm sliding down to the small of her back. Liliane pointed over to where I was standing, and I ducked behind the plant. When I peeped through the stems to check on them, Jacques was on his phone again and Liliane was striding over to me.

'He said we could wait for him upstairs,' she said. Her cheeks were pink; her pupils were two large dots. 'He has to make some calls first. Look, I have the key!' She dangled the plastic card in front of me.

'Who is he talking to?' I asked.

'Oh, a patient or someone, I think.'

*His wife, more like.*

Liliane tucked her bag under her arm. 'Shall we go up? He said he's reserved the best room.'

She had no clue that this was the most danger she'd ever faced. The 'best room' in this sumptuous hotel might be her final resting place.

Liliane skipped along the corridor as we searched for the room, calling out the numbers on the doors with ever-increasing delight. She squealed at everything: the stylish lampshades, the ornate handles, the vases spaced at precise intervals that brimmed with artful displays of aromatic flowers.

She paused to sniff a bounteous spray of gardenias and glanced back at me. 'Isn't this fantastic?' She tossed her hair like she was in one of those commercials Diana was always trying to ape. '*And* he said he's left a gift for me on the bed. A gift! Can you believe it?'

'No,' I said. 'I can't.' I stopped at a hulking oak door. 'I think this is it.'

Liliane jumped up and down. 'Wow! How do I …?' She waved the room key around aimlessly, and I had to intervene or else we would've been there all night.

'Let me.' I took the key from her and swiped it across the sensor. A light flashed green and the lock clicked.

'Honestly, Inès,' she said. 'I don't know what I'd do without you.'

'There's no need to say that.'

'No, I mean it.' She clasped my hand and looked into my eyes. 'I know Diana is your best friend, but I hope you consider me a true friend too. I'd never have been brave enough to do this without you.'

Her earnestness sparked a twang of pity. It wasn't her fault that she'd been born so perfect and had lived such a charmed existence. And maybe I *had* helped her; maybe she *wouldn't* have been brave enough to meet Jacques by herself – a distinct possibility, given that she couldn't even manage to open the door to their room.

But then I remembered that the blondes were liars. They loved nothing more than to beguile people, and I wasn't there to fall victim to her deceit. I was there to secure the prize the gargoyle had promised I'd receive when the deed was done.

I turned the handle and pushed open the door.

'After you,' I said.

As she bounced into the room I made sure to hang the do-not-disturb sign on the door handle. This was definitely not a night for interruptions.

The suite was like something from a baroque fairy tale. It had parquet floors, high ceilings with embossed mouldings, and intricate gilt work and textured panels on the walls that I could not resist putting my hand out to touch. The colour scheme was pastel blue, with the pale yellow fabrics of the cushions and the canopy above the bed giving a pleasing contrast. At one end of the suite was a table with several chairs arranged around it, and at the other were a large sofa and two armchairs. Facing the enormous bed were doors leading out onto a balcony, on which there was an additional, smaller table and chairs, where I assumed Jacques had imagined himself breakfasting with Liliane in the morning, the two of them admiring the view as they glowed from their night of unbridled passion.

Liliane cooed over everything, picking up vases, flicking lamps on and off again, examining the elaborate candelabra and staring into the mirrors, before finally flopping into an armchair, panting as if so much opulence had left her breathless.

Just when I thought she might, at last, be lost for words, Liliane sprang up and went to investigate the bathroom. 'Inès,' she squawked, 'you *must* come and see this!'

I ignored her and sat on the bed. The sheets were scattered with rose petals, and positioned between the pillows was a blue box tied with a satin bow. I ran my fingers over it as I listened to Liliane bumbling around in the bathroom, opening cabinets and raving about the toiletries, the plush robes and the softness of the towels. Maybe Christophe would bring me to a luxury hotel when Liliane was gone – when it was I, not she, who was the one. Maybe we would have breakfast together on a terrace. Maybe we would make love on luxurious sheets.

Liliane poked her head around the bathroom door.

'You *have* to look in here,' she said. 'You can see the Eiffel Tower!'

'In a moment.' I held the box out to her. 'I think you should open your gift.'

She shrieked and scuttled towards the bed. 'Oh wow!' She snatched the box and swooned over the name of the designer embossed on the lid. 'I've never had anything from this boutique before.'

'Fillings and dentures must be lucrative,' I said.

Liliane blinked at me, as if it had never occurred to her to question whether her paramour could afford all this extravagance.

'Tell me ...' I leant back on my palms. 'Have you fucked him yet?'

She turned crimson and stared at the carpet, shifting awkwardly from one foot to the other, and I couldn't help but smile.

'You *haven't* ...' I said.

Now the bank-breaking hotel suite, the rose petals and the gift from the fancy boutique all made sense.

I got to my feet. 'I shouldn't be here. This is supposed to be your special night. I'll leave you to it.'

'No!' Liliane looked at me imploringly. 'Please don't go. Not yet. I'm so nervous.' She put a hand to her stomach, as if to calm the butterflies. 'This feeling ... it's wonderful and terrifying at the same time. Will it always be like this?'

'Yes,' I said. 'If it really is love.' I sat down again and nodded at the box. 'Open your gift.'

Slowly, she untied the ribbon. She prised open the lid and gasped as she peeled back the layers of tissue paper.

Inside was a silk scarf – white, with an ochre trim – and as Liliane lifted it out reverently, any lingering doubts I had about Jacques's marital status disappeared. For wives, there were budgets and practicalities, but for mistresses, no expense was spared, and no sum was too extortionate, even for a scrap of fabric with a microscopic logo embroidered on the hem.

'It's so elegant.' Liliane pressed it to her cheek. 'I never dreamt I'd own one of these.'

'Try it on,' I said. 'It will look wonderful on you.'

She moved to the full-length mirror propped up against the wall. 'It's the most amazing gift I've ever received,' she said, for once not enraptured by her own face, but by the fine silk. 'I can't believe it's for me.'

She was mistaken. The scarf wasn't a gift for her, from Jacques. It was for me, from the gargoyle.

I stood behind her. 'Allow me.'

She was stock-still as I took the scarf from her and draped it around her neck.

'It's as if it was made for you,' I said. 'As if it was designed with you in mind.'

'Do you think so?' she said.

'Certainly. The choice could not have been better.'

Liliane twisted to admire herself from every angle. 'Inès?'

'Yes?'

Her eyes met mine in the mirror. 'You said everyone is obsessed with something … What are you obsessed with?'

'Me? Haven't you guessed?'

'No,' she said. 'Tell me. It's been so long since we shared a secret.'

I dismissed her lie – it would be her last – and started tying the scarf into a knot. 'Isn't it obvious?'

She stared at me blankly.

I smiled at her. 'I am obsessed with *you*.'

I spun her round to face me. At first she was puzzled, two furrows appearing between her brows, but then she caught the glint in my eyes and the reptilian part of the brain that concerns itself with danger, with survival, took over. In an instant her expression switched from confusion to terror.

She lunged for the door, but I was too quick. I grabbed her arms and pushed her onto the bed and held her down. Cushions flew onto the floor as she kicked and clawed. She screamed for me to let her go, but her pleas had no effect and her cries barely registered. I was aware only of myself, of my own strength. It was as though my body were made of pure muscle and my heart were made of stone – as though there were two of me, one observing the unfolding obscenity and another carrying it out.

Liliane tried to sit up, and I shoved her onto her back. It was easy; she was light as a feather, and I was a force of nature. Now, all the power was mine.

I climbed onto the mattress and straddled her. I could've crushed her ribcage with the lightest squeeze of my thighs. But that was not how death was supposed to come for her.

I grasped the ends of the scarf in my fists. The noises she made, the sobs, the pleas and the entreaties, were all in vain.

'No one can hear you,' I said.

No one except the gargoyle. It was up by the north tower, watching her writhe and flail, but its assistance, its intervention, was only for me.

She started begging and bargaining, but the things

she offered in exchange for her life were not the things I wanted.

'I want him,' I said. 'Don't you see? *Him.* It will only ever be *him.*'

Her eyes grew even larger as the realisation dawned on her, but it was too late. The good fortune that had blessed Liliane throughout her life was about to desert her.

I tugged the scarf as hard as I could, but merely an ounce of my strength would have sufficed. Her eyes darted wildly in their sockets as she fought for breath. One of her arms flapped towards the telephone on the bedside table; the other scratched at my cheek. It did not stop me. Nothing on earth could stop me.

It seemed to take only a matter of seconds for her legs to stop twitching and her arms to cease thrashing. A matter of seconds, and Liliane was gone.

I gazed down at her. Her skin was mottled, and the whites of her eyes were bloodied by burst vessels. Her tongue, swollen and purple, lolled from the corner of her mouth. But she was still beautiful. Still perfect.

I got off the bed, straightened her dress and smoothed her hair. Her dead eyes stared at me as I kissed my fingertips and pressed them against her lips.

# 11

The Inès who left the hotel suite alone was not the same one who had entered it with Liliane. I was now fractured, disparate. Mired in the horror of the crime I'd committed.

I staggered down the staircase, gripping the handrail, and ducked my head as I crossed the lobby. Jacques was at the reception desk, fussing over some detail or other. He didn't notice me as I passed him, but my hands, which a moment before had been so steady, began to shake. And my legs, which had been strong and powerful, no longer felt capable of taking my weight.

I teetered out onto the street, and the gravity of my actions pressed down harder on me. *I have taken a life.* I had crossed a boundary into a dark hinterland, and there was no route back. I was forever changed, reborn in the gargoyle's image.

I couldn't face boarding the Métro and retracing the steps Liliane and I had taken together. So I decided to walk, hoping that the long trudge home would make my despicable act seem distant. But Paris was more glorious than ever, the lights from the buildings reflecting off the river, and the romance and beauty of the city only exacerbated my own ugliness. At the Quai des Tuileries,

I had to stop and lean against the wall as Liliane's last moments rushed through my mind: how she had struggled and begged, how I had ruthlessly extinguished her existence as easily as snuffing out a flame.

When I reached the academy, my chest was burning and my head was swimming. I took off my shoes before I went through the gates, so the sound of my heels tapping on the cobblestones wouldn't wake anyone. I was grateful that the installation of security cameras was 'pending' on Christophe's long list of promised 'refurbishments'. The only eyes I feared observing me were human ones.

As I tiptoed across the courtyard, I paused and looked up at the dormitory building. The lights in every room were off, but no window appeared darker than Liliane's.

I wanted nothing more than to try to forget what I'd done, to hold Théo close and pretend that nothing had changed – that *I* hadn't changed – but his concerned expression as I entered my room only fuelled the maelstrom of torment inside me.

'Where've you been?' he said, climbing off the bed.

I couldn't meet his eyes. The room spun, and I kept my gaze on the wall, like we did in class when we were twirling, faster and faster.

'Inès?'

My shoes slipped from my grip and the thud as they hit the floor seemed to come from far away.

'Inès, what's happened? What's wrong with you? I

was worried … You've been gone for so long.'

I had no idea what time it was. It might have been midnight, but it might have been noon – I couldn't tell. In the hotel suite, the laws of time hadn't applied.

'Inès, come on. Please.'

Théo gripped my arms, like I had Liliane's. Shortly before I … before I *killed* her.

I shoved Théo away and stumbled into the bathroom. He followed, leaning against the sink as I hunched over the toilet and retched.

'Have you been *drinking*?' he said.

I wiped my mouth and shook my head. I wished I had been drinking. I wished that was the worst of it.

I tore off my clothes and stepped into the shower cubicle. I stood there for a moment, my palms splayed on the cracked tiles, hoping I could wash away my mortal sin.

The tap squeaked in protest as I turned it on, and I yelped as the freezing shower spray hit my skin.

'He keeps promising he'll get the thermostat fixed,' Théo said. 'Your darling *Christophe*. He promises so many things …' He sat on the edge of the bath and folded his arms. 'Where *have* you been? You look terrible.'

'It doesn't matter.' I closed my eyes as the water warmed, but snapped them open as Liliane's face came to me again. 'Tell me what I missed.'

Théo took a cigarette from the top pocket of his shirt and put it between his lips. 'The usual. Hélène masturbating, Diana bragging. Oh, and Veronica was looking for you. She knocked a few times.'

My eyes snapped open. 'She knocked? For me? You didn't answer, did you?'

'Of course not.' He threw me a sulky glare. 'I would never break your precious *rules*. She was very persistent though. You know what she's like.'

'Veronica must have made a mistake.' Or she was up to something. 'What about Christophe? Did he go out?'

Théo exhaled a stream of smoke and watched it drift up to the ceiling. 'Yes. Shortly after you did.'

'Where?'

He shrugged. 'Probably to grovel to his rich sycophants. Who cares?'

'I care, Théo.'

'And how I wish you didn't.'

I turned off the shower. Théo slid the towel from the rail and swaddled me in it.

'You can't scrub it off, you know,' he said.

'Scrub what off?'

'The stain of whatever it is you've done.'

I looked into his eyes and saw Liliane fighting for breath. I saw the evidence that drew an arrow pointing to me: the fingerprints I'd left on the walls, the fibres from my clothes on the yellow sheets, the indent of my heels on the parquet, my skin under her nails.

The white scarf tied around Liliane's neck.

I thought I'd lost the ability to cry long ago – I thought I'd wept the last of my tears in that room underground.

I thought I could contain it, let nothing show, but when I put my head on Théo's shoulder, all the sorrow, the shame and the disgust, came rushing back to me. *Everything* came rushing back to me.

The nuns' voices. Their punishments and their warnings, the things they had called me. Abomination, diabolical, monstrous. Unholy.

*Nothing will become of you, Inès. Nothing.*

# 12

Even after all the crying, and despite the crushing fatigue I felt, I couldn't sleep. Voices and images whirled through my head – a hurricane of noise and pictures. Dawn broke, and I listened to the academy stirring. Floorboards creaked, pipes clanged, toilets flushed and footsteps beat along the corridor as the blondes surfaced from their rooms. I lay still, dreading the moment they discovered that our unlucky thirteen had been reduced to twelve.

'Girls!' Diana's shrill voice penetrated the thin walls. 'We need to get a move on. Veronica? Where is Veronica?'

There was a squeak of hinges, and then Veronica's voice announced, 'Here!' She sounded as if she was panting. 'Bad hair day. Sorry.'

'So you should be,' Diana said. 'Now, let me look at you all.'

'Why?' Veronica said.

'Because,' Diana replied, '*someone* has to make sure we adhere to Christophe's standards.'

They went through this routine every morning before class: sniping at each other over the most inane foolishness. From what I could hear, today seemed to be no exception.

'Roxane,' Diana said, 'what on *earth* is that mark on your leotard?'

'It got dirty,' Roxane replied with a snivel.

'How?' Diana said. 'Did you soil it? That often happens to *babies*, so I understand.'

Déborah and Cécile snickered. Their amusement was as much a part of Roxane's torture as was Diana's goading.

Beside me, Théo's eyelids fluttered. He yawned and rubbed his chin. 'Why are you listening to this stupidity?' he whispered, hooking his leg over mine. 'It's like a play I've heard so often I know every line.'

'Not today.' *Today there's been a change to the script.*

Théo raised his head to give me a quizzical look. I put a finger to my lips to hush him.

'You can't very well go to class like that,' Diana said. 'It looks revolting, not to mention slovenly.'

'But I can't find my other one,' Roxane said.

'Then you must buy more. Do it today. We'll come with you.'

'You will?' Roxane said. 'Why?'

She was wise to be suspicious. The blondes' only motivation for accompanying her would be to ensure that she purchased the ugliest, most ill-fitting garment. The entire thing was a farce anyway – they had probably snuck into her room and hidden her leotards. They thrived on those kinds of spiteful tricks.

'Aren't we going to be late?' Hélène said.

'We can't go downstairs yet,' Diana said. 'Not without all of us present.'

I knew they weren't referring to me. I was never included in this tomfoolery.

'We have to wait for Liliane,' Aurélie said.

'Perhaps she's not coming to class today,' Cécile said.

'I don't want to be late just because she can't be bothered to get out of bed,' Déborah said.

'Me neither.' Hélène sounded distraught. 'He'll expel us if we're late.'

'Will you all be quiet,' Diana scolded. 'Liliane cannot possibly have overslept. Not with this frightful racket you're making. Now, has anyone actually *seen* her this morning?'

There was silence.

'Well?' Diana said, and I pictured her in her schoolmarm pose, tipsy from the taste of authority. 'Has anyone at least knocked for her?'

'We didn't like to,' Élodie said. 'In case she's with Christophe.'

'If she's with Christophe then she won't come to the door, will she?' Cécile said.

'What about if he's in *her* room?' Déborah said. 'Stranger things have happened.'

There was a burst of laughter from Nathalie. 'Not *that* strange.'

'What would you know?' Maëlle said.

'More than *you*,' Nathalie replied.

'Come on, guys.' Veronica's drawl was unmistakable.

'Let's just knock on her door now. Or we'll be late.'

'We *can't* be late,' Hélène said.

'What are you so afraid of?' Françoise said. 'He's hardly going to throw us out for being a few minutes behind schedule.'

'How do you know what he'd do?' Hélène said. 'We must be on time. It's the rules.'

'Don't worry,' Veronica said. 'I got this.'

Feet clomped along the corridor – they had to be Veronica's; for a dancer, she could be so ungainly – and then there was a knock.

'Liliane?' Veronica paused. 'Liliane?'

'Maybe she really is with Christophe,' Aurélie said. 'Maybe she's fallen asleep in his four-poster bed or something.'

'Maybe he's already given her the lead and she doesn't need to bother coming to class any more,' Françoise said.

'He wouldn't just *give* her the lead,' Diana said. 'She has to earn it. Like the rest of us.'

'Liliane!' Veronica banged on the door so hard the wood rattled in the frame.

'She's not with Christophe,' Roxane said.

'It speaks!' Déborah said.

'What are you on about?' Diana asked. 'Have you seen her?'

'No,' Roxane said, 'but I heard him get up. Hours ago. He was definitely alone.'

'What should we do, then?' Élodie chimed in.

'We have to go to class,' Hélène said. '*Now.*'

'I agree,' Diana said. 'There's no point jeopardising our futures for the sake of Liliane's lie-in. She wouldn't do it for us.'

'But what if she's in trouble?' Veronica said. 'Or she's sick? Shouldn't we kick the door down or something?'

'Oh *please*,' Diana said. 'We do not kick down doors here, Veronica.'

'Sure you don't,' Veronica said. 'Instead, you stand outside them and have *conversations* and do absolutely zero. Where's your sense of sisterhood? Of solidarity?'

'This *is* solidarity,' Diana said. 'Come on, girls, let's go.'

Veronica's final protest was smothered by the blondes' stampede to the staircase. A few seconds later, I heard Veronica run off to join them.

As soon as their footsteps faded, I leapt from the bed.

'Where are you going?' Théo said.

I groped on the floor for my clothes. 'If I run down to the studio now, I can have Christophe to myself.'

And if I could just see him, alone, have that sacred time with him, then surely it would purge my guilt. His presence would make me clean.

'What about breakfast?' Théo said.

'I'll skip it.' It wasn't as though I hadn't gone hungry before.

'Inès, you need food. You need sustenance.'

'And you need to go back to your room.' I pulled on

my boots and stuffed a clean towel into my bag. 'Preferably without anyone seeing you.'

'There's no one here now except us,' Théo said. 'And the ghosts.'

'There are no ghosts here, Théo.'

'There are always ghosts. *Always.* And it's not only buildings that are haunted. People are too. You, me … we carry so many ghosts inside us.' He turned onto his side. 'Something is happening here, Inès. Something … something I can't explain. Something bad.'

My blood froze in my veins. 'Here?' I said. 'In the academy?'

'No.' He touched his chest. '*Here.*'

I sat down on the bed. 'Théo, I—'

'I know,' he said. 'You love him. Or so you tell yourself. But I would do anything for you, Inès. For us. You saved me. One day, I'll save you in return.'

I tucked my head onto his shoulder. 'I don't need you to save me.'

'You don't have a choice. That's how love is.'

'This isn't love, Théo.'

'It will be,' he said, lifting his arm to pull me into him. 'You will see.'

# 13

The blondes were not the only residents at the academy who had a morning routine.

Each day, Christophe rose at five and crept downstairs to the studio. In interviews, he'd often remarked that dance was his first love, and throughout his career it had reciprocated his affections, winning him as much acclaim as his acting. But perhaps the critics were right when they pontificated that his best might yet be to come, for alone in that small space, Christophe danced with even more grace and power than he had on Paris's most prestigious stages, as though he'd saved his best performances for when he no longer had an adoring audience.

Or so he thought.

Whenever I could, I'd sneak down after him to watch through the glass pane in the door. My breath would catch in my throat as he glided across the floor. He'd turn, and jump, and raise his arms as if he were reaching to pull heaven upon him; he'd arch his back and kick his legs, his eyes closing as the music carried him away. As he spun and leapt, my heart would take flight with him. The more I watched him, the more I loved him, and I ached for a time when there was no glass between us — when he would see me, *love* me, and there was nothing in the way of us being together.

And now that time had come.

That morning, rather than standing outside and hiding in the shadows, as I always did, I pushed open the door and let myself be seen.

Christophe was lost in motion, spinning and whirling, his eyes shut tight. It took a moment for him to sense that his solitude had been breached, that someone was in the room with him. He paused mid-turn, his eyes opening slowly, like he was awakening from a fugue state, and saw me sitting on one of the chairs opposite the long mirror.

'Inès.' He put his hands on his hips, his chest heaving. 'Keen to make a start?'

'Keen to watch you.'

It was a thrill to tell him something so true, so personal, but my confession elicited little more than an arch of his brows.

'How did you know I was here?' he said.

'Open secret.' One I guarded very carefully.

He reached for the towel hanging from the barre and dabbed at the perspiration on his forehead. 'I'm so rusty these days,' he said. 'And age is not being kind to me.'

Christophe was forty-seven – 'still in his prime', they'd said when he'd retired, lamenting the years of brilliance he had ahead of him. But in our profession, the years were measured using a different scale.

'You are better now than ever,' I said.

'You think so?'

I nodded. 'But you know that, surely.'

Christophe draped the towel around his neck and came to sit beside me. I could smell his sweat, and the woody tang of his cologne. If I shifted my legs, just an inch, our knees would touch. If I moved my arm, just a fraction, it would graze his. My whole body thrummed with desire, and I wondered if it was palpable – if my need for him would give me away.

He inclined his head as he studied me, and I managed to return his scrutiny. Steely blue eyes – cold and calculating, Théo had once remarked. To me, they were warm and inviting.

'You are a curious creature, Inès,' he said. 'I've never been able to figure you out.'

'You always say we should maintain an air of mystery.'

He mused upon this for a second, stroking the stubble on his cheek with his thumb, and then laughed. I had never heard him laugh like that before – deep, throaty. *Hard.* Everything about him was so raw, so masculine, and every word I spoke to him felt like taking a step on a tightrope stretched across a deep precipice. One wrong move and I would be falling, falling …

'Well, you have excelled yourself,' Christophe said. 'There is no one as mysterious as you.' He rose from the chair, his movements as dexterous as when he was dancing. 'Are you keen enough to help me set up for class?'

'Of course,' I said, and Théo's favourite saying drifted

into my mind. *I would do anything for you. Anything.* And I had. For Christophe, I had done the unthinkable. And it had been worth it.

'You know,' he said as we began arranging the chairs into a circle, 'after your audition, I thought about you. You were the one who stayed in my mind. When you entered the room you had this manner about you – an aura. A *force*. And for a while, I …' He put down the chair he was carrying and looked at me. 'I couldn't get you out of my mind. I couldn't think of anything else *but* you.'

Sometimes you wait so long for something, spend so long picturing it, that when it is finally within reach, the tension is unbearable.

'And now?' I said.

'And now …' He nudged the chair with the side of his foot. 'Now I feel I'm getting to know you. There is something about you, something that …'

Christophe lowered his chin to his chest, the way he did when he was evaluating our performance. 'Who would you choose? If you were going to pick the lead. Excluding yourself,' he added as my mouth opened to reply. 'Who would it be?'

'Is this part of the class?'

He chuckled. 'Everything is part of the class, Inès.'

I didn't have to think about it. As before, there was only one real choice.

'Liliane,' I said. 'She's the one who will change everything.'

He became thoughtful. 'Have you told the others about our conversation from the other night?' he asked. 'About the future of the academy?'

'No. I thought it was between us.'

'Yes. Yes, it was. I hope you were not disappointed, Inès.' He placed his palms on my shoulders. 'You have every chance if I change my mind about the lead.'

The warmth of his hands spread through me like lava. Heating me, filling me, giving me new life. It took all my resolve to keep my voice steady.

'Does that mean you've made your decision?' I said.

Christophe peeled his hands away. 'As a matter of fact, yes. I have. I feel I can trust you … Can I?'

'Most definitely,' I said, wanting to add that he could trust *only* me.

He paused for a brief moment, and then shrugged. 'It won't be a secret for much longer anyway. You're right, Liliane *will* change everything. She'll be the lead in the showcase – my star, the face of my academy. It could only be Liliane. Without her …' He spread his arms and let them drop to his sides. 'Without her, I'd have to start from scratch.'

'And that would be a travesty.'

'It would be a *disaster*,' he said. 'I'm walking a very fine line between success and failure. My future depends on all of you just as much as yours depend on me.'

I visualised the satisfaction on Liliane's face as Christophe announced his choice, and then I remembered she was dead. My throat closed up, as if I were the one being choked. I coughed and stared at my hands.

'What is it?' he said. 'Is there something I should know? Inès?'

*You should know that I love you. That I worship you. You should know that Liliane is dead and I killed her. For you. For us, and the future we could have together.*

I took a deep breath and released it slowly. 'Liliane is the perfect choice.' As she had been for me.

He nodded, and I knew this was part of the class too.

'I'm glad we had this conversation,' he said. 'We don't get much time to talk, but I feel that if we did, if we had more opportunities to—'

We were on uncharted territory, on the cusp of a seismic shift in our relationship. But then the door burst open and Veronica barged in and ruined everything.

'Oh, sorry,' she said, although there was nothing apologetic about the way she stood in the doorway, goggling at us. 'Didn't realise you guys were having a private conversation. I can come back …?'

'No, no,' Christophe said, motioning for her to enter. 'Come in and warm up. Inès and I were just getting things ready. Where are the others?'

'Finishing breakfast,' she said, stomping into the studio and dropping her bag in the corner. 'I had a smoothie. Easier to digest. Have you tried the kale and spinach one, Inès? It's a-*mazing*.'

She unzipped her hoodie and I turned my back

to pull off my boots, but she kept yammering about superfoods and protein shakes. It was almost a relief when the rest of the blondes trickled in, polluting the room with the floral stench of the pink-bottled deodorant they all used (not, I noted, the kind once advertised by Veronica). They dumped their bags next to hers and continued their vacuous chatter. As Françoise and Nathalie started bickering about whose hips were the most flexible, Christophe clapped his hands.

'Enough,' he said. 'Time to focus.'

The hubbub ceased, and it became quiet enough to hear the mice scrabbling about beneath the floorboards. Christophe scanned the blondes' faces, and I noted his dismay when he saw that his favourite student, his 'star', was absent.

'Where is Liliane?' he snapped.

The resulting silence made my ears buzz.

'Well?' Christophe's gaze settled on Diana. 'Where is she?'

'No idea,' she replied. 'We waited *ages* for her. We knocked on her door and everything, didn't we?'

The blondes murmured in agreement, except for Veronica, who glared at her.

'Maybe Inès knows,' Maëlle said.

I was doing some stretches to warm up, and I froze as, unbidden, Liliane's corpse flashed into my mind.

'Why would I know?' I asked.

'Someone must know,' Christophe said. 'She wouldn't

just fail to come to class.'

'Maybe she's eloped,' Élodie said. 'With her lover.'

'She hasn't *got* a lover,' Nathalie said. 'That's just a rumour.'

'Maybe the ghost has taken her,' Roxane mumbled.

'Maybe the ghost *is* her lover,' Françoise said. 'Like in that book.'

'Which book?' Déborah said.

Diana tapped her foot. 'There is no ghost. And there is no lover.'

'She has to be somewhere,' Christophe said. 'She can't have disappeared.'

Just as they were turning to me again, Théo sloped into the studio. His hair was even more tousled than usual, and his shirt was untucked, his unbuttoned cuffs sticking out of the sleeves of his blazer. He looked like he'd just got out of bed. I hoped it was not obvious that the bed in question was mine.

'Sorry,' he muttered. 'I overslept.'

Christophe eyed him with patent displeasure. 'Evidently.'

Théo kept his head down as he took his seat behind the piano. He positioned himself on the stool and began arranging his music sheets.

'Have you seen Liliane?' Christophe said.

It took Théo a few moments to realise Christophe was addressing him.

'No,' he said quietly.

'We should start without her,' Diana said.

'Maybe she has an appointment at the doctor's and didn't want to tell anyone,' Aurélie said.

'Maybe she's pregnant!' Cécile said.

'Or maybe,' Maëlle said, 'she—'

I was relieved when Christophe interrupted.

'I'm sure Liliane will arrive very soon,' he said. 'You should be taking advantage of this chance to get ahead.'

His appeal to their competitive natures took effect instantly. The blondes stood straighter; Maëlle tied her hair into a neater bun, and Diana, Françoise and Veronica jostled for prime position at the front of the class, leaving Roxane and Hélène to drift to the back.

Théo regarded me over the top of the piano, his eyebrows raised questioningly. I glanced away from him.

'Right,' Christophe said. 'Let's begin where we left off yesterday.' He turned to Théo. 'If you would, please.'

Théo started to play, and I closed my eyes as the first bars of the piece we'd been practising for weeks filled the studio. I kept them closed as I danced, letting the music lift me out of the studio, out of the academy and high above the Paris rooftops. I was light and lithe; I didn't need to think about how and when to move – it came instinctively. Christophe's instruction was an incantation, and I responded to it like a snake to a charmer. I wove into the gap where Liliane would usually be and danced right under his nose. Now, at last, he would *see* me. He would understand that it was all for him.

The extra space Liliane's absence provided did not appear to be working so well for everyone else. The blondes seemed disorientated, and where I was free and fluid, they were uncoordinated and maladroit. Christophe chided them for their poor concentration, but he was just as distracted, his attention frequently straying to the door. As the lesson went on with no sign of Liliane, his face became etched with worry. I wondered how much time he'd allow to elapse before he started asking questions again. Before he began to panic.

In the end, there was no need for further inquiry. Events took care of themselves.

When the class was into its second hour, Christophe called a halt to proceedings and posed the question yet again.

'Are you *sure* no one has seen Liliane?' he said.

A second later, as if in response, the intercom buzzed.

Théo took his hands from the piano keys. The blondes' feet stilled and they stared at each other, perplexed by the disruption. Other than potential benefactors and patrons, the academy did not receive many visitors, and never during class unless they had been invited to observe a lesson.

The intercom buzzed again.

Christophe went to the panel of buttons by the door and pressed one. 'Yes?'

A male voice answered. 'Mr Leriche?'

'Yes?' Christophe said warily.

'It's the police. We need to speak to you urgently.'

'Police?' Christophe's wariness became alarm. 'What for?'

'Sir, please let us in.'

The blondes swapped glances, clearly wondering what was going on.

I had no need to wonder. The police had come because they knew. They had found the reams of evidence I'd left behind, and they'd come to arrest me. I had put my faith in a gargoyle, a thing that could not be real, and because of it I'd committed a heinous crime. And now I was to face the consequences.

Christophe collected himself before he cleared his throat and said, 'Come in. First door at the end.' His hand quivered as he pressed the button to allow the officers to enter.

'Should we leave, Mr Leriche?' Nathalie said.

Christophe shook his head. 'I have nothing to hide from you. We should have no secrets from each other.'

'I bet this is about Liliane,' Élodie said. 'I *knew* she had run off with her lover.'

'Will you shut up about that?' Aurélie said.

'Yes,' Diana said. 'I'm so sick of those puerile rumours.'

'They are not rumours,' Françoise said. 'She definitely has someone.'

On and on they went, talking themselves round in the same circles. Christophe paced alongside the mirror, his hands on his head, and I prepared what I would say. I wouldn't bother with a defence, for there wasn't one I could offer. I couldn't tell them about the gargoyle, not only because they'd never believe me but because I wasn't sure I believed it myself.

The police officers entered the studio – two grizzled, thickset men, one notably taller than his colleague. Christophe darted over to them and shook their hands.

'How can I help you, gentlemen?' Christophe said. 'Although, actually, I am hoping you can help me … One of my students has not yet arrived for class. I know she hasn't been gone long enough to be considered a missing person, but it is unusual for her not to be here.'

One of the officers coughed. The other, the taller of the two, stepped forward and said, 'Monsieur Leriche, I'm afraid we have some upsetting news. Perhaps we could go somewhere private …?'

Christophe rattled through the usual spiel about how we were a family, a collective, and how if something had happened then we should hear it together. The officers did not appear entirely comfortable with this, but reluctantly complied.

They were more sensitive than their gruff exteriors suggested. They broke the news gently, choosing their words with care. But there was no sanitised way to say that Liliane had been found dead in a hotel suite.

It took a few moments for it to penetrate. Then Françoise let out a screech so loud I thought the mirrors might crack. Hélène swayed and covered her mouth with her hand, as if she was about to vomit. Déborah howled and clung to Cécile. Veronica stood still, her kohl-rimmed eyes like saucers. Roxane keened and rocked back and forth. Diana was rendered mute, capable only of gawking at the officers in astonishment.

Christophe's face turned so pale it was almost grey. I'd never seen him so stricken – not even when he was on-stage, playing a father who'd lost a daughter. He shook himself and went to Françoise, who was shivering from head to toe, and curled an arm around her shoulders. She crumpled into him, sobbing on his shirt and saying, 'No, oh no, no!' over and over again.

Christophe signalled to Maëlle. 'Take Françoise upstairs,' he said. 'And Roxane.'

Roxane was now catatonic, her eyes glassy. Maëlle took her hand and tried to pull her towards the staircase, but she was so inert that Aurélie and Élodie had to come and assist.

Christophe waited until they had gone before speaking again.

'She's dead? Liliane is dead?' He looked as if he was about to faint. 'What … *How?*'

'I'm afraid we can't disclose that detail at this point,' the taller officer said. 'But we have opened a murder investigation.'

'Murder?' Christophe almost bellowed the word, and Déborah howled again.

'I don't …' Christophe screwed his eyes shut and pinched the bridge of his nose. 'Do you have any suspects?'

'We do,' the shorter man said.

I readied myself, certain they were about to mention how a woman matching my description had been seen entering the hotel with Liliane. I waited for them to list the witnesses who saw us on the Métro, the testimony of the doorman and the concierge, and the innumerable fingerprints found in the room.

My heart knocked against my ribcage as the shorter officer took a photo from his inside pocket and held it in front of Christophe. 'Do you recognise this individual?'

Christophe took the picture and studied it. 'No.'

'Perhaps we could ask your students?' the taller officer said tentatively, as though he were anticipating that his request would be denied.

But Christophe simply nodded and said, 'Go ahead.' His shock was evident, like he, too, wanted to fall to his knees and sob.

The photograph was passed among the blondes. Each shook their head as they glanced at it.

'You should ask Inès,' Nathalie said. 'She and Liliane were very close.'

'What?' I said. 'I don't think—'

The two police officers came and stood on either side of me. They smelled of menthol and cigarette smoke.

'You were her best friend?' the shorter one said.

'Not at all,' I said. 'I hardly knew her.'

He thrust the photograph at me. 'Do you know this person?'

I was sure it was a trick, and I almost cracked and admitted everything rather than be confronted with a picture of my own face. But I forced myself to look, and there I saw not my miserable countenance but that of the dentist — Jacques.

He was wearing the same grey suit, only now the fabric was wrinkled, and there was blood on his collar. There was a scratch on his right cheek, and his lips were parted in what appeared to be disbelief, as if he had only realised in the instant the photo was taken that the price of his night with Liliane might be higher than he could ever have estimated.

I tried to hide my relief as I gave the photograph back to the officer. 'I don't know him.'

'Are you sure?' he said. 'Do you want to take another look?'

I did, but only to make sure I wasn't hallucinating.

There was no mistaking it: it was Jacques, Liliane's first, and last, love.

'I have no idea who he is,' I said. 'Is he the killer?'

'He is a suspect,' the taller one said. 'Although, if it reassures you, there's a lot of evidence against him.'

'Really?' I asked, hoping my incredulity was not obvious. 'Like what?'

'Forensics, mostly. Prints, fibres, blood, that sort of thing. We found traces of her skin under his nails.'

'She fought him, then.'

'She fought the *suspect*.'

'But you're not looking for anyone else.'

'Not at this stage.'

I let it sink in: the 'evidence', the unusual speed of the investigation and the fact that, so far, my name didn't seem to have been linked to the crime.

The shorter officer tucked the photograph into his pocket. 'Did she have a boyfriend?'

I pretended to think about it. 'Possibly. She was very secretive.'

'And did she mention she was going out last night?'

'No. But she wouldn't have confided in me. As I said, I hardly knew her.'

'*What?*' Diana said. 'You and Liliane—'

'Diana, please,' Christophe said. 'Let the police talk to Inès.'

The officer nodded his gratitude. 'We understand your desire to protect your friend,' he said. 'But if you know something – anything – you must tell us.'

'I don't,' I said. 'Really.'

'Did you see her leave the academy yesterday evening?'

'No.'

The other man took out his notebook. 'May I ask where you were last night?'

'In my room,' I said. 'All night. I saw nothing. No one.'

'Nothing at all?'

'No,' I said.

Théo stared at me over the top of the piano. I did not dare to meet his eyes.

# 14

Classes were suspended. Christophe retreated to his room, and in the days that followed we caught only fleeting glimpses of him, when he was forced out of seclusion to give statements to the authorities and answer routine enquiries. He didn't respond to the hordes of press who were camped outside shouting questions at the closed gates, nor did he speak to us, other than to suggest we go home to be with our families. None of the blondes – not even Roxane – elected to do so. On the contrary: not one of them ventured further than the courtyard, as if they shared Christophe's instinct to isolate from the rest of the world. Instead, as the grisly details of Liliane's death began to trickle out, the blondes piled into each other's rooms to analyse the tragedy from every conceivable angle.

'You'd think they'd have grown tired of dissecting it by now,' I said to Théo as we sat on wicker chairs in a cheap brasserie the blondes would never frequent, even if they hadn't chosen to cloister themselves inside the academy.

'Why?' Théo said. 'It's only been a week. Their friend was murdered. Her death was brutal, and sudden. That's a lot to process, don't you think?'

'Liliane wasn't their friend. She wasn't anyone's "friend".'

He looked at me. 'She was *your* friend.'

'You've become as insane as them.' I touched the back of my hand to his forehead. 'Or perhaps you're coming down with flu and it's made you delirious.'

He swiped my hand away. 'Are we going to talk about it now, Inès?'

'We are talking about it. We hardly talk about anything else.'

Théo shook his head. 'We've talked *around* it, as if it's something that's happened to strangers in some distant place. But we haven't addressed the most glaring question of all.'

'Which is?'

'Which is …' His gaze focused on me. 'Why did you lie to the police about where you were?'

'Because it's irrelevant,' I said. 'And anyway, the police have their suspect. What difference would it have made if I'd told them where I was?'

'Why can't you tell me?' he said.

For a brief moment, I forgot my awful deed and the reason behind it. The beseeching look in Théo's eyes made me want to tell him everything. To beg him to forgive me, absolve me. But it could not happen. Would never happen. And so I told him what I sensed he'd never believe.

'I was nowhere,' I said.

Lying to him felt wrong, but the truth had to stay

hidden. I had to protect him. Not just from the atrocity I had perpetrated but also from the source that had inspired it.

The enormity of the blondes' grief was disturbing. They shuffled around the dormitory like zombies, their pallid faces devoid of make-up, their hair limp and greasy. At Aurélie's urging, they took to wearing black, and this symbolic gesture seemed to plant a seed in their minds, and mourning became a creative exercise.

They sketched pictures of Liliane; they crafted collages and posters. They wrote poems dedicated to her, detailing how talented she was and how much she meant to them. It was hard to keep up with their fevered outpourings, but I forced myself to go along with it, if only to ensure that my plan – the gargoyle's plan – really had worked and I was not under suspicion.

I joined them as they gathered one afternoon to discuss what they could do next. It was a miserable, wet day, and the rain hammering against the window and the dreary skies matched the blondes' moods as they sprawled on the pink cushions and beanbags in Françoise's room. The ponderous quiet was broken by the occasional sniffle from Roxane and sighs from Élodie. Déborah laid her head on Cécile's shoulder, and Diana twisted a strand of frizzy hair around her index finger as she gazed vacantly at the film posters Françoise had tacked to the walls.

It was jarring to be that close to them – to be there,

among them, but not one of them. Though the blondes were wan, subdued by their sorrow, this was still a viper's nest, and I was careful not to let my guard slip.

'We could raise money in Liliane's name,' Maëlle said. 'For charity. One close to her heart.'

The idea was so ridiculous I struggled to contain my laughter. The only thing Liliane held close to her heart was herself.

'Or …' Hélène said, her cheeks reddening as the others turned towards her, 'we could lay a wreath.'

Veronica pounced on this suggestion. 'Yes!' she said, snapping her fingers. 'We could go to the flower market. Pick out something super special. We should ask Christophe to come with us. He'd want to be a part of it, and he ought to have a say in which flowers we choose. After all, it's his academy.'

'We are quite aware of that,' Diana said.

'Well, then.' Veronica got up from her chair and moved to the door. 'I'm going to ask him.'

'Right now?' Hélène said, with a note of panic.

'Yes, *now*. Why not?'

'You can't just interrupt him,' Françoise said. 'We should wait until he's ready to talk.'

Veronica put her hands on her hips. 'He might never be ready. So it's up to us to show some maturity. He's obviously in pain, right? We should help. Reach out to him.'

'We simply *cannot* intrude like that,' Diana said.

'Christophe is grieving too. I would imagine he's probably even more upset than we are.'

'Liliane *was* his favourite,' Déborah said with a smirk, and Cécile tittered in agreement.

'We shouldn't talk about Liliane like this,' Hélène said. 'It's not right.'

'Why not?' Nathalie said. 'She can't hear us.'

'Maybe she can,' Roxane said. 'Maybe she's one of the ghosts now.'

'Will you shut up about bloody ghosts?' Diana said. 'Will you all just shut up about *everything*?'

Roxane shrank back, chastened.

'What do you think?'

It took me a second to realise Diana was talking to me.

'*Me?*' I was baffled at being consulted on this when they never asked my opinion about anything. 'Why are you asking me?'

Diana frowned. 'Pardon? Because you know about these things. About all things.'

Élodie gave another sigh, one apparently exaggerated for Diana's benefit. 'Are we going to buy these flowers or not?'

'We are,' Veronica said. 'And we'll do it *with* Christophe.'

With that, she flounced out of the room, leaving Diana fuming and the rest of the blondes stewing in their disquiet. They all stared at me, as if they were expecting me to intervene. I slunk back against the wall, keeping my eyes on Françoise's sparkly rug. Not one of them uttered another word until Veronica returned.

'Well?' Diana said as the door opened. 'What did he say? Tell us!'

'It was awful,' Veronica said. Her gusto had vanished, and she collapsed onto the bed as if she were drained by the whole encounter. 'He was so … *sad*.'

'Of course he was *sad*,' Diana said. 'What did you expect? Pirouettes? Cartwheels?'

Veronica contemplated the glow-in-the-dark stars Françoise had glued to the ceiling. 'Oh God, he's a mess. He's always so strong, you know? He always has the answer. But now he seems … *broken*.'

'We're all broken,' Aurélie said.

'And no one has the answer for something like this,' Maëlle added.

'So he's not coming with us, then?' Diana said.

'He said he couldn't,' Veronica said. 'He looked *terrible*. He hasn't shaved or anything – for days, it seems like – and his eyes were all red and puffy. He gave me this.' She uncurled her fist and a few tattered banknotes fell out. 'He said he trusts us to choose something appropriate.'

Nathalie snatched the money and held it up. 'Is that it? *That's* his contribution?'

Even knowing Christophe's despair, they still did not have it in them to show some gratitude.

Veronica, having now appointed herself as the group's

official bereavement coordinator, organised a collection. I was reluctant to contribute, not only because I couldn't afford to be generous but because of the obvious hypocrisy (not that the issue of hypocrisy appeared to bother the blondes, none of whom had particularly cared for Liliane when she was alive). On balance, though, I decided it was better not to draw undue attention to myself, and I added what little I could spare to the pool of cash.

As promised, Veronica went to the flower market and purchased a large and inevitably garish wreath. Together, the blondes laid it outside the academy gates, and when several members of the public bolstered their display with bouquets and teddy bears, it inflamed their need to demonstrate their grief.

They left flowers outside Liliane's room, and beneath the barre in the studio. They drew pages of hearts and pasted them onto the walls. They stuck one of her headshots on the noticeboard in the library and scattered rose petals in the courtyard. They were discussing releasing a dove in her honour when Christophe finally ventured out of his room and ordered them to stop.

He bore no resemblance to the nervous wreck Veronica had described. He had obviously not shaved in some time, and yes, his hair was longer than usual and appeared dry and wiry, but he was still handsome. Still the same god I had worshipped for so long.

'You have to stop this,' he told them. 'It's not helping anyone.'

'It's helping *us*,' Maëlle said, but only after he had disappeared back into his room and locked himself in again.

Liliane's parents came to the academy. I had expected them to be older versions of her, but there was nothing reminiscent of their daughter about them. Her mother was a petite woman with lank hair and pudgy features, and her father had a stoop and a large domed forehead that was made more conspicuous by the lopsided toupee he wore. It was as if Liliane had been gifted to them by beings from another planet.

Christophe managed to compose himself enough to meet with them, and I watched from my window as they huddled in the courtyard, wiping their eyes as they surveyed the array of tributes.

With no body to bury until the police were willing to release it, her parents did not stay in Paris long, allowing Christophe to recede once more into his solitude and the blondes to recommence their conjecture.

As well as memorialising Liliane, the blondes became obsessed with Jacques Robineau. They devoured the numerous reports about him, all of which presented a scathing account of his failing dental practice, precarious financial situation and gambling debts. They spent hours scrutinising the photographs of him, fascinated by how such an ordinary-looking man could commit such an atrocious crime. Over breakfast one morning in the rather ambitiously named 'dining hall', the blondes examined the latest images of Jacques, which a journalist had uncovered through sources she was 'not at liberty to disclose'. Here, Jacques was scowling and sinister, and looked much older than he did in real life.

'Forty-five!' Élodie said. The blondes were appalled and aroused by Jacques's age.

'More than twice her age,' Veronica said. 'A father figure.'

'I bet he was good in bed,' Déborah said.

'Age does not equate to expertise,' Françoise said.

'Not that you would know,' Nathalie said.

'Neither would you,' Cécile sniped.

'I think it's romantic,' Roxane said.

Maëlle almost spat out her coffee. 'What, being strangled with a scarf?'

'At least it was an Hermès scarf,' Françoise said. 'Better that than a nasty tie.'

'Or a piece of old rope,' Aurélie said.

Hélène shuddered and put a hand to her throat. 'Don't talk about it like that.'

I helped myself to another hunk of bread, wishing they wouldn't talk about it in any manner.

'I think it's *disgusting*,' Diana said. 'He's a filthy old pervert.'

'You're just jealous because you don't have an older lover of your own,' Nathalie said.

'Or *any* lover,' Françoise added.

But I could tell that what piqued Diana was that Liliane's beautiful face was now everywhere. She was eulogised almost daily by the press and had become a symbol of stolen potential – a reminder of the fragility of youth and how easily it could be defiled. Death had granted her wish: Liliane was famous, her name known to everyone. A few journalists even began calling her 'The Angel of Paris'.

Jacques Robineau's legacy was less flattering.

It turned out that he was indeed married, and had four children, the oldest not that much younger than Liliane. It should've bothered me that his offspring would grow up with a killer for a father, but after days of hearing nothing but the story of this 'tragedy', I had become numb to it, and my actions seemed to have less and less to do with me. Liliane's murder and her death were two distinct things, one of which I was responsible for and one I wasn't.

The catalogue of evidence against Robineau was extensive and, they said, 'conclusive'. His sentence was expected to be lengthy, and the public clamoured for the harshest possible punishment – some called for the return of the guillotine.

Robineau's wife vowed to stand by him, but was photographed moving out of their home in the suburbs just days after his arrest. Despite this betrayal, Robineau continued to proclaim his innocence.

I was probably the only person in France who believed him.

# 15

The hiatus from classes, and the absence of the routine that had ordered our days, made the blondes supine and listless. They whiled away hours lounging in the dormitory corridor, their limbs slack and idle. Diana had tried to rouse them from their torpor, but she was too discombobulated to exert any influence. Thus it was left to Veronica to rally them. She encouraged them to do some light practice to keep their muscles strong, and to take walks to help ease their minds, but her efforts came to nothing. The blondes preferred to wallow in melancholy, and the only activity that stirred any real enthusiasm was reliving the trauma of their loss.

Fighting a losing battle against their lassitude, Veronica vowed to 'take ownership of the situation'. She declared that the best thing for everyone was for the academy to get back to something close to normal, and the key to this, she told us, was Christophe. And so she decided to install herself as his confidante.

She went about fulfilling her role with typical brashness and zeal. She brought him fresh bread from the bakery, handmade truffles from the chocolatier and the finest cheeses from the delicatessen. She'd knock on his door 'just to say hi', and eventually, to my horror, he invited her in.

'How is he?' the blondes asked when she returned, desperate for news on his condition.

'Still pretty bad,' she told them. 'He looks like he hasn't slept in forever.'

'He probably hasn't,' Diana snapped.

Although it was edifying to watch Diana simmering with resentment as Veronica's stature rose within the group, I shared her frustration. *I* was the one Christophe trusted; *I* was the one he confided in, and I had patiently borne the agony of not being able to see him, or hear his voice, believing that he would come to me when the time was right. But Veronica was behaving as though she knew him better than anyone else.

As the days rolled on, the periods of time she spent in his room grew longer – first mere minutes, then hours at a time. Her latest visit lasted a whole afternoon – I was counting each excruciating second – and the blondes were desperate to find out how it had gone. For them, the snippets of information Veronica gleaned were like valuable treasures to be hoarded and curated. Even though it pained me to hear them, I had begun to rely on these updates too.

As the blondes walked across the courtyard to the library, not to study but to pick over the most recent news, Théo and I followed. We kept a distance close enough to eavesdrop but far enough that we remained unnoticed.

'Does he ever mention Liliane?' Roxane spoke her name in a whisper.

'Only occasionally,' Veronica said. 'He's really depressed. It's like he's too sad to even mention her.'

'What does he say?' Maëlle asked. 'Is he racked with guilt? Does he blame himself?'

'Why would he blame himself?' Hélène said. 'He didn't kill her. That *monster* did.'

'Christophe feels responsible,' Veronica said. 'He's our custodian.'

'He is our teacher,' Nathalie said. 'That is *all*.'

'Assuming he ever teaches again,' Déborah said.

'Of course he will,' Veronica said. 'A brilliant man like him can't *not* teach.'

Françoise shook her head. 'That doesn't even make sense.'

'Liliane's death has sent him completely mad,' Diana said. 'It's the only explanation.'

'The only explanation,' Veronica said, 'is that he is a genius.'

'What would *you* know about such things?' Maëlle said.

Veronica's smile was revoltingly smug. 'More than you think. Christophe is an awesome teacher and a wonderful guy. He knows what's best for the academy, and what's best for us. We have to have faith in him.'

As Veronica crowed about Christophe, Théo looked at me, and I knew what he was thinking.

It was as though Veronica was reciting from a script I'd written. She had stolen all my lines.

Seventeen long days after Liliane's death – or her murder, depending on how you chose to view it – Christophe emerged from his room, clean-shaven and dressed in tailored trousers and a light blue shirt, and announced that classes were to resume immediately.

His metamorphosis revived the blondes. They went from languid to hyperactive, laughing and joking as they skittered around, and suddenly the academy was buzzing again. Even Théo was intrigued by the transformation.

'The way Veronica described it,' he said as we met for a quick cigarette in our secluded spot in the courtyard, 'it sounded like your beloved Christophe Leriche had something of a breakdown.'

'She's exaggerating,' I said. 'As always.'

'She's become close to him. And he's become dependent on her.'

'Of course he hasn't. She's exploiting Christophe's vulnerable state. Trying to use Liliane's death to her advantage.'

Théo eyed me carefully. 'What about you?'

I flicked ash onto the ground. 'What about me?'

'Well,' he said, 'you can't deny that it's better for you now Liliane isn't around. Whoever killed her did you a great service. And the academy has never had so much publicity.'

In that, he was correct. In the days after Liliane's demise, several prominent Paris figures had made hefty donations, and the academy had received a flurry of interest from potential investors. According to Veronica, who had taken it upon herself to field these enquiries, even Justine Deschamps had made time to offer her personal condolences to Christophe.

'Things have to move on,' I said, avoiding his eyes. 'It's just how it is.'

Théo stared at me until I met his gaze. 'But what if they don't move on in the way you want? What then?'

Above us, there was a loud thump. A pigeon had crashed into one of the dormitory windows – Veronica's, I thought – mistakenly seeing a clear path when, instead, there was an obstacle blocking its route.

If the loss of Liliane had diminished Christophe in some way, it was evident that he was now renewed, and reenergised.

'The academy has been wounded,' he said when we reconvened in the studio. 'Wounded, but not fatally. We will heal.' He paced inside the circle we had formed around him, his hands clasped loosely behind his back. The blondes were rapt, their lips parted in awe.

Christophe cast his eyes over them. 'We are carrying a terrible pain, every one of us,' he said. 'But our grief can make us stronger. *Better.* It can bring us closer together.'

Overcome with emotion, Roxane wept. Hélène's eyes,

too, were moist with tears. Cécile cheered, while Déborah put her fingers in her mouth and whistled. Françoise and Aurélie burst into applause. Not to be outdone, Diana joined in, clapping harder and louder than anyone else.

Christophe was focused on Veronica. She grinned proudly at him, and as he nodded at her, I wondered if those were her words he had spoken – if *she* had coached him.

He raised his palm and the jubilation dwindled gradually – no one wanted to be the first to end the celebrations. Christophe motioned for us to sit, and one by one we settled onto our chairs. Théo rested his forehead on the top of the piano and pretended to drift off to sleep.

'During this horrendous time, I have asked myself many questions,' Christophe said. 'I have been torturing myself, agonising over why it happened, why our dearest, treasured Liliane …'

Christophe's voice seemed to ebb away as my hands began to tingle. My fingernails dug crescents into my palms, as if I were once again tugging the white scarf around Liliane's neck, watching the light fade from her eyes as the breath left her lungs.

'I have no answers to these questions,' he said. 'No explanation as to why we must endure this terrible loss, this sadness that we each feel so acutely. However, I've come to realise that the most crucial question we must ask ourselves is not the one that causes us further hurt but the one that empowers us. We must ask, how?' He put his hands on his hips. '*How* do we start again?'

There was a ripple of anticipation and a sharp intake of breath from the blondes. They murmured to each other excitedly, but I kept my eyes on Christophe.

'I must tell you,' he continued, 'Liliane was to play the lead in the showcase.'

Despite the circumstances, the blondes couldn't suppress their disapproval, and I waited for Christophe to look at me, to acknowledge that we had shared this secret and that I had kept his confidence – that I, not Veronica, was the one he could rely on. But he did not glance in my direction.

Diana's hand shot up. 'I can do it.' She thrust out her chin. 'I can play the role much better than Liliane ever could.'

Aurélie and Hélène gaped at her. Roxane cowered, as if she were trying to curl into a ball to escape the scene.

'She has *no* shame,' Françoise whispered to Nathalie, who nodded in agreement.

Belatedly registering her faux pas, Diana blushed as she tried to backtrack. 'What I *meant* was,' she said, with much less bluster, 'may Liliane rest in peace and everything, but I could do it better. I really think I could.'

A muscle pulsed in Christophe's jaw. 'The role has been rewritten,' he said, and I was pleased to see a hint of distaste on his face. 'I have made some fundamental changes to the script. New scenes, new lines.'

'Rewritten?' Diana said. 'I liked the old script.'

'Good. But you will like this one better. So, let's get started.'

The blondes were flummoxed, their excitement replaced by apprehension.

'What, *now*?' Diana said. 'Aren't you going to tell us more?'

'What changes?' Françoise said.

'What new scenes?' Maëlle said.

'Will there be new choreography?' Nathalie said.

Their questions rained down like hailstones, each whinier than the last. Christophe rubbed his brow and gave a weary sigh.

'The academy is to have a change in direction,' he said.

'Will there be another selection process?' Déborah asked.

Hélène blanched. 'Will we need to audition again?'

'Your places at the academy are secure,' Christophe said. 'Each of you is here because you deserve to be. Because you have potential.'

The blondes' relief was manifest. Maëlle blew out her cheeks and exhaled deeply, Aurélie fanned herself with her hands, and Déborah and Cécile high-fived each other. I knew – because I knew *him* – that the reprieve from their anxieties was not to last.

'However,' Christophe said, 'there *will* be auditions, although not the kind you are used to. And they have already begun. From this moment onwards, every single thing you do, every aspect of your conduct, from how you tie your shoes to how you make your beds, will be part of the assessment.'

Roxane subtly lowered her hands to cover the stain on her leotard.

'I don't understand,' Aurélie said. 'What does making our beds have to do with it?'

'Don't pretend you actually make yours,' Cécile said with a giggle.

'If I were casting right now, Cécile,' Christophe said, 'your name would be the very last on the list.'

Cécile's amusement vanished as her face dropped. She did not utter another word for the remainder of the class.

'The greatest art,' Christophe said, 'defies convention. It sets its own mould. Starts its own trend. And therefore, for our showcase, I am looking for something different. Some*one* different. I am seeking a lead who can excite people – who can excite *me*. A lead with flaws, with mystery. A lead who is not afraid to be ugly. No, more than that … who *wants* to be ugly. Who knows the dark side of herself and embraces it. Who *feels* it inside her.'

I felt a shiver of triumph. Christophe must have reflected on the conversation we'd had the night I'd gone to his room and realised it was me that he wanted – me that he *needed*. And now he was describing me so clearly he may as well have mentioned me by name. I closed my eyes and thanked the gargoyle for helping me to get what

I wanted, for giving me the courage to take those 'extra measures'.

Diana piped up again. 'Do you have any tips on how we can prepare? Any hints on what we can do to get in character?'

'She is not a *character*,' Christophe said. 'She is a person. She is *real*. You cannot prepare. Either you are her, or you are not. It's as simple as that.'

Diana stuck out her bottom lip and her forehead creased into a deep frown. How satisfying it would be, I thought, to lean over and tell her not to bother. She was not the one Christophe had described, and she wasn't the one he wanted – none of them were. I was. *Me*.

'So,' Christophe said. 'Does everyone understand?'

They nodded to assure him that, yes, they did – I merely smiled – but it was obvious that the blondes had never been more confused. They couldn't comprehend what he was seeking, and even if they plumbed the depths of their souls, they would never find it inside them. But it was in me, and all the blondes had to do if they truly wanted to see that darkness, if they really wanted to 'prepare', was to turn around and look into my eyes.

'I want to make this the best showcase Paris has ever seen,' Christophe said. 'The *best*.' He nodded at Théo. 'Start with the first six bars.'

Théo took a quick glance at me and started to play. I went to step into Liliane's space, but Veronica was quicker. She barged past me and positioned herself in front of

Christophe. She danced with her head held high, as if she believed she was in with a chance.

'Excellent, Veronica,' Christophe said. 'Excellent. Everyone, watch what Veronica is doing, how she's moving. This is what I want. *This.*'

A new fear gnawed at me. I told myself there was no need to fret – that I was home free, that my time had come. And as for Veronica, well, she was just as clueless as the others.

Never show your hand, Christophe had told us. But it was different when, at long last, you held all the cards.

# 16

This time, I was prepared. I planned what I was going to say; I washed my hair and styled it so that it hung in a sleek sheet. I applied moisturiser and my boldest make-up; I put on my favourite dress. This time, I was ready.

I knocked once, then twice. The words I'd practised were on the tip of my tongue, but when Christophe's door opened I was forced to swallow them whole.

'Inès?' Veronica seemed as shocked to see me as I was horrified to see her. 'What are you doing here? And why are you all dressed up?'

I could've asked her the same thing. She had surpassed her usual polished appearance and had switched – effortlessly, it appeared – to startling glamour. The kohl remained around her eyes, but she had swapped her normal attire of designer leggings and crop tops for a low-cut turquoise sheath dress. Her hair was out of its customary bun and pinned into an elegant chignon, and her lips were painted fire-engine red, like a Hollywood screen siren.

Christophe called from the bathroom, 'Who is it, V?'

A burst of outrage fractured my veneer of composure. '*V?* So you have nicknames now?'

'He thinks it's cute,' she said, her eyes shining. 'It's only Inès,' she yelled back at him.

*Only Inès.* I clenched my fists to curb the mounting urge to scream.

Christophe's footsteps echoed on the floorboards as he came to stand at Veronica's side and slotted in next to her naturally, instinctively, as if he were at ease there. He looked sublime in black trousers and a charcoal shirt, a bow tie hanging loose around his neck.

'Ah, Inès. Are you all right?'

*No. And I wonder if I will ever be.*

'I wanted to speak to you,' I said. 'But it can wait. Actually, it doesn't matter.'

I turned to leave but Veronica caught my arm.

'It's okay,' she said. 'We have time. We don't mind, do we, Chris?'

*Chris?* I was sure I was going to be sick.

He smiled – at her rather than at me. 'Not at all. Please, come in.'

Veronica pulled me inside and began filling my brain with noise and words – so many *words*. She perched on the wingback chair, the one in which I'd sat as I listened to Christophe tell me I was gifted. That I was the best.

As Veronica droned, I watched Christophe. He was now at the mirror, fastening his bow tie. He met my eyes, and I had to glance away. It was too much; history seemed to be repeating itself.

'I can't tell you how psyched I am that you've stopped

by,' Veronica said. 'I mean, I wanted to tell you before, please don't think I didn't. But it was never the right time. I could never catch you alone, and you know what this place is like … There's always someone listening. *Spying.* The others are total sieves – they can't keep anything to themselves. You're the only one I can count on not to blab.'

'V's always telling me what a good friend you've been to her,' Christophe said.

'I think that might be an overstatement,' I said.

'Don't be modest!' Veronica said, her bracelets jingling as she sliced a hand through the air. 'If it weren't for you, I'd have been totally lost here. I probably would've gone home *months* ago.'

She noticed my eyes widen.

'Yeah, I know,' she said. 'It's a shocker, right? Me, quitting! Don't worry, Christophe knows the whole story.'

Christophe eased his jacket from its hanger and threaded his arms through the sleeves. 'Veronica was even more homesick than Roxane,' he said. 'She used to come crying to me almost every day.'

'For sure,' Veronica said. She considered me with a disturbing fondness. 'But then you took me under your wing, and I can't tell you how grateful I am that you did. I told Christophe about how you showed me around Paris … how you sat with me for hours and helped me learn those stupid verb conjugations. Some of which I still don't get, by the way!' She laughed. 'Seriously, Inès …

without you, none of this would've happened.'

A dull ache began in my temples. My brain was a swirling fog; my thoughts were fragments of a picture I couldn't piece together.

'And I appreciate how you never told Diana about it,' Veronica said. 'God, she would *love* to find out how I struggled. Just tell me one thing … Did you help her with her French? She's gotten good pretty damn quick. Was that you, too?'

The room was spinning. I wanted to ask her if she'd lost her mind, but I couldn't make myself speak.

'Yeah, I get it.' Veronica winked. 'You'd never tell. I respect that.'

'I told you,' Christophe said with an enigmatic smile. 'Inès can keep a secret.'

He made himself comfortable on the arm of Veronica's chair and laid a hand on her shoulder. That they matched was undeniable: the glossy American blonde with her glamorous dress and vertiginous heels, and the debonair Frenchman in his tailored suit. As they gazed at each other my mouth filled with a metallic taste.

'Let's tell her now,' Christophe said. 'She should know.'

'You tell her,' Veronica said. 'It ought to come from you.'

'As you wish.' Christophe linked his fingers together and clasped his knee. 'I have chosen Veronica as the lead.'

Veronica's face split into a toothy smile that evoked

the joyful delirium of her deodorant advert. 'Isn't it the most awesome news? I am *so* stoked about it, and I'm super happy now I can share it with you.'

'V is perfect for this role,' Christophe said. 'She embodies everything I'm looking for.'

I seemed to be dissolving from the inside out, as if I would soon be nothing more than atoms.

'But what about the auditions?' I said. 'You said you'd be watching to decide who's the most suitable.'

'Actually …' Christophe chuckled. 'Actually, it was you who inspired me to say that. Our little chat got me thinking about how I could push my students harder, how I could get the best out of them. I said all that simply to motivate them, but I'd already chosen Veronica. She's the right girl to fill Liliane's shoes.'

Veronica stretched across and took my hand. 'Thank you, Inès. I truly mean that. *Thank you.*'

'You understand that we must keep it a secret for now,' Christophe said.

'Oh, yeah,' Veronica said. 'The other girls can't know yet. They'd go batshit.'

My head was light. I feared I might faint, drop like a stone onto Christophe's plush rug.

'I should go,' I said, prising Veronica's fingers from my skin. 'You clearly have more pressing things to attend to.'

'It's just drinks with donors,' Christophe said. 'A bigger production means we need more funding.'

'Which Chris will *totally* be able to get,' Veronica said, grinning at him. 'He's the best.'

I edged towards the door. 'I hope your evening is a success. And well done, Veronica. I hope this role brings you everything you deserve.'

Veronica leapt from the chair and flung her arms around me. 'I won't forget what you've done for me. Ever.'

Trapped in her sticky embrace, I was a ball of fury. This was not supposed to happen … I was supposed to be in that room with him; *I* was supposed to be at his side. I had taken the 'extra measures', but I was further away from him than ever.

I needed an explanation. I needed to know what to do.

There was only one place where I would find the answer.

# 17

The cathedral loomed before me, its splendour enhanced by the glow of the full moon and the stillness of the empty streets.

I crossed the road and strode past the spot where, by day, the queue for the towers would form. As I approached the entrance, the gates swung open with a squeak that sounded like a question, and I thought I heard the gargoyle's gravelly voice asking, *Well, are you going to come in?*

Without hesitation, I entered.

There was no one manning the souvenir shop, and a dim light illuminated the merchandise, casting shadows onto the walls. I hurried to the spiral staircase and found it as I'd never seen it before.

Candles had been placed on every step – by whom, I did not dare to wonder. Each one extinguished the instant I passed it, as though some unseen presence had blown it out. If I changed my mind and turned back, I'd have to feel my way down those narrow, winding steps in the darkness, and if I made it to the bottom without breaking my neck – which was unlikely – I was certain I'd find the gates locked. The gargoyle would let me leave only when

I had listened to what it had to say.

And that night, there was much to discuss.

The gargoyle was leaning back against the parapet, its arms folded and its horns twitching.

'*There* you are,' it said. 'I knew you'd return. They always do.'

My skin prickled. '"They"?'

'People like you, people not like you …' It shrugged. 'There's always a queue to get up here, isn't there?'

'Not tonight.'

The gargoyle smiled and opened its wings. 'Come and see the view. It's even better at night. Darkness sharpens the vision, makes you see so much more. Come on, take a look.'

I took a tentative step across the platform and peered over the edge of the parapet. Far beneath us, the city blazed with light. People were now everywhere – snapping photos of the cathedral, relaxing at tables outside restaurants and cafés, walking briskly along the pavements. Traffic clogged the roads as usual. Paris was alive again.

'Where do they all disappear to when I come here?' I said.

'Nowhere,' the gargoyle replied. 'Perhaps the question is, where do *you* disappear to? Ah, over there, look … that car …' It extended a finger towards the quay. 'That's Christophe and Veronica.'

My stomach rolled. 'That can't be them … You can't be sure.'

'I am *always* sure, Inès. He's taking her to Le Meurice to meet some of his contacts. He networks in all the best places, you know. Don't you ever wonder how he can afford so much extravagance?'

'It's an investment. If you want to attract money, you have to spend money.'

The gargoyle laughed. 'It's as though you are repeating his exact words.'

I was, of course, and I sensed that it was well aware of that.

'Are you showing off?' I said. 'It must be amusing for you to perform your tricks.'

The gargoyle's features contorted into a venomous glare. 'The notion that I perform "tricks" implies that I am involved in deception, which is insulting. I reveal the purest of truths.' Its head turned to the quay. 'There they go, Christophe and Veronica … Tell me, do you think he has reserved a room at the hotel as another "investment"?'

'Why ask me? Surely you know the answer.'

'But where's the fun in that? Tell me what *you* think. Yes or no … Is Christophe planning to seduce dear Veronica – V, as he calls her – in a sumptuous suite tonight? Or will she seduce *him*? Go on, Inès, think about it. I dare you.'

The scene floated into my mind all too easily. Veronica sitting astride Christophe, her nails burrowing into the hair on his chest. Veronica with her arms wound around him. Veronica kissing him until her lips were raw. Veronica pressed against him, her heart beating in time with his.

'How does it make you feel?' the gargoyle said. 'Envious? Or perhaps'—it came closer, its hibernal breath on my neck—'*murderous.*'

It let out a vicious cackle as I shrank away from it.

'You should have come to me sooner,' the gargoyle said. 'I've been so looking forward to congratulating you. You did a very good job with Liliane. I'd say you were a natural. I should applaud, make you feel at home.'

'I don't deserve applause,' I said. 'I failed. It didn't work.'

'Liliane is dead, isn't she? And the police have their perpetrator.' The gargoyle tipped its head to the side. 'How do you feel about poor Jacques Robineau taking the punishment for strangling "The Angel of Paris"?'

'She was no angel. An angel would not have been in a hotel suite with a married man.'

A vile grin spread across the gargoyle's face. 'I think that answers my question. You have no guilt at sending an innocent man to prison for the rest of his life, and none for killing your fellow student. Or do you …?'

I thought of Liliane's face as the scarf cut off her oxygen. I thought of her as she had been – mesmeric, luminous – and I thought of her as she might be now: lying in a morgue with telltale red marks on her neck, a testament to the despicable act I had inflicted upon her.

I swallowed hard. 'Remorse won't change anything.'

'And would you want to?' the gargoyle said. 'Would you want to undo what you've done?'

The events in the hotel ran through my mind in reverse, and I saw myself unwinding the scarf from Liliane's neck and her eyes snapping open. I saw us going back to the academy together. I saw her returning to being Christophe's favourite student and me fading into the scenery.

'I did what needed to be done,' I said. 'All I regret is that I have to join in with the blondes' performative grief, just so they don't suspect me.'

'No one will *ever* suspect you,' the gargoyle said. 'Except maybe your pianist friend.'

'Don't mention Théo. This has nothing to do with him.'

'As you wish. But he wouldn't tell anyway. He would take your secrets to his grave.'

'I don't want him to keep our secrets.'

'*Your* secrets. I am just a gargoyle.'

'I think you are more than that.'

'See for yourself. Touch my face. Go on …'

I didn't want to, but at the same time I *had* to. It was peculiar to experience so many conflicting feelings at once: disgust, foreboding, compulsion, fright and, most powerful of all, curiosity.

It nodded encouragingly as I stretched out a hand and touched my fingertips to its cheek. The shock of the cold stone made me gasp, and I wrenched my hand back.

'See?' it said. 'Just a gargoyle.'

'And yet, here you are. Talking to me.'

'And yet, here *you* are. Talking to *me*. So, about Liliane – why do you insist that your plan failed?'

'Because look where I am now. Look where *he* is now. I did everything right. I waited, I gave Christophe time. He *needed* time. And it seemed to work at first – when he announced his requirements for the lead he *had* to have had me in mind. But Veronica manipulated him. She got the lead. She got *him*.'

The gargoyle peered intently at me. 'You're surprised?'

'And I suppose you're not.'

'Not one bit.'

'But you said if I got rid of Liliane he'd be mine. It was your idea. Your plan.'

The gargoyle's nostrils flared. 'I said no such thing. And it was *your* idea, and your plan. Yours. What I *did* say was that tall flowers must be cut down. Tall *flowers*. Did you really think it would be that simple? That you'd only need to remove one of them?' It gave that malicious laugh again. 'Poor Inès. Well, there's still a chance. The situation is far from irredeemable.'

'What are you implying?'

'I'm not "implying" anything. I'm merely offering my opinion. My advice.'

'Do people follow it?'

'Yes. They always do. Although, regrettably, some do not act until it is too late. I see it all too often. They vacillate, weighing things up from every possible angle, waiting for "signs", for the "right moment".' The gargoyle grimaced. 'I don't want you to succumb to folly like them. Next time, do not leave a vacuum.'

'*No.*' I shook my head. 'No! I can't do it again.'

'Yes, you can. The first one is always the hardest. But if you can do it once, you can do it twice. I'll protect you. I'll make sure you're in the clear. Unless there's something else you're afraid of …'

'I'm not afraid.'

'Are you sure?' The gargoyle glanced skyward, its palm out as if it were checking for rain. When its bleak stare returned to me, its eye sockets were two piercing red orbs that burned through me, penetrating my flesh and searing my soul.

'Maybe it's your feelings for Théo that are holding you back,' the gargoyle said.

'I have no feelings for Théo. We might be … close, but it doesn't mean that I love him. You should know life is not that simple.'

'Indeed I do. And are you still in love with Christophe?'

'I wouldn't be here if I wasn't.'

'Really? Are you certain of that?' The orbs glimmered. 'The heart is deceitful. Can you really trust it? You must be sure it is Christophe you want, that you love *him* and not the futility of wanting him.'

'You're being absurd.'

'I'm being *wise*. Sometimes wanting what you can't have is easier than being disappointed.'

'Wanting Christophe is *not* easy,' I said.

'Very well then.' The gargoyle nodded. 'You must complete what you have started.'

'I can't,' I said. 'Not again.'

'You can. You have it in you. I see it now, when I look at you.'

'What? What do you see?'

'The darkness. The darkness that makes us see things much more clearly. That makes the view so much better.'

I looked across the city. The sky was dotted with red lights that matched the gargoyle's eyes, giving me the uncanny feeling that it was everywhere – that there was no escape from the things it knew, the things it could see.

Christophe was out there somewhere, with Veronica. Talking, laughing, unaware of how much I longed for him.

'Christophe told me I had an aura,' I said. 'That there was a force about me.'

'Maybe there is,' the gargoyle said. 'You should choose your methods wisely. If you need me, I am here. I will *always* be here.' It flicked a hand towards the staircase. 'Go, now, and do what you must.'

'How?' I asked. 'How will I do it?'

'It will come to you. Just as it did before.'

The sky was now the colour of burning coal. It was no longer night, but something even darker.

'I have lit a path for you,' the gargoyle said. 'Follow it, and you will not fall. It's a long way down if you fall, Inès. A very long way down.'

# 18

Veronica was putting on quite the act. Day after day, we practised for the showcase, and day after day, her performance only got worse.

She bungled the choreography, tripping over her own feet and colliding with the other blondes, testing even Hélène's patience. She stammered through the dialogue, causing rehearsals to be lengthy and tedious. Once the eternal optimist, her consistent 'failures' transformed her into an infernal pessimist, and she bleated constantly about how Christophe was never going to pick her.

Her despair deepened with each class.

'It's no use,' she said as the blondes sat around a table in the library. 'Did you see the way he looked at me after I messed up again?'

The blondes must have noticed Christophe's frustration at Veronica's sudden incompetence – they were watching as carefully as I was – but it seemed she'd fooled them into believing they were in contention, that it was still a competition and not a fait accompli. The clues were there, if you were paying close enough attention: the sneaky glances she gave Christophe – who was apparently complicit in the farce – the way she held his gaze for a fraction too long, how her face grew red and her lips twitched whenever he mentioned the lead role. But the others had been completely hoodwinked.

Maëlle flung an arm around Veronica's shoulders. 'Don't worry,' she said. 'We're all finding it hard to keep up. And you weren't *that* bad.'

'Yes, I was,' Veronica said, wringing her hands. 'I think he's going to kick me out of the academy.'

'He would never do that,' Hélène said.

'He might,' Diana said.

Françoise stared at her in astonishment. 'Can't you be sensitive for once? Veronica is upset!'

'I said he *might* throw her out,' Diana said. 'It's a possibility. It's a possibility for *all* of us. I didn't say he would actually do it.'

'Try saying nothing,' Nathalie said, and Diana glowered at her.

'Thanks, you guys.' Veronica took the tissue Roxane offered her and blew her nose with a loud honk. 'I really do appreciate your support. It means a lot to me. I just …' She exhaled. 'I want the lead so badly. You know?'

Diana reached across to clasp Veronica's hand.

'Of *course* you do,' she said. 'And you have every chance of getting it. Every chance in the world.'

'You think so?' Veronica said.

'I know so,' Diana said, although the only way she'd admit this was if she was confident it would never come to pass.

It was obvious to me, if not to them, that Veronica revelled in her secret – I could see how pleased she was with herself, even if they couldn't. She thought she was so clever, so superior. But the thing with having a secret is that, eventually, it becomes a burden, and the only way to relieve it is to share it with someone. Someone you think you can trust.

I had my prey, but no opportunity to snare it. Veronica never seemed to be alone: if she wasn't surrounded by the other blondes, she was with Christophe. The days grew longer as each passed with no opportunity to get near her, and I was starting to worry that she might elude me indefinitely.

But then, one afternoon, I was taking a languorous walk around the quartier, contemplating the sobering prospect of going back to the gargoyle to admit that I'd failed again, when I heard a bell chime. The sound made me jolt and lift my gaze from the ground. I stopped and looked across the street. There was Veronica, sitting in splendid solitude on the grass in the park behind Notre-Dame. I glanced up at the towers. This was my reprieve – my one and only chance to 'do what must be done'. I would not delay, like those 'others' the gargoyle had spoken of. I would not leave a vacuum.

Veronica was sprawled inelegantly next to a rosebush on a small stretch of lawn that bordered the fountain. There was a towel spread beneath her and a box of grapes by her feet, and she appeared oblivious to everything except the magazine she was holding up close to her face. She didn't sense the shadow falling over her as I approached. I lit one of Théo's cigarettes, and she started in surprise as the lighter snapped.

'Gosh, Inès ...' She puffed out her cheeks and sat up. 'You scared the bejesus out of me!'

'You should pay more attention to your surroundings,' I said. 'Anything can happen out here.'

'Yeah, well ...' She placed the magazine down on the grass, laying a palm on it as a gust of wind rustled the pages. 'I was just catching up on some reading.'

'So I see. Looks intense.' I tilted my head to read the title of the article that had so engrossed her. '"Ten Ways to Tell if He's into You." And? Is he?'

'Can't say for sure yet, I'm only on point number two. But'—Veronica winked—'it's looking good so far.' She shifted position and smoothed out the towel. 'You wanna sit? Plenty of room for your skinny butt on here.'

'I don't think you're supposed to be on the grass.'

Her face scrunched. 'I hate this city sometimes. There are so many rules and regulations.' She flapped a hand to bat away the cigarette smoke. 'You still haven't quit the coffin nails, huh? Did you even try those patches I got for you?'

'What patches?'

'Thought you'd say that. Well, they're your lungs, I guess.' She picked up the box of grapes and held it out to me. 'Want one?' She shrugged as I shook my head. 'Whatever. Hey, if you're not doing anything, shall we go get a coffee? At that cute little café? I could really use one of our chats.'

She looked at me hopefully, and it hardly seemed worth the effort of responding to her latest peal of unreality. I had an antidote to her madness, a cure that would quash it.

I slid my hand into my pocket and felt the pills I'd been carrying around with me in anticipation of a chance as golden as this one.

With pleasure, I accepted Veronica's invitation.

Veronica insisted on going back to her room to change her clothes first.

'You never know who you might meet,' she said as she tugged on a pair of brown suede boots. 'My mom taught me to be ready for the unexpected.'

She went to the mirror to comb her hair while I gazed around trying to take in everything and nothing. Her room stank of perfume and was cluttered with useless trinkets and mementos. There were teddy bears on the dresser with 'good luck' embroidered on them, and cards emblazoned with messages like 'Missing you' and 'Break a leg!' On the shelf, there were framed photographs of Veronica with her arms around an assortment of young women with broad, gleaming smiles – all blondes like her. So many blondes … so many, it made my brain hurt.

'You never talk about your family,' Veronica said. 'You know everything about mine, and I know zip about yours.'

'I don't have any family.'

She put down her comb. 'Seriously? Wow, that must be tough. What happened?'

*They left me. They left me in that awful place, and I don't know who I am.*

'Doesn't matter,' I said. 'The past is irrelevant anyway.'

She shook her head. 'The past is *everything*. It makes us who we are today. To understand someone, you have to know their history. Don't you think?'

I turned away, pretending to read the 'inspirational' quotes she'd tacked up alongside a collage of photographs of yet more people. Life was so easy for her with her connections, money and support system. If my past had been like hers, then perhaps I might want to keep reminders of it everywhere. But if you don't have the past then you have only the future, and that was my 'everything' – the life that lay ahead of me once another blonde had been snipped from the collage.

I took my cigarettes from my pocket and held the packet out to her. 'Go on. Live a little.'

'Live?' She laughed. 'You're offering me something that could kill me and you're telling me to live? Inès, you're a trip.'

'But it won't kill you. At least, not right now, not at

this moment. And this moment is all we have.'

'And what a wonderful moment it is.' Veronica crossed the room and took my hands. 'I'm here with you, and Christophe has chosen me. *Me!*'

Unfortunately for Veronica, he wasn't the only one.

The first café we came to was along a busy street, a typical tourist trap that was crowded enough for our presence to be unremarkable – perfect for my purposes. Veronica's buoyant mood deflated as I led her towards it.

'This isn't the one we went to before,' she said, taking in the plastic tablecloths and the menu in the window offering a generic selection of dishes. 'That one was way nicer.' She lowered her voice, for once trying to be tactful. 'And you told me you can't stand these overpriced places that cater for people from out of town.'

I smiled. It was something, at least, that the version of me she had concocted seemed to have good taste.

There was only one free table on the terrace, and she followed me to it with obvious uncertainty. She sat down gingerly, cradling her bag on her lap as though she was anxious someone might snatch it. The man sitting at the adjacent table was reading a newspaper. On the front page was a photograph of Jacques Robineau. Veronica flinched and turned her back to it.

'God, his face is everywhere,' she said. 'I swear I'll go crazy if I see his evil eyes one more time. You can just tell he's sick, right? Some people have it written all over them.'

The media described him as a monster, but Liliane's besotted paramour had struck me as nothing more than a nondescript man who'd started something that probably, somewhere inside him, he had known would end badly. Although admittedly not *that* badly.

'You should get used to seeing his picture,' I said, taking the chair opposite her. 'There's still the trial to come.'

Despite the warmth of the afternoon sun, Veronica shivered. 'Do you think we'll have to give evidence?'

'What for?' I snatched a menu from the centre of the table and scanned the list of drinks for a suitable option. 'We don't know anything.'

'We knew Liliane. And you knew her better than anyone.'

I opened my mouth to correct her but was interrupted by the arrival of our waiter.

Despite Veronica's tendency to vaunt her language skills, she had a complex about speaking French in public. So she played dumb and let me order our drinks. Normally, her wilful helplessness would have annoyed me, but today it was extremely useful.

I chose something sweet for her, something that would mask the taste of any additional ingredients.

'Hot chocolate,' she said. 'You remembered! You're not having the same? I thought it was your favourite too.'

'Not today,' I said.

I wasn't that stupid. When our drinks arrived, hers

came in a tall glass, whereas mine was in a cup and saucer. There was no way I could mix up the two.

Veronica sat back, her hands in her lap. 'How do you do it?'

My gut lurched as an image of Liliane on the hotel bed, the white scarf knotted around her neck, popped into my mind. 'Do what?'

'How do you always manage to be so, I don't know … *composed*.' Veronica stirred her drink and licked the spoon. 'You were so brave when the cops came to tell us about Liliane. So damn brave. Françoise totally went to pieces. And for a while I was, like, a total wreck too. I couldn't think, couldn't eat, couldn't sleep. If it weren't for Christophe …' She inched forward, resting her elbows on the table. 'I think we healed each other, you know? His grief was so intense it pulled me out of mine. And then I was able to help him. He said he couldn't have gotten through it without me. Liliane's death brought us together.'

A foul taste flooded my mouth, like something was rotting on my tongue. I took a swig of tea, but it failed to wash it away.

'So you *are* together then,' I said. 'You and him.' I couldn't bear to utter his name in her presence.

'Christophe? Well, yeah. Kinda. In a way. He says I'm his muse.' She blushed, as if she were embarrassed, but it was clear she was proud of it. 'He's based the new scenes around me.'

'But if Liliane were here we'd still be doing the old version.'

'I can't think about it like that,' Veronica said. 'Everything happens for a reason. I'm here now. She isn't.'

'That seems harsh.'

Veronica's mouth set into a hard line, and I caught a glimpse of what she might look like when she got older. *If* she got older.

'I'm sad for her,' she said, 'but it is what it is. I can't feel guilty because I'm happy. Because I'm alive and Liliane is dead.'

A car sped past, music thumping from its open windows. Veronica watched it merge into the queue of traffic waiting to cross the bridge.

'It's such a relief to be able to talk about this with someone,' she said. 'It's so tiring having to fake everything. You know, Christophe is right about you. You really can keep a secret. You kept Liliane's, didn't you?'

I said nothing.

'I bet it's hard for you,' Veronica continued. 'Being without her. You two were so close. Hey,' she said, just as I was about to dispute this, 'you don't have to pretend. Diana's not here. And I won't tell her.'

'What does it have to do with Diana?'

'Are you kidding me?' She laughed. 'Diana would lose her shit if she knew I was talking to you like this. She doesn't know we're out together, by the way, so don't worry. But doesn't it bother you that she's, like, super possessive?'

White dots flashed in front of my eyes. Her madness was giving me a migraine.

'Diana was so jealous of Liliane,' Veronica said. 'She knew you two hung out together. That you had a secret friendship. She used to talk about it a lot, and it was clear she didn't like it. She wants you all to herself. We all do.' She cast a bashful smile at me. 'But Diana is *fanatical*. Do you actually like her, or is being pally with her a tactical thing? I could understand that. Ultimately, we're all in competition.'

'Not any more,' I said. 'You're the lead now. The competition is over.'

'But *they* don't know that. I keep asking Christophe when he's going to tell them, but he says the uncertainty is good for them.' She lifted her glass again. 'God, I can't wait until the showcase is over. The sooner that happens, the sooner we can leave.'

The white dots became a blizzard. 'Leave?'

Veronica gave a sharp nod. 'Uh-huh. Christophe said we could have a really good future together. But, naturally, we'll have to move to the States once things take off. I mean, we can't stay *here*.'

'And what does he think about that?'

'I haven't told him yet. But I'm sure he'll agree. He's totally open to my ideas. You have to go where the industry is, right? And everyone knows the heart of theatre is Broadway.'

She had spent all that time with Christophe and

hadn't learnt a thing about him. Christophe would never leave Paris. He was one of its greatest stars – he belonged in Paris. *To* Paris. She had truly disconnected from reality.

She slurped her drink and wiped a speck of foam from her top lip. 'Man, that's good.'

'It must be cold by now,' I said. 'I'll get you another.'

'That would be so nice. Will you have another as well?'

'Why not? We have nothing to rush back for.'

Veronica reached across and put her hand over mine. 'Thank you for everything you've done for me. Without you, I probably wouldn't be here right now.'

She was so blatantly unhinged that, for a second, I felt something close to pity for her. 'It's nothing,' I said, sliding my hand away. 'Don't mention it.'

Veronica pushed back her chair and stood up. 'I'm going to the restroom.' She pointed into the café. 'Is it through there?'

'Yes, upstairs, on the right,' I said, gambling that in a place like this it was probably downstairs and hoping that the diversion would give me enough time to do what was needed.

'Hold that thought,' she said, and stepped confidently inside. She always moved with purpose, as if everything she did, even just taking a shit, was of vital importance. Well, I had a purpose too, and nothing was more important than carrying it out.

Once Veronica had disappeared inside the café,

I signalled to the waiter and ordered another round of drinks. As soon as he'd gone, I took the pills from my pocket.

There were ten in total. The man who'd sold them to me had spoken little French, so we'd conducted our business in English. I'd spotted him hanging around a side street close to Gare du Nord, and took shelter in a doorway to smoke a cigarette and watch him work. No doubt he thought he was being surreptitious, but years of hustling and struggling had taught me what to look for – *who* to look for – to get what I needed. People like me, people like him ... we recognised others who were doing whatever was necessary in order to survive.

I finished my cigarette and went over to him.

He told me his name was Ruslan; I told him mine was Veronica. There were no pleasantries, no pretences. His opening gambit was to name his price.

'For how many?' I said.

'For each.' He seemed agitated and kept glancing around, as though he feared someone was hiding behind the bags of fetid rubbish piled on the kerb.

'How many will I need?' I asked.

'These are very strong. To get high you need no more than two.'

'What if I want to do more than get high? What if I want to get high enough to leave the planet?'

Ruslan, which I assumed was as much his name as Veronica was mine, wedged his hands into his pockets and shifted his weight from one foot to the other.

'Could be dangerous,' he said. 'Myself, I would not take more than two. And two is for expert. You should not take more than one.'

Precisely what I wanted to hear.

'Show me,' I said. 'I want to see them.'

With obvious reluctance, he took his hand from his pocket. Nestled in his palm were ten tiny pills. They seemed to glimmer in the street light, little stars shining on Veronica's destiny.

'I want them all,' I said.

Doubt had clouded Ruslan's face, but business was business and cash was cash. It's the same in any language.

Veronica was still inside the café when the waiter brought our drinks. The pills were in an envelope, all ten painstakingly crushed into a fine powder. I dropped them into Veronica's hot chocolate and gave it a stir. I had just placed the spoon back on the saucer when she returned.

She'd loosened her bun, and it made her look less austere, offering a glimpse of an alternative version of her. Her lips were freshly glossed, her cheeks dusted with some kind of shimmery blusher.

'Did I miss anything?' she said, sliding into her seat. 'Oh goody, my hot chocolate.'

She picked up the glass and I held my breath as she took a gulp, watching her throat bob as she swallowed. I waited for her to grimace, or fuss about there being a funny taste. But instead, she smacked her lips together and sighed.

'That is good,' Veronica said. 'Like, *insanely* good. You wanna try some?'

'No,' I said, too quickly, but my reluctance didn't appear to temper her enthusiasm.

'Yeah, I should probably stick to tea as well. God knows how much sugar they put in this stuff.'

'But it tastes good, doesn't it? That's the main thing in life. Pleasure.'

She considered this, and then smiled. 'You're right. Screw it.' She clinked her glass against my cup.

'We should totally do this more often,' she said, flicking her hair over her shoulders. 'I get that it's hard for you because of Diana and everything, but I'd like us to be real friends. You know, like *proper* best friends?'

I agreed. At that point, with the pills coursing through her system, I could promise her anything.

As Veronica chattered about her plans and her goals, I wondered how long it would be until the pills took effect. Ruslan, when I'd asked, had been vague about the specifics.

'Depends,' he'd said as he counted my money and pocketed it. 'Someone like you … would be quick. Takes longer if person is bigger.'

'What about someone smaller than me,' I said. 'Thinner. Shorter.'

He shrugged. 'Do not know.'

'You must have an idea. A professional opinion.'

Ruslan looked alarmed. 'An hour, maybe more. For two.'

'What about for the whole lot? For all ten?'

'You are crazy,' he said, shaking his head and moving on to his next customer.

So I had no idea what to expect. I assumed it would be a slow descent into oblivion, but it was only a few minutes before Veronica abruptly stopped talking and clutched her stomach.

'What is it?' I said.

'I'm not sure. I …' Her hand flew up to her mouth. 'I don't feel so good.'

'You do look rather off-colour,' I said, although that was an understatement. Her face had turned the colour of granite, and her skin was glistening with dots of perspiration. 'Perhaps we should go back.'

'No … I'm fine, I just need …' Her chest juddered. 'Oh God, I think I'm going to puke.'

I stood up and held out my hand. 'I'll take care of you.'

Veronica looked up at me, her eyes watery. 'You will, won't you? You always have.'

I put my arm around her and helped her out of her chair. There was a woman sitting near the door, reading a different newspaper. Liliane's photo stared at me from the front page. I wondered how long it would be until Veronica's replaced it.

# 19

Getting Veronica back to the academy proved harder than poisoning her. She lumbered along the pavement like she was drunk, attracting far too much attention. I debated hailing a taxi – that would've been the logical thing. But I was compelled to take the scenic route past the cathedral and parade my handiwork to the gargoyle, even though it had surely already seen it.

'Are we nearly there?' she croaked.

'Nearly,' I said, manoeuvring her around a woman carrying a tiny dog in a Chanel bag.

The woman stopped and looked at us with concern. 'Do you need help?'

'No, no,' I said. 'She's fine. Just had too much to drink. I'm taking her home.'

Veronica's sweaty fingers clung to my sleeve. 'Inès …'

'It's okay.' I wound an arm around her. 'I'm here.'

Progress was arduous. Veronica became more lethargic with every step, and I feared she might keel over right there on the street. It would be typical of her to make such a public exit, and it was troubling enough that there were already dozens of witnesses. Still, I hoped the gargoyle was impressed by my ingenuity.

I hoped it would keep its promise and protect me.

When at last we neared the academy, Veronica was no longer capable of coordinating her limbs, and all I could do was drag her across the courtyard. I had a string of explanations ready in case anyone saw us, but somehow we made it to the dormitory entrance without being spotted.

I propped Veronica up against the wall while I hastily opened the door, then shoved her inside. She managed to shuffle forward a metre or so, but halfway up the stairs her legs gave way. She lay prostrate across the curve where the staircase curled upwards, and let out a long moan.

'Just leave me here,' she said. 'I can't go on.'

I tucked my hands under her armpits. 'Come on, Veronica. Up.'

'No!' she yelled.

I glanced up at the landing, expecting to see Élodie or Cécile peering over the banister – or, worse, Diana.

No one came.

Veronica whimpered as I yanked her upright again.

'Almost there,' I said. 'And then you can rest. You won't have to do any more.'

'I won't?' Her head sagged, as if it were too heavy for her neck.

'No,' I said. 'Soon, it will be over.'

We made it to the top of the staircase, and I was

reassured to see the corridor was empty. I steered her towards her room, desperately hoping the coast would remain clear, and that the blondes wouldn't hear her groans, or her boots scraping along the floor. She slumped against the door as I searched in her bag for her key. The bag contained the usual detritus – tissues, tampons, chewing gum, torn Métro tickets and crumpled receipts – but hidden in an inside pocket were a few surprises: her passport, several hundred dollars in cash and a plane ticket to New York with an open date.

I held it up in front of her. 'What's this? Were you planning a little trip?'

Veronica sputtered in response. Her eyelids flickered, and a stringy line of foam trickled from the corner of her mouth.

'Never mind,' I said. I had an idea of how those items had got there.

I bundled Veronica into her room and laid her on the bed. I removed her jacket and tugged off her boots, and fanned her hair out across the pillow in a way I thought she'd appreciate. She drooled, her eyes half closed, and called softly for her mother.

'Your mother's coming,' I said. 'She's on her way right now.'

I took Veronica's passport and the plane ticket from her bag and dropped them into the top drawer of the bedside table.

Her lips peeled back into a rictus grin. 'You'll like my

mother,' she croaked. 'You have a lot in common.'

'I very much doubt that.'

Veronica dug her fingers into the sheets. 'Where's Christophe? Where is he?' She beat her legs on the mattress and rolled onto her side.

'You need to be still,' I said, turning her onto her back. 'To be calm and quiet. It will be better for you that way.'

Her fingers clamped around my wrist. 'Don't leave me, Inès. Stay with me, please. Stay with me.'

Only an hour before, Veronica's skin had been luminous, her eyes clear and bright. Now her face had a yellow tinge, and the whites of her eyes were riddled with burst blood vessels. Even her lips seemed to have thinned, and there were deep lines around her mouth.

'What's wrong with me?' she murmured.

I sat on the bed and stroked her forehead, running my finger through the beads of sweat. 'Perhaps it was something you drank,' I said. 'I told you to pay attention to your surroundings. But you didn't listen … You never just *listened*.' I stood up. 'I have to go now.'

'Where? To call someone? Christophe?'

'Christophe isn't coming,' I said. 'You're not the one.'

Veronica made a mewling sound. 'I love him. I really love him. I love him, I love him …'

She mumbled it over and over, until the words became unintelligible. By the time I reached the door it seemed as if she were saying, 'I love you, I love you.'

I took one final look at her.
'I love you too, V,' I said.
She gave me a grateful smile and closed her eyes.

## 20

*I love you, I love you …*

Veronica's incantation looped round in my head as I darted across the corridor. Although it was still light outside, inside my room it was inky black, and cold.

Cold as stone.

The hairs on the back of my neck rose. That feeling came again. A presence. Someone was there. Some*thing*.

A figure lurked by the window. On the wall behind it, I could make out the shape of two horns extending from the crown of its head and the curve of two wings on its back.

'You,' I said. 'You're here.'

Two red orbs pierced the darkness.

'Of course,' came the reply. 'I said I would be.'

That voice … Where had I heard that voice?

The light seeped in all at once, as if an eclipse had just ended. I put my hands up to shield my eyes. When I took them away, there was only Théo.

He stared at me inquiringly. 'Did I scare you? What's wrong?'

'Nothing, I …' It was him, it was Théo – his face, his voice. 'How did you …? Wait.'

I went to the window and checked behind the curtains. I looked under the bed, in the wardrobe, in the bathroom. Théo watched as I scoured the room, his arms folded.

'What have you lost?' he said.

'Nothing. No one.' *Just a gargoyle.*

I pinched the bridge of my nose. 'How did you get in?'

'You left the door unlocked. Don't worry, the "blondes" have gone out. To the cinema, I think. What about you? Where have you been?'

I unbuttoned my coat and tossed it onto the chair. 'Out.'

'Out where?'

'Just out.'

'They were looking for you,' Théo said. 'I heard them calling before they left. They looked for Veronica too. Have you seen her?'

*I love you, I love you …*

My fingers felt clammy. I rubbed them on my dress. 'I expect she's hiding somewhere. She probably couldn't bear to spend an entire evening with Diana and Françoise.'

I flopped onto the bed and gazed at one of the spidery cracks on the ceiling, unable to decide if it was new or if it had always been there and this was just the first time I'd noticed it. There were cracks everywhere in the academy – yet another issue Christophe had assured us would be addressed 'in due course'. I wondered how deep and how large a crack it would take to bring the whole building down.

'Théo, can I tell you something?'

'Since when did you ask permission?' He lay down alongside me, his body parallel to mine. 'What is it?'

I put my head on his chest. 'I think the blondes have gone mad. They imagine things. Things about me.'

'Are you sure?'

'Positive. They've been spewing all sorts of nonsense. Outright *lies*. I'd assume it was just one of their stupid jokes, but they seem so sure. It's disturbing.'

'No, Inès, I mean …' Théo stroked my hair. 'Are you sure they're the ones imagining things?'

I raised myself onto my elbows to look at him. 'You're taking their side?'

'I'm on *your* side. I always will be. You know nothing could ever change how I feel about you.'

'Feelings can always change,' I said. 'It takes only a second to go from love to hate.'

'Could I change how you feel about Christophe? Could I tell you something that would make you stop loving him?'

'Like what?'

'That he is a horrible person. That you shouldn't risk your heart – your *soul* – for him.'

There was a moment when I believed him, when I was tempted to tell him about the corpse in the room across the corridor – about *everything* – but it passed as quickly as it had arrived. I curled into him and told myself that the ending – the one I deserved – more than justified the means.

# 21

Maëlle's screams were loud enough to wake the whole quartier.

Doors burst open, and the blondes came thundering out of their rooms. I'd intended to remain in bed and listen to the drama play out, like I had before, but Théo was awake and regarding me questioningly.

'Aren't you going to see what's happened?' he said. 'Unless, that is, you already know …'

He watched me closely as I leant across to retrieve my robe from the back of the chair.

'Be careful, Inès,' he said. 'Be very careful.'

But it was too late for caution: in the corridor, pandemonium reigned. Maëlle was shaking and crying; Nathalie and Françoise were trying to console her. Déborah tore past me and disappeared into Aurélie's room, only to re-emerge a second later. Élodie loitered outside Veronica's door, her hand cupped over her mouth. Cécile was lying on the floor, her limbs splayed at odd angles, like a broken doll. Beside her was a puddle of steaming vomit.

Hélène was pressed against the wall. She was hugging one of her slippers as if it were a teddy bear; the other was wedged onto the wrong foot.

'What's going on?' I asked.

'It's Veronica,' she said, staring at the skirting board. 'She—'

'She won't wake up,' Françoise said. 'We don't know what's wrong with her.'

'She's dead!' Maëlle said. 'I keep telling you, she's dead!'

Diana shook her head. 'She *cannot* be dead. It's impossible.'

'Why?' Élodie said. 'Liliane's dead, isn't she? Anything is possible now.'

Françoise's attention shifted to the end of the corridor, and she heaved a deep sigh of relief. 'Oh, thank God,' she said. 'He's here.'

Christophe's arrival both soothed the blondes and increased their distress. They clamoured at him as he came striding towards us, grabbing his shirt and wailing, begging him to do something, anything, to help Veronica. To help *them*.

'Go back to your rooms,' he said. 'All of you.'

His instruction did not appear to sink in. Hélène didn't move away from the wall, and Cécile remained prone on the cold floor. Maëlle was now hysterical, and Françoise abandoned her attempts to offer comfort and began to sob. Diana watched Christophe as he tentatively entered Veronica's room, and then trailed after him. I hovered in the doorway, queasy at the knowledge of what Christophe was about to find.

'I said go to your room.' Christophe's voice held steady, but their mania was like a virus, and from the growing apprehension in his tone, it appeared he was not immune to it.

'She's dead,' Diana said in a chilling monotone. 'Isn't she?'

I'd done my best for her, but Veronica must have struggled as she met her end. Her hair was matted, a clump at the front twisted into a curl, as if she had tugged on it in her last moments. Contrary to my instructions, she had rolled onto her side, and her cheek rested in a pool of viscous green liquid. Her mouth was open, her eyes rolled back in the sockets.

The stench was nauseating. Christophe covered his mouth and nose with one trembling hand and reached out with the other to check Veronica's neck for a pulse.

'Call an ambulance,' he said.

'Is she dead?' Diana said. 'Tell us!'

'Call an ambulance!'

Maëlle screamed again.

I shifted out of Diana's path as her legs began to pump, propelling her away from the awful tableau, but after only a second or two, she stopped and turned in a circle.

'Where …'

'My room,' Christophe said, tossing his keys at her. 'My phone is on the shelf. Go. Go *now*!'

In her haste, Diana skidded on the vomit, and I

marvelled at how people run even when there's no life left to save, how they still call for help when it's clearly already too late.

Christophe sat on the bed and gazed at Veronica. He smoothed her hair from her face and whispered into her ear. I would've killed her again to learn what he said.

Diana returned with Christophe's phone in her hand and tears flowing down her cheeks. 'I don't know, I don't know …' She was almost incoherent through her frantic blubbering. 'I don't know what to dial!'

Nathalie snatched the phone from her and punched in the number. The blondes fell silent as she gave the operator a halting summary of Maëlle's grim discovery.

Christophe gripped Veronica's shoulders and shook her.

'Wake up,' he said. 'Wake up, Veronica. Wake up! Wake up, wake up!'

I had to go to him. This time, it had to be me he turned to for solace.

I came up behind him and prised his hands from Veronica's lifeless body.

'She's gone,' I said. 'She's gone.'

He looked at me, his eyes wide and trusting, and I saw that Veronica had gone from them too.

## 22

When the news broke about the latest tragedy to strike the Leriche Academy, questions were immediately asked about what exactly was going on inside it: were the two deaths a terrible coincidence, or was there something more insidious at play? All manner of wild theories were posited, until the authorities disclosed that a search of Veronica's room had uncovered not only the plane tickets but also several bottles of antidepressants. Shortly afterwards, her death was pronounced a suicide.

'We had no idea she was struggling so much,' Veronica's mother said in a television interview from the family's palatial home in New York. 'If only she'd come to us … If only she'd reached out, we would've supported her. She was so excited to go to France to train with Mr Leriche … We never thought it would come to this.'

The blondes followed the coverage zealously. They spent hours glued to their phones, scrolling through the same stories. Hélène even started clipping articles from the newspapers and sticking them into a scrapbook, in spite of Diana's objections.

'It's morbid and serves no purpose,' Diana said.

But it served a purpose for Hélène. She was trying

to make sense of it – they all were. Liliane's murder, although shocking, had been easier to comprehend: the innocent young woman slain by a predatory older man was a danger they had long been warned about. But the notion that Veronica, who'd seemed so strong-willed, so unfailingly positive, had despaired of her life so much that she'd decided to end it stirred a miasma of emotions too intricate for the blondes to process, and reopened a wound that had not yet healed. Their renewed grief made them jittery, and with Christophe once again sequestered in his room, they had no one to anchor them. Their histrionics left unchecked, wild ideas took root.

Talk started up once more about the ghost.

'It must be the ghost,' Roxane said as they sat in the now-disused studio, the mirrors on the walls reflecting their apprehensive expressions. 'There is something bad here. An evil presence. What else could have caused this?'

'Thirteen was a bad number,' Maëlle said. 'We were cursed from the beginning.'

'It was suicide,' Déborah said. 'Unless the ghost told her to do it …'

'She was upset about Liliane,' Françoise said. 'Her murder pushed her over the edge.'

Nathalie snorted. 'She hated Liliane.'

'So did you,' Cécile said.

'And you,' Nathalie said. 'Don't act like you were her friend.'

'I am not,' Cécile said with a petulant scowl. 'I am

simply saying—'

'Would you both stop,' Diana said. 'Would you *all* stop. None of us liked Liliane. Not even you, Roxane – *especially* you, Roxane, so don't look so shocked. And none of us cared much for Veronica either. But the fact is, they're both gone now. We have to make the best of it.'

Aurélie shot her an accusing glare. 'How can you be so cold?'

'I'm being practical,' Diana said. 'We need to move on. Like we did before.'

'Well, I can't,' Roxane said. 'I can't be practical. I can't move on.'

Diana scrambled to her feet and marched over to Roxane, waving a finger at her. 'You have to try! You have to pull yourself together! And you have to stop talking about this bloody ghost. Liliane was murdered by her pervert lover, and Veronica killed herself. That's *it*. There's nothing else.'

'It's more than that,' Hélène said. 'Something is stalking us. Something wicked.'

'No!' Diana stamped her foot and looked around at the others. 'I will not hear another word of this balderdash. Do you understand? This silliness has to end right *now*.'

The blondes acquiesced, and no more was said about it – at least, not within earshot of Diana.

Later that day, while I was browsing the shelves in the library, I heard Françoise asking Roxane and Hélène about the ghost, and how they could protect themselves from it.

Hélène said the answer was prayer, and she took to wearing the large silver crucifix her mother had sent to her.

'Ghosts aren't scared of crosses,' Déborah told her.

'And Liliane and Veronica weren't killed by vampires,' Cécile said.

'How do you know?' Hélène said.

'This place is evil,' Roxane said. 'I want to go home.'

Now, the blondes agreed with her. They all claimed they wanted to leave, but not one of them did.

Veronica's parents did not travel to France. The blondes intercepted the message they sent to Christophe, which thanked him for giving their 'beloved daughter a chance to do what she loved most' and expressed regret that they 'did not have the strength' to visit the academy. That was just as well, for Christophe was refusing to see anyone, but the blondes were disappointed – particularly Hélène, who had hoped to convey her condolences in person.

Through the press we learnt that Veronica's body was to be flown back to New York, and the funeral to be held in an old church on the Upper East Side, which Hélène duly located on a map and showed to us as we huddled in her room.

'It's only a few hours on a plane,' she said, pointing to the red dot on the screen that marked the church. 'We could be back in a couple of days.'

'We can't go to New York,' Françoise said.

'We have classes,' Aurélie said.

'No, we don't,' Nathalie said. 'And who knows if we ever will again?'

'Of *course* we will,' Diana said. 'Christophe just needs ...' She pursed her lips as she gazed around Hélène's room. Cluttering the shelves and filling the walls were statues and paintings of saints that roused a shadowy memory from the recesses of my mind.

'What?' Élodie said. 'What does he need? What would Veronica do?'

*She would intervene*, I thought. *She would go to him.*

But someone already had.

The night before, I'd gone to his room and slipped a note under his door. In it, I told him that the academy needed him, and it needed catharsis. *Something ought to be done*, I wrote, *to remember Veronica, but also to signal that the Leriche Academy is still operational, and to reassure our patrons and donors that their investment remains sound. We need to show that we believe in the work we're doing, and that we still have faith in each other.*

*I still have faith in you.*

A day later, Christophe's door opened, and he informed the stunned blondes that he had arranged a memorial service for Veronica.

The venue was to be Notre-Dame.

The cathedral was packed. Sitting in the front row, looking august but sombre, was Justine Deschamps. She gave

Christophe a thin smile as we took our seats. He nodded solemnly in return. The scrutiny on him was intense, and though it was obvious that he was doing his best to remain composed, I noticed his hand shaking as, for the third time in as many minutes, he reached into his inside pocket to retrieve the eulogy he'd written. The blondes tried to mimic his poise and stoicism, but they couldn't quite manage it.

Roxane and Hélène wept as soon as they glimpsed the photo of Veronica displayed near the altar. This set off Françoise, whose noisy sobs punctuated the opening prayers, and one by one all the blondes dissolved into tears. Diana was the last to break down, succumbing as Christophe began the eulogy, and once she started crying, she did not stop for the rest of the service.

Théo and I sat at the end of the pew. There were fewer blonde heads between us and Christophe now. Once or twice, he even glanced over, nodding at me as he had to Justine. I nodded back, and my heart skipped a beat as something passed between us.

The service drew to a close. The blondes were squeezed together, still weeping. Théo and I remained apart from them, watching people lining up to offer Christophe their sympathies. First to get to him was Justine Deschamps, as impressive as ever in high heels and a black suit that enhanced her flawless skin. She laid her hand on Christophe's arm and kept it there as she spoke. It was too noisy to hear what she was saying – the organ was still playing – but whatever it was caused Christophe's eyes to mist with tears.

'I bet he's fucking her,' Théo whispered to me.

A sharp pinch of envy made my fingers curl into my palms. 'She's not his type.'

'She's exactly his type. *Rich*. I read about her, and her family … She could buy the academy several times over. She could make his silly, self-aggrandising dreams come true.'

'You're jealous of him,' I said. 'That's why you say such terrible things.'

'Yes, I am,' Théo said. 'But it doesn't mean I'm wrong.'

When the formalities were over, we stood in the square outside. People continued to approach Christophe to pledge their support, some of whom he appeared to know well and others who seemed to be strangers. They shook his hand and told him it wasn't his fault – that he was treasured, and Paris needed him.

The blondes clustered around him in a broken circle, shuffling their feet and staring at the ground, as if they wanted to avoid acknowledging the glaring spaces where Liliane and Veronica should be. Diana tugged at Christophe's sleeve.

'What do we do *now*?' she asked.

'We go on,' Christophe replied. 'You heard those people … Paris needs us. But today, you must rest. Take some time for yourselves. Classes will resume tomorrow. *We* will resume tomorrow.'

'Rest?' Diana said, her face a picture of bewilderment. 'But—'

'Come on,' Françoise said, taking her arm. 'Let's go back. We can do facials or something.'

'Manicures,' Déborah said.

'And pedicures,' Cécile added.

The blondes wandered off, leaving Théo and me behind. I glanced up at the gargoyle, wondering how it had done it. I had to know. I had to ask it.

Théo took his cigarettes from the pocket of his blazer and slipped one between his lips.

'Want to get a coffee?' he said, pointing to the brasserie across the road. 'I might even buy you lunch.'

'I can't. I have something I need to do.'

Théo followed my gaze. 'Don't you get bored staring at the same view every time?'

'It's never the same. That's the point.'

'I'm relieved to hear there *is* a point to you going up there so often,' he said. 'Maybe one day you will tell me what it is. Or maybe I should go and see for myself.'

The thought of Théo up there with the gargoyle brought a stab of panic. 'You must never do that. Promise me, Théo.' I took his wrist, my fingers digging into his flesh. 'Promise me you will never go to the towers.'

His expression was inscrutable as he looked at me, sucking on his cigarette. 'I saw you that night.'

Fear bloomed in the pit of my stomach. 'Which night?'

'You went out after midnight. You thought I was asleep, but I wasn't. I followed you, Inès. I saw you at Gare du Nord, talking to that guy. Who was he?'

'You shouldn't spy on me.'

'Why not?' he said. 'What is it you don't want me to see?'

*Me. I don't want you to see* me.

I snatched the cigarette from Théo's fingers. 'Forget what you saw. It was just a means to an end.'

'And what is that end?' Théo said. 'Him?' He gestured at Christophe, who was shaking hands with a tall man with dark hair. As the man walked away, Christophe's eyes found mine.

'Quick,' I told Théo. 'You have to—'

Théo lifted his palms in surrender. 'I'm going, I'm going.' He gave me a light kiss on the cheek – a chaste, platonic kiss – and trudged off towards Saint-Michel.

I puffed on the cigarette as Christophe came over to me, knowing I shouldn't be smoking in front of him but needing something to calm the butterflies in my stomach. He smiled at my attempt to wave the smoke away.

'Sorry,' I said, holding the cigarette behind my back. 'Bad habit.'

'Disgusting,' he said, an impish twinkle in his eyes. 'Do you mind if I …?'

It took me a second to work out what he wanted.

'Oh,' I said. 'Oh yes, of course.'

My hand quivered as I gave the cigarette to him, and a tingle ran down the length of my spine as he took it. His chest swelled as he held the smoke in his lungs.

'Yes,' he said, exhaling slowly, 'it's the most disgusting habit. I had almost forgotten how good it feels to do something so bad.' He considered the glowing tip. 'I gave up when I became serious about dancing, but it still tempts me.'

'Don't worry,' I said. 'I won't tell anyone.'

'You wouldn't, would you? You are very good at keeping my secrets.'

His ice-blue eyes drilled into mine, and I became effervescent. Being in his presence made me sparkle, made me shine – made me better, so much better, than I was. Given time, it would make me *perfect*.

'I should thank you,' he said. 'For today. It was a good idea.'

'It was your idea.'

He shook his head. 'Without that note you sent me, I wouldn't have thought of it. I wouldn't have thought of *anything*. I would have gone under. I was drowning, Inès. Drowning in guilt. Your words were like a hand reaching to pull me out of the water. What you wrote … about having faith in me.'

'I meant every word,' I said. 'I believe in you.'

'You think there is still something worth believing in? Even after everything that's happened?'

'*Especially* after everything that's happened,' I said. 'We have to make it count for something.'

I watched, mesmerised, as Christophe took another greedy drag on the cigarette. He was smoking like a pro now, like he'd never given it up.

'What's your opinion of what the others are saying?' he said. 'About this "ghost".'

'I think it's absolute nonsense.'

'It is. But I must admit, sometimes …' He toed the ground. 'Sometimes I feel as if something is at work inside the academy. Something dark. I wonder if it's my fault. If I caused all this.'

'It's not your fault,' I said. 'You mustn't think that.'

He winced. 'That's what she used to say – Veronica. "None of this is down to you, Chris," she'd tell me. Over and over, until I began to allow myself to believe it. And now …' A shadow crossed his face and I longed to relieve him of his remorse, to tell him the lengths to which I was prepared to go for him.

'Do you miss them?' I asked. 'Liliane and Veronica?'

'Every day.' He pulled at his tie, loosening the knot. 'You must miss them too. I know you were close to both of them.'

I shifted on the spot and glanced over my shoulder, half expecting to see Liliane and Veronica leaning on the railing outside the cathedral. 'Not especially.'

Christophe frowned, and handed the cigarette back to me. 'I'd better stop before I get hooked again. It's so easy to become dependent on something.'

'Yes,' I said. 'It is.'

As I took the cigarette from him, I noticed a powdery smudge on the sleeve of my coat. It was the same colour as the crushed pills, although it couldn't have been from them. *Could it …?* I tried to brush the smudge away, but my efforts only ground it deeper into the fabric. I lowered my arm to conceal it from Christophe, but fortunately he appeared not to have spotted it.

'Do you ever feel as if you'll never get what you want?' he asked, rubbing his chin thoughtfully. 'That no matter how much you try, how hard you work, how much you sacrifice, your desires will always be out of reach?'

'All the time.'

'And?' He raised an eyebrow. 'What do you do about it? How do you conquer the fear that you will never be fulfilled?'

'I fight it. I do whatever it takes, whatever I need to. Even things other people might not understand.'

'I do too, but … but it still feels as if it's not enough.'

I inched closer to him. 'Then fight harder,' I said. 'Go further, deeper. It's easy to get overwhelmed by all the options, but sometimes what we need most is right in front of us and we can't see it.'

He studied me with the same intensity as he had on the day of my audition, his eyes searching mine, seeking something I desperately wanted him to find.

'How did you become so wise, Inès?' he asked.

'Not through choice, I assure you.'

Christophe touched my arm. 'I should go. I need to make some calls, go over the script … get us back on track. Do something nice for yourself this afternoon, yes?'

My lips curled into a smile – my first of the day. 'I will.'

And I knew exactly what it would be.

This time, there was a woman behind the counter in the souvenir shop. Her hair was snow white, her face scored with lines, her body thin and bony. As she heard my footsteps she gave me a wide, toothless grin.

'You're here.' Her rasping voice did not fit her frail exterior. She extended a liver-spotted hand to me.

'Come,' she said. 'The conditions are perfect today.'

The keenness of her instruction, the urgency of her tone, made me want to turn and run. Instead, I found myself walking towards her.

Her grin broadened. She seemed as old as the cathedral itself, but her black eyes were sharp and alert, studying me with a malignant fascination that siphoned all my thoughts, so that inside my mind there was only darkness.

The woman held a ticket out to me, and I rooted in my pockets for the money I'd taken from Françoise's purse.

'There is no charge,' the woman said. 'Not for you. You are almost part of the place now.'

I was about to ask what she meant, but her gaze drifted to the postcards in front of her. She picked up a stack that bore the image of the gargoyle – my gargoyle – and moved them to a more prominent position.

'Go on,' she said. 'It's a long way up, and an even longer way down. But you know that already. You know *everything*.'

'I don't understand,' I said.

'You will,' the woman replied. 'In time.'

Her eyes glazed over. Her arms hung flaccidly at her sides and her expression turned slack, as if she were no longer staring at me but through me. As if I had become part of the scenery.

The gargoyle flashed me a devilish grin.

'I thought you might come to congratulate yourself,' it said.

'Actually,' I said, breathing hard from the climb, 'I came to congratulate you.'

'Me?' It touched one of its long, pointed fingers to its chest. 'You did all the work. And, I must say, you did a magnificent job. The pills were a masterstroke – pure genius. Anything else, if you'll excuse the expression, would have been overkill.'

I shuddered as it snickered at its own joke.

'You arranged it all,' I said. 'The plane tickets, the pills ... that was you, wasn't it? Some kind of ... illusion.'

The gargoyle rested against the parapet and inclined its head. The gesture was unsettlingly human.

'I deal in reality, not illusions,' it said. 'I'm not a magician.'

'If you're not a magician, then what are you?'

'Just a gargoyle. As you well know.'

'I don't know anything about you.'

'There's nothing *to* know. Your friend—'

'She wasn't my friend,' I said.

The gargoyle's smile was mocking. 'Your *acquaintance*, then. Veronica had been battling depression since adolescence. Her difficulties in acclimatising to Paris only exacerbated her condition.'

'I don't believe you. You put those props there so they would work to your advantage.'

'I think they worked to your advantage rather than mine, wouldn't you say? Everyone's convinced their "beloved" Veronica couldn't cope any more and took her own life. I gave you my word that no one would suspect you, and no one does.'

The wind picked up; the temperature plummeted.

'Théo suspects me,' I said. 'That night I went to get the pills … he saw me.'

'And I saw *him*, skulking around after you. What surprised me was that you, of all people, didn't think to check whether he had followed you.'

My cheeks coloured. Now that the gargoyle had pointed it out, it seemed an obvious mistake.

'Oh, don't feel foolish,' it said. 'And don't worry about Théo.'

'But I do.' The words escaped my mouth before I could stop them.

'Yes, you do, don't you?' the gargoyle said. 'Are you *sure* it's not him that you love?'

I curled my arms around my waist, shivering at the cold. 'I know who I love. Did you see Christophe and me just now? Do you hear how he talks to me? How he trusts me? I wrote him a note … I stepped into the vacuum. He said I saved him from drowning. It's just a question of time now, isn't it?'

The gargoyle fixed its stare on me, its horns moving like antennae.

'You did see,' I said. 'Didn't you …?'

'I have no choice. My eyes are always open.'

'There you are then,' I said. 'You're aware of how it's coming together. I wanted to thank you. For helping me. For showing me what needed to be done. For making my dreams come true.'

The gargoyle ran a hand over the thatch of moss on the stone beside it. 'That sounds like goodbye. Surely you're not planning to stop now?'

'What are you suggesting?' I said.

'You know what I'm suggesting.'

'But they're gone. The tall flowers. I cut them down. There's no threat now. You heard what he said … how moved he was by my note.'

The gargoyle drummed its fingers on the parapet. 'Don't be misled by flattery when what you need is certainty. Are you *sure* the path is totally clear? Tall flowers are like weeds – when one is uprooted, another grows in its place. Don't get complacent. Not now, after all your good work.'

I saw them in my mind's eye. Liliane and Veronica, their bodies stiff and slowly decaying – their eyes snapping open, their arms lifting and reaching out to me, trying to pull me down, down …

'I'm not …' My teeth began to chatter. The temperature on the viewing platform was now arctic. When I spoke, my breath formed a cloud in the air. 'I'm not complacent.'

'You *are*. I can see it on your face. I can hear it in your voice. Are you prepared to risk squandering the progress you've made? You must act now while you have momentum. The balance of power shifts quickly. And when it does, you can never claw it back.'

The thought of what the gargoyle implied was horrifying, and yet … and yet.

'Who?' I said. 'Who should it be?'

'I can't tell you that. Trust your instincts.'

'But you know … you know which one. You know how it ends.'

'I am a gargoyle,' it said huffily, 'not a clairvoyant.'

'You're more than that. A mere gargoyle couldn't do what you've done. Couldn't see everything, couldn't be everywhere. Couldn't *be* at all. What are you?'

The sky darkened. The gargoyle turned towards

Paris and put its chin on its palms, appearing as it did on the postcards sold in the shop far below us.

'Show me your face,' I said.

'This is my face,' the gargoyle said.

'Your true face. I want to see it. I need to.'

The gargoyle's head swivelled like an owl's and it looked at me. 'Why? You believe in me. I'm real enough to you, aren't I? Of what do you require proof?'

'I want to see what you really are,' I said. 'Show me.'

'Maybe one day. When you're ready.'

'When will that be?'

'When the final act is about to begin.'

'So you *do* know how it ends,' I said.

The gargoyle smiled, enjoying its dominion over me. 'I know about *you*.'

I was afraid what the answer would be, but I had to ask.

'Tell me,' I said. 'Tell me that it ends well. Tell me that he does love me. That I get to be with him.'

Two red orbs formed in the gargoyle's eye sockets.

'It depends upon which path you take,' it said. 'If you were to give up, to wait for him to come to you, then I couldn't tell you how it ends. But if you continue along the route I have shown you, then your ending, when it comes, will be spectacular. You will get what you want, and Christophe will be more obsessed with you than you are with him. Can you conceive of that, Inès? Can your imagination stretch that far?'

'Yes.' It was all I had imagined since I had first seen his picture.

'And? Is it everything you desire? Are you sure Christophe is the one you want?'

'Yes,' I said. 'It's him. He's the one.'

It nodded. 'Then you know which path to choose, and what you must do to ensure you get the ending you deserve.'

The gargoyle's red eyes glowed bright. Lighting the way.

## 23

Those two red orbs were burned onto my retinas. The ground spun, and my ears rang with the gargoyle's words.

*You must act now while you have momentum … The balance of power shifts quickly.*

I stumbled from the eerie gloom of the towers and out into blazing sunlight. Diana was standing on the corner reading a street sign as though she had no clue where she was – as though she were lost in every sense of the word. She stepped off the kerb, almost crashing into a passing cyclist, and glanced around. Her face lit up as she spotted me, and she lifted her arms and scissored them above her head.

The orbs faded from my vision as Diana scampered over the pedestrian crossing and ran towards me.

'Inès!' Her moon-face zoomed in close to mine and some of her cheer dampened. 'Golly, Inès, are you all right?'

'I'm fine,' I said.

'Really? You look awfully pale. And you were muttering to yourself.'

I was aware that I should just leave, or at least offer an excuse to allow me to slink back to the safety of my room, but I couldn't think of one. I couldn't think of *anything*. My mind was a void, and I was falling, falling …

Diana frowned. 'Are you *positive* you're okay?'

I swerved out of range as she reached out to touch me. 'Just tired, that's all.'

'What a hellish day it's been,' she said. 'I went back to the academy after the service, but I couldn't bear the atmosphere and had to get out again.' She rubbed her instep along her calf to dislodge a smear of dirt from her shoe. 'He said I'd probably find you around here – the pianist. You know Roxane has a thing for him?'

My ears popped, as if the air pressure had changed. '*Roxane?*'

'Scandalous, isn't it? We were just as shocked when we found out. It appears she's obsessed with him, whatever his name is. Thomas, or something …?'

I rubbed my temples as I tried to process this information. 'Roxane is in love with Théo?'

Diana snapped her fingers. 'Théo, that's it. She claims to be completely and utterly in love with him. It's pathetic, don't you think? Utterly *pathetic*.'

'How do you know?'

'Well, the other night, Françoise and Déborah found some letters she'd written to him on this silly pink paper. Honestly, they were quite obscene. She seems so innocent, but the things she wrote …' Diana shuddered, as though merely remembering was distasteful to her. 'Even Cécile was shocked. I said we shouldn't read them without you, but Françoise couldn't resist.'

'What things did she write?'

'Oh, all sorts of debauched claptrap about how she wants to kiss him. *Where* she wants to kiss him – where she wants him to kiss *her*.' She stuck out her tongue and jabbed two fingers at her open mouth.

'Where does she want him to kiss her?'

'Where do you think?' Diana made a vague motion towards her groin and shuddered again. 'Can you imagine anything more repugnant?'

Sweat trickled down the back of my neck. I knew what it was like to be kissed like that by Théo, to feel his soft hair brush against my stomach, my thighs, and the cool wetness of his tongue on the heat between my legs.

'There were pages and pages of it,' Diana said. 'Lewd ramblings about how she dreams about his … Ugh, it's so ghastly. I would *never* write about putting some stranger's private part in there – or in *anywhere*, for that matter. Roxane is clearly quite unwell. She must've been fantasising about him for ages. Heaven alone knows why. He's such a scruff, and he absolutely *reeks* of cigarettes.' Diana sucked in her cheeks. 'And the most absurd thing is that she's never spoken a single word to him. I thought she was going to pass out when Déborah threatened to show him the letters.'

My mouth became dry. 'And? Has she?'

'Not yet, no. But the others are all for it. Oh, except for Hélène, who insists we've violated Roxane's privacy.' Diana made a face. 'She can be so *pompous* sometimes. But I told them we should wait for you. That you should decide what we do with the letters.'

'*Me?*'

'Well, yes! I said you always know best, and the others agreed. What should we do? Should we tell Christophe?'

It was almost too much to take in. First the disturbing revelation about Roxane, and now the risible assertion that the others cared about my opinion. But intuition told me that playing along with her charade could prove to be useful.

*Trust your instincts …*

I walked over to one of the nearby bollards and sat down to ponder the most advantageous course of action. Telling Christophe was out of the question. He had enough to deal with already and did not need to be troubled further by this inanity. And what about Théo? If I told Théo, it would probably amuse him and nothing more, but he'd want details. He'd ask me what I thought, whether I was jealous. He would, I was certain, make more of the whole affair than was warranted, and he might want to see the letters for himself. I could not allow that to happen.

'Burn them,' I said. 'Take the letters, and burn them. Then we can all just forget about it. It's the best outcome for everyone.'

Diana grinned. 'I *knew* you'd have the solution. I'm so glad we waited for you. We miss you, you know. I miss you.' She plopped herself down next to me, squeezing onto the bollard. 'We rarely spend time together these days. And, yes, I'm aware it's my fault because of how I behaved. I realise now that I overreacted. Totally overreacted.'

My ears started to ring, and my head throbbed. I couldn't listen to any more of her deranged waffle. I got up and began walking towards the river, only for Diana to follow and fall into step alongside me.

'You were right,' she said. 'I *was* acting like a jealous lover. I had no right to be so demanding, and of *course* you are entitled to have other friends, I do see that, but it was difficult for me. I was so upset, Inès. We were so close and, well, Liliane and Veronica … It felt like they were trying to take you from me. As though we were in competition for you as well as for everything else. I couldn't stand it.'

I stared at her, trying to work out why she was saying all this. Yes, she would benefit from manipulating me, from fabricating stories and twisting reality, but I had an inkling that there was more to this deception than trying to wear down the competition. Something I couldn't see, a truth that eluded me.

'Diana'—I spat out her name as if it were a maggot in an apple—'I was *never* friends with either of those two buffoons.'

'It's quite all right,' she said. 'Don't feel obliged to spare my feelings. I'm past all that now, and not simply because they are both …' She paused. '*Absent.* I miss your friendship. I miss *you*. Can we go back to how things were?'

I crossed the bridge and headed for the Latin Quarter, hoping to shake her off. But Diana was like a wasp that had caught the scent of something sweet.

'It won't be like before,' she said, her thumb and forefinger circling my wrist. 'I promise. I've changed, I've learnt my lesson. Please. Give me another chance.'

Her eyes were wide and pleading. Her mascara was ruined from all the crying, her hair frizzier than ever. Her maroon lipstick, borrowed from Françoise, was inexpertly applied and made her look like a cartoon villain.

'Please,' she said. 'Can we just forget about it, like Roxane and her nasty letters? Pretend it didn't happen.'

'It didn't, Diana. *Nothing happened.*'

She clasped my hands. 'Oh, Inès, thank you. You don't know how much this means to me.' She threaded her arm through mine. 'Say, shall we go to a tearoom or something? It would be *super* to catch up properly.'

'I have plans,' I said.

Her maroon mouth drooped. 'Oh yes, right, you must have. But maybe we could start practising together again? I've *so* missed that. You've probably seen the pickle I've got myself into since you stopped helping me. It would make all the difference if you could tutor me, like before.'

I was about to point out that I had never helped her with anything, and that there had been no friendship, but I wanted to choose the right path – the one in which Christophe was mine and I was his, where we were indelibly linked to each other. And now, here was Diana, offering herself to me.

'All right,' I said.

Diana's chin lifted. 'Really? You mean it?'

'Yes. I'll help you.'

'Great! When shall we start? How about now?'

'I told you, I have plans,' I said, vexed by how incapable the blondes were of listening. 'There is something I need to get in order. And something *you* need to get in order.'

She gave me a quizzical look.

'Roxane's letters,' I said. 'Burn them. Burn every single one.'

She crossed her fingers and held them up to show me. 'I promise. I'll do it as soon as I get back.'

'Make sure you do.'

Roxane's sordid fantasies had to be reduced to ashes. And Diana's rabid delusions had to be laid to rest.

# 24

A few days later, Christophe instructed us to assemble in the courtyard after class. No explanation was given, but as we'd been told to wear our smartest clothes, we assumed it was in aid of something notable. The blondes were already there when Théo and I arrived – separately, despite his objections. As we took our place behind them, Diana gave me a thumbs up, which I did not acknowledge. Roxane was staring into space, as if she were unmindful of Théo's presence. But I knew differently. I may have dismissed her before, but she was in my sights now.

Christophe was dressed in a navy suit which, from the look of the quality and how it was cut, was obviously expensive, and bespoke. The motive for such an extravagant purchase, and for the interruption to our classes, was standing beside him.

For this occasion, Justine Deschamps had fixed her hair into a low ponytail. Her lips were painted a bright shade of pink, which should have clashed with her complexion but instead increased her allure. The blondes gawped at her with reverent fascination, and for once, I could not blame them. Justine Deschamps was stunning.

'My dear students,' Christophe began. 'The academy

has been through a terrible time. And while we're carrying on as best we can, it is only right that we do something to honour Veronica and Liliane, as a sign of our love for them, and of our strength and unity.' Christophe motioned behind him, where a makeshift curtain had been hung across the wall. 'Madame Deschamps has generously donated this plaque, which will serve as a memorial to our absent friends. Madame Deschamps, please, if you would.'

Justine smiled kindly at the blondes, and they craned their necks to get a better look at her.

'First, may I say how sorry I am for your losses,' she said, 'and for the sorrow you have endured. Thank you for allowing me to be here with you and to help you come to terms, however you can, with what you have suffered. It is with great honour …'

Justine was a paragon of sympathy. Her voice dripped with concern as she reeled off some already stale platitudes about how the two blondes would be missed, how we would never forget them, and how their legacy – whatever that was – would live on. When Justine spoke of how honoured she was to be one of the sponsors of our upcoming showcase, Théo stifled a yawn. Roxane peered over her shoulder and gave him a shy glance. It was quick – blink and you'd miss it – but enough for me to recognise the pain on her face, the agony of her unreciprocated affections.

Justine pulled back the curtain. The blondes gasped

as the plaque was revealed. A few began to cry, causing Justine's green eyes to moisten. But, in spite of her elegant tears and Christophe's efforts, the dead girls would amount to nothing more than memories.

Afterwards, the blondes drifted back to their rooms. Théo and I stayed behind – he to smoke and me to inspect the plaque. I ran my hands over the two names etched into the brass. Two girls we had known. Two threats I had eliminated – tall flowers I had cut down.

'Let's hope that's the end of it,' Théo said. 'Any more death would ruin us.'

'It's not like you to fret about the academy,' I said.

'I couldn't care less about this place,' Théo said. 'I meant us. Any more misfortune will ruin *us*.' He held my eyes. 'We are bound together.'

'That's not how it ends. You know that.'

Théo dipped his head as though he were about to kiss me. But right at the last moment, he changed his mind and walked away, leaving me alone with the dead blondes.

# 25

I was on my way to buy the knife when I saw Roxane perched on the low wall that bordered the hedgerows opposite Notre-Dame. The square was busy, filled with raucous groups of youngsters and tourists milling around the cathedral entrance, consulting travel guides and posing for photographs in front of the famous facade. Despite the bustle, Roxane appeared to have tuned out of her surroundings. Her eyes were closed, one hand resting primly on her knee, the other on the posy of flowers beside her.

My head was brimming with my plans, and I nearly kept walking and left her in her repose. But as I crossed the road and got a clearer view of her, I thought of those letters – 'pages and pages of them', Diana had said – and on a whim I changed direction and headed her way.

Roxane was completely immersed in her thoughts, making it all too easy for me to creep up on her.

'Penny for them,' I said.

Her eyes snapped open, and she gave a startled cry.

'What do *you* want?' She glared at me reproachfully. 'Why are you talking to me?'

'What a peculiar question.'

Roxane tensed as I sat down beside her. 'My mother said I shouldn't trust you.'

'You've been talking to your mother about me?' I put my elbow on my knee and placed my chin on my palm. 'How intriguing.'

'I tell her the cruel things you do,' she said. 'How you hide my things, play tricks on me … how you make fun of me.'

'I think you're confusing me with the others,' I said. 'And those awful girls play tricks on me too, you know. They invent all kinds of stories about me. I think they're trying to convince me I've gone mad.' I nodded at the posy. 'What's that for?'

'It's for Liliane and Veronica.'

'For the memorial in the courtyard?'

She nodded and shivered, although the sun was out and it was an unseasonably warm day.

'That's very decent of you,' I said. And so typical of her: even though both Liliane and Veronica had never shown her a shred of kindness, Roxane still wanted to lay flowers for them.

'They would do the same for me,' she said.

I couldn't contain a hoot of laughter. 'They wouldn't have done anything for anyone. Neither of them. They were concerned only with themselves.'

Roxane squirmed. 'You mustn't say things like that. They were kind. *They* were decent.'

'Sure they were. If there was something in it for them.'

I put a hand in my pocket and found Théo's cigarettes. 'I think we need to have a talk. Don't you?'

'A talk?' She eyed me suspiciously. 'About what?'

'I think you have a secret,' I said. 'And I think you want to share it with me.'

'I would *never* confide in you. Not after what happened before. You told everyone. *Everyone.*'

'Roxane, I don't—'

'It was only that one time!' she blurted. 'Just once! It was my first night away from home … I'd never slept in a strange bed before. I was frightened, I missed my mother, and I … I …' Her gaze dropped to her lap. 'You said you were my friend. I went to you for *help*. And you told all the girls, Inès. *All of them.* Every day, Élodie says, "Pissed yourself yet, Roxane?" They will never let me forget it. Never.'

'Don't listen to Élodie,' I said. 'She teases you in order to deflect attention from her own issues. The next time she makes fun of you, ask her about her chronic constipation, and the cream she puts on her piles every night. That will shut her up.'

Roxane's mouth fell open. 'How do you know that?'

I was about to answer but found my mind was empty. I had no idea where that information had come from – none whatsoever – but I was certain it was true.

'It doesn't matter how I know,' I said. 'What matters is that now you know too. So if she teases you again, tease her back. That's how the world works. Tit for tat, eye for eye, tooth for tooth. If you don't stand up for yourself, no one else will. And, anyway, you're mistaken. It wasn't me. I didn't tell.'

I moved to touch her arm, but Roxane wrenched it away. 'It could only have been you. You were the only person I told.' She got up, holding the posy in front of her like a bride. 'I really must go now.'

'I know about the letters, Roxane. Diana told me.'

Her face drained of colour.

'So, you see,' I said, with a smile I couldn't suppress, 'I'm not the one who can't be discreet. You're in love with Théo, aren't you?'

Her mouth formed a perfect 'O'. Her salacious secret was out, its sticky threads pinning her in place. Her head dipped and she said, so quietly I could barely hear her above the youths laughing and the mopeds streaking past, 'Please don't laugh at me.'

A breeze blew across the Seine, lifting Roxane's blonde tresses off her shoulders. The traffic quietened and the city noise receded until there was only the rustle of the leaves on the trees along the riverbank and the sound of an old bell ringing. Each chime was a signal. A command.

'I would never laugh at you,' I said. 'Because I understand. I understand completely.'

I rose to my feet and linked my arm through hers. 'Shall we take a stroll?'

It didn't take long for Roxane's reserve to crumble. As we walked, she gushed like a broken pipe, as if she'd been yearning for a willing listener to whom she could vent her pent-up feelings. And now, she had one.

She talked of how her heart fluttered whenever she saw Théo, how her knees became weak, how her head felt dizzy and her pulse raced. She told me there were times when she feared she loved him too much, and how she worried that one day her emotions would consume her completely.

'Like a fireball?' I said.

She looked at me in surprise. 'Yes. Exactly like that. How did you know?'

Because I lived it. Every day, every hour, every minute, I lived it.

We went over the bridge and I saw her glance at the padlocks that people persisted in fixing to the metal grille. I wondered if Roxane had added to them: if she'd bought a lock and etched her name and Théo's onto it.

'How long have you felt this way?' I said.

'Since the first moment I saw him. It was love at first sight.'

'And you've never told him? He has no idea?'

She shook her head. 'I'm too scared to speak to him. I think I'd die if I did. Sometimes in class I feel faint just knowing he's watching me from behind the piano.'

'He's not watching *you*. He's reading the music.'

Two pink blotches appeared on her cheeks. 'Well, yes, I know, but … He's the only reason I can bear it. I hate Paris. I *hate* it. And I hate the academy, too. It's a malicious place. If it wasn't for him, I'd have run away. Although sometimes I dream …' She stopped as we reached the quay. 'I dream that we run away together. That he tells me he's in love with me too, that he's always been in love with me. And then we leave. Just the two of us.'

'Théo is a Paris boy at heart,' I said. 'He'd never leave.'

Roxane gawped at me. 'You *know* him?'

'A little. I could put in a word for you.'

'You'd do that?' Her expression brightened for a second, but then she seemed to clam up again. 'This is another of your cruel jokes, isn't it?'

'I never joke. But I promise you that it isn't. I do need to know more, though.'

'More?'

'Yes,' I said. 'Much more.'

We descended the steps and sat side by side on one of the benches by the Seine. It was a glorious day, the sunshine making the river gleam. There was no one else around to enjoy the fine weather, and we had the idyllic spot all to ourselves.

'Tell me how you feel about Théo,' I said.

'I already did.'

'Tell me the things you wrote in your letters.'

I felt her body stiffen.

'The letters were just daydreams,' Roxane said. '*Private* daydreams. I'd never have sent them.'

'Of course you would. Why write them otherwise? You wanted him to know. You wanted him to know so that he would do those things to you. I don't blame you for that.'

'You don't?'

'Not at all.'

I shifted closer to her. 'Do you think of him touching you, Roxane? Are you unable to think of anything else but him? His smell, his skin …?'

Her thighs clenched. Her chest rose and fell rapidly; her breath came in short, shallow rasps. A long moan escaped her lips, and she closed her eyes. When she opened them and saw me, she jumped up as though she'd been electrocuted.

'No!' she said. 'I won't fall for it. You're going to tell everyone.'

'I won't tell a soul. This is between us. We'll take it to our graves.' I rose from the bench. 'I need to see the letters. Where are they?'

She backed away, edging towards the river. 'Diana took them. She burned them all.'

*Good girl.*

'That's a shame,' I said. 'A terrible shame. Do you think you'll write more?'

'I don't know …' Roxane rubbed her forehead and took another step backwards. 'I don't know. Maybe. No!'

'That's right,' I said. 'You won't. Oh dear, you forgot this.' I picked up the posy and thrust it into her arms. 'You'll need it.'

'Need … need it for what?' she stammered, shuffling ever nearer to the water.

'For when you see Liliane and Veronica. One of us ought to visit them, and I think it should be you.'

I clasped her shoulders. Her brow wrinkled, and I could see from the fear on her face that she wanted to run, but she was too afraid, too meek, to save herself.

'Go to them,' I said.

It required only the lightest of touches – the tiniest amount of force. One gentle shove, and Roxane toppled like a skittle.

She barely made a splash as she hit the Seine. There was a momentary thrashing of her arms, her head bobbing up through the waves once or twice, and then a watery scream that was quickly smothered as the current dragged her under. For a few seconds, there were bubbles. Then, there was nothing.

The posy floated to the surface, commemorating Roxane before she had even begun to be missed.

My hands were shaking as I lit one of Théo's cigarettes and stared at the river, expecting – *hoping* – to see her pale arm pierce the surface, or hear her voice cry out for help so that I could dive in and save her … save myself. I stared and stared for any sign of her, but there was only the whoosh of the wind through my hair, the whisper of the gargoyle's voice in my ears and the emptiness in my soul. My hateful, rotten soul.

As the Seine carried the flowers away, I turned and resumed my quest to buy the knife.

When the idea of the knife had come to me, I knew it couldn't be just any knife – not the quotidian kind found in a typical kitchen. It had to be special. It had to fit the task. Fortunately, a life of constant desperation had taught me to be resourceful, and a series of tenuous connections had led me to Olivier, whom I was assured could be trusted to procure almost anything.

Due to the unexpected dispatch of Roxane, I was late for our rendezvous, and I arrived at the address flustered and sweating. Olivier was already in our agreed meeting spot, looking harried and impatient as he loitered on the kerb in front of what was surely one of the ugliest buildings in Paris, an attempt at modern architecture that served the notion that the past was not only better than the present, it was also preferable to the future.

Olivier surveyed me as I approached, his head framed by the wash of colourful graffiti on the wall behind him. When we'd spoken on the telephone, he'd given me a brief description of himself, which I saw now had been disarmingly honest. 'I'm hideous,' he'd said. 'You'll know me.'

I felt my palms tingle from the feel of Roxane's velvet jacket as I'd pushed her into the Seine, and thought that the same was true of me. *I'm hideous. You'll know me.*

I shoved the thought aside and walked towards him. 'Olivier, I presume?'

His eyes were bloodshot but beady, and almost buried by the lines and wrinkles that ravaged his sallow complexion. They narrowed as he regarded me.

'Who's asking?' he said. The depth of his suspicion was reassuring.

'Roxane,' I said, wondering if the name I'd given to secure the meeting had been a coincidence or an omen. 'Have you got it?'

Olivier slipped into the alleyway beside him. He turned his back to the street and opened his jacket. Tucked in one of his many inside pockets was a knife.

'Is this what you wanted?' he said.

He took it out and passed it to me, and I had to smile.

The blade was the optimum size; the handle was smooth and comfortable in my grip. I ran my finger along the serrations on the blade and the power, the potential, seemed to flow into my skin. Although it was just a knife, it was easy to see how it could, with a mere flick of the wrist, be so much more.

I dropped it into my bag and took out an envelope of cash.

Olivier eyed it with measured interest. 'It wasn't easy to find that, you know. In fact, it's a credit to my skills that I managed to get it at all, especially at such short notice.'

'No need for the speech.' I gave him the envelope. 'There's a little extra in there in acknowledgement of your efforts.'

Olivier counted the money quickly. Content it was all there, plus the bonus I'd promised, he stuffed it into his pocket and took out a packet of cigarettes. 'You've gone to a lot of trouble. The knife must be for a very particular purpose.'

I hitched my bag onto my shoulder, pressing it tight against my body with my elbow. 'I'm making a fruit salad. You know how tough watermelons can be.'

The trough between his bushy eyebrows deepened, making his face appear even craggier. 'It'd better not come back to me, Roxane. I don't like fruit salad. Usually, I don't go near it. I'm allergic. You understand?'

'Don't worry,' I said. 'There will be no repercussions for you. I will make sure of that.'

## 26

As darkness fell that evening, the blondes lounged in the corridor, scrutinising the latest iteration of Christophe's script. Sitting as far away from them as I could, I leafed through my own copy, enduring their burbling in order to keep up appearances, and so I wouldn't be outfoxed by any sly manoeuvres. There was a renewed sense of competition in the air, for Christophe had warned us that preparations for the showcase were to be accelerated and that we would be working even harder than before. The blondes were reinvigorated by this news, and the shift in focus from the stalled lives of their ex-classmates back to their own futures lifted their malaise. So much so that as they obsessed over casting permutations and swapped vivid daydreams about being 'discovered', not one of them noticed Roxane's absence.

'I like this version better,' Diana said, her head bent over the page as she highlighted one of the key monologues. 'The lead is much more challenging.'

'He's certain to choose you,' Aurélie said. 'I can't imagine who else could perform it.'

Diana's lips twisted into a smile so conceited, it made me glad of the knife.

'I shall never get my head around all the changes,' Françoise said.

Christophe's script had undergone several brutal rewrites since the loss of two cast members, but the flood of donations to the academy had allowed him to expand his ideas and make the performance more elaborate than previously planned. I listened to the others trying to get to grips with the new scenes and the additional dialogue, and wondered how they'd cope when it was discovered that another actor had departed and the script would have to be rewritten yet again.

'The previous version was less complicated,' Déborah said. 'I preferred it.'

'Because *you* are less complicated,' Élodie said, and Déborah stuck her tongue out at her.

'Christophe is a wonderful writer,' Hélène said, sighing as she ran her fingers over the title page.

'Naturally,' Cécile said. 'He is a brilliant man.'

Diana looked up and tucked her pen behind her ear. 'What do *you* think of it?'

It took a few moments to register that she was talking to me, and that every blonde head had turned in my direction. As they stared, I saw it happen again in slow motion: the surprise on Roxane's face when I'd pushed her, and her terrified expression when she'd hit the water.

'Why do you care?' I asked.

'Of *course* we care,' Nathalie said. 'What's got into you?'

'Normally you would have told us by now,' Maëlle said. 'We wouldn't even have to ask.'

'Yes,' Élodie said. 'You usually enjoy telling us what to think.'

'She doesn't *tell* us what to think,' Diana said. 'She gives us her *opinion*. And we are extremely grateful for it.' She got up and scurried towards me, almost tripping over Nathalie's outstretched legs.

'You always make the right choice, Inès,' she said, sounding unusually humble. 'We respect your judgement. We *need* your judgement. Without you we would just …'

'Drift,' Nathalie said, dipping her chin and gazing at me from under her fringe.

Diana touched my arm and lights flashed before my eyes. Suddenly there was only Liliane, Veronica and Roxane in the corridor, torn pages of Christophe's script scattered around them like confetti.

I jumped to my feet, the script rolled up in my fist like a baton. 'I know what you're doing.' I edged away from them – the blondes who were there in the flesh and the ones in my head. 'Your plan is to send me mad, so that I'll leave the academy. Leave Christophe. That's what it's always been about … your lies, your fanciful stories. You're trying to twist everything.'

'Inès, no, we didn't mean to—' Diana reached for my arm again, but I batted her hand away.

'Do *not* touch me. *Never* touch me.'

I fumbled in my pocket for my keys, and my fingers

brushed the handle of the knife.

'You might have a plan,' I said, staring into her startled eyes. 'But so do I. So do I.'

My dealings with the blondes and their fallacious fantasies unnerved me, and afterwards I sat in my room unable to concentrate on the script, or on anything. I was cradling the knife in my palm and admiring the sharp blade when Théo knocked on the door – soft, then loud, then soft, the code we'd agreed from the very first night. The sound revived me, and I stuffed the knife under the mattress and got up to let him in. Although I'd heard the girls drifting into their rooms an hour or so before, as I opened the door I glanced along the corridor to reassure myself that no one was there to see us. Théo watched me, his mouth puckered in disapproval.

'You must know by now that I'd never betray you,' he said. 'But still you don't trust me.'

'It's not you I don't trust, Théo.'

I closed the door and locked it. Théo reached for the book on the bedside table, flipping through it to find his place.

'I thought they were never going to settle tonight,' he said. 'Christophe's pretentious opus has got them all worked up. They were like a cloud of hornets.'

'They always are.'

He looked pointedly at me. 'I didn't see Roxane around this evening.'

My flesh began to itch, as though the hornets Théo spoke of were crawling on my skin.

'I don't want to think about the blondes,' I said. 'Not tonight, at least.'

But they wouldn't let me rest.

Sleep was even more elusive than ever. Whenever I closed my eyes, I saw Veronica's skin turning yellow and Liliane gasping for air. I saw the events of the afternoon: Roxane sinking into the river, dying how she had lived – barely making a splash. Three blondes gone now. Three lives snatched away by my hands. When would it end? *How* would it end?

The hours ticked by, and the images of Roxane's last moments became more vivid. Eventually, I couldn't take it any more. I left Théo to his dreamless sleep and slipped out of bed. I dressed as quietly as I could, tiptoed out of my room and slunk across the courtyard, like the ghost Roxane had feared, and made my way to Notre-Dame.

The souvenir shop was deserted. Candles of every conceivable size and shape were dotted everywhere: thick pillar candles that dripped hot wax down their lengths; thin, tapered candles housed in ornate holders. Votive candles and tealights, placed decorously along the surfaces and shelves, formed a trail of light leading to the spiral staircase. I wondered who – or what – had positioned them all there.

The night was at its darkest point as I stepped out onto the platform that ringed the two towers. The gargoyle was standing with its arms folded, one foot tapping the stone.

'Can't sleep?' it said. 'Insomnia has always plagued you.'

'How do you know how I sleep?' A wave of alarm engulfed me as I considered what it might know not just about my future but about my past. 'How long have you been watching me?'

'Since the beginning. I watch over all those who need me, especially those with your potential. I am eternal.'

'Nothing is eternal. You were created, just like the rest of us. Someone made you. Before that, you didn't exist.'

It snorted, two tendrils of smoke shooting out of its nose. 'I am my own maker, Inès. So, tell me about your little episode today ... Poor, sweet Roxane. Drowning makes for a horrible death. What did she ever do to you?'

'You told me they were all threats,' I said. 'That I shouldn't take any risks. I was only following your instructions.'

The gargoyle regarded me inquisitively, its ears wiggling. 'Are you sure? From up here it appeared as though Roxane's death — no, Roxane's *murder* — had nothing to do with what we discussed. You killed her not because you feared she might have a chance with Christophe but because of her affections for Théo. Your conscience is pricking you not because you killed Roxane but because of *why* you did so.'

The hairs on my arms rose. 'No.'

'Then, what is it? What do you need from me?'

The gargoyle rested on the parapet, and as it studied me with its hollow sockets, memories began to unspool in my mind. Images I thought were buried, scenes I thought were excised, visceral feelings I thought were lost in the tangle of the past, came rushing into the present.

*The descent into that deep hole underground. The dank air, the musty smell. The slam of a metal door, the turn of an old key in a rusty lock.* Please, no, please ... *The growl of hunger, and a desperate thirst. Guilt, disgust, shame. A shroud of shame, covering me from head to toe. The clicking of beads and the rhythmic repetition of prayers, on and on, day and night.* For your soul, Inès, for your soul. *What soul? What could remain? Only the darkness of this tiny space, only the dampness of the ground seeping into my bones. Only the hand that beckons to me with fingernails like talons, and the eyes that gaze upon eternity, and the voice that promises me everything and tells me nothing that I see or know is true.* Trust me, *it says*, only I will tell you the truth.

'I ...' The words crawled around my skull like cockroaches, but I couldn't speak them. I daren't.

The gargoyle's horns flexed. First one, then the other. 'You need feel no shame up here,' it said. 'Nor guilt.'

An icy coldness spread up my spine – the chill not just from the night air but from that hole underground all those years ago. 'I keep thinking ... about what the nuns used to say. What they told me I was. Maybe they were right. Maybe I deserved those punishments. Perhaps I *should* be locked up.'

'But they let you go,' the gargoyle said. 'If they truly thought you were an abomination, a curse upon the world, why not keep you locked up?'

'So you *do* think that's who I am.'

It smiled knowingly, showing its jagged teeth. 'All that counts is who *you* think you are.'

My head throbbed. 'I don't know. I'm not sure I ever will. These thoughts, these feelings …'

'You needn't fear them,' it said. 'You needn't fear anything.'

I looked at the gargoyle, wanting so badly to trust it. 'What *are* you? Maybe you're not even real. Maybe I've imagined you like the blondes imagine things … Liliane spoke as if we were friends. Veronica told Christophe I helped her. Diana insisted we used to practise together. Even Roxane made up some story about how I told everyone she wet the bed. Why do they come to me with their crazed fantasies? Have they all gone mad? Are they trying to send *me* mad? Tell me the truth.'

'Reality is a spectrum,' the gargoyle said. 'We each find our own place within it.'

'Then how can I ever believe in you? I don't even know what you are.'

'And as I keep telling you, I am what I am. Nothing more, nothing less. You are here with me, talking with me. You *know* I'm real.'

The gargoyle came to stand next to me. Its breath was like a blast of winter.

'I saw the knife,' it said. 'And that's why you've come, isn't it? You need something. Something only I can give you.'

I stifled my trepidation and met its desolate gaze. 'I want a guarantee.'

'For what you did today?'

'Not just for today. For what I might do. For the future. I … I'm out of control.'

'Really? I would say this is the most composed you've ever been. But, very well …' The red orbs appeared in its eye sockets. 'No one will know that you killed Roxane. No one will know it was you. As for the knife, well, as we speak now, it is just a knife. Nothing more.'

'But you know what it could be. What it might become.'

'By your hand and not mine,' the gargoyle said. 'Your choices are your own.'

Far on the horizon, the first shards of light filtered through the clouds, heralding the arrival of a new day. But above Notre-Dame, the sky remained pitch black.

'The idea of the knife came to me from nowhere,' I said. 'I saw how it would happen as if I were watching a film. I saw myself using the knife, and I thought, "How could I do such a terrible thing?" But I did not stop. At the end of the daydream – the *nightmare* – I was covered in blood.'

The gargoyle nodded, its tongue flicking out like a snake's. 'There will be a lot of blood. Even more than you imagine. But this is the path you have chosen.'

'Did I? Perhaps you made me choose it.'

'A seed can only grow in fertile soil.'

'Then the nuns *were* right.'

'If that's how you choose to think of it,' the gargoyle said. 'Who will you believe, Inès? Those nuns, who crushed you, who damned you, who thrust you down into the pit and forsook you? Or the one who tells you the truth, who wants to take away the pain? The one who will never abandon you, and who knows you deserve the ending you so badly crave.'

I gazed across Paris, my eyes drawn to its outer fringes. I hadn't returned to the orphanage since my ignominious expulsion, but I knew it was still there. I knew the room underground, with the metal door and the iron bars, remained. I knew it was still dark inside it, still damp, and that those rosary beads still clicked as prayers were chanted for my soul. Somehow, I *knew*.

'How much blood would you spill for him?' the gargoyle said. 'For love? Perhaps that will tell you who you are.'

I turned my back on my past and looked at the gargoyle. At my future.

'Am I getting closer?' I asked. 'Am I near to reaching the end?'

The gargoyle's smile was wider than ever.

'You're almost there,' it said. 'And your ending, when it comes, will be *spectacular*.'

It had been dark and deserted when I entered the towers, but I came out to find that dawn had broken, and Paris teemed with its usual morning activity. I hurried back to the academy and headed straight for the studio. I peered in through the glass panel on the door and saw that rehearsals were in full swing, but the blondes seemed agitated. Aurélie was taking her turn at dancing the lead role and kept bungling the steps, and even from outside I could sense Christophe's irritation. His eyes shifted to the door as I turned the handle, and everything stopped. The music ceased mid-bar, legs halted and feet stilled.

'Sorry,' I said, slipping off my coat and adding it to the pile. 'I overslept.'

There was a hum of anxiety in the room that my entrance seemed to have exacerbated. As I took my place behind the blondes, Théo watched me from over the piano.

Christophe put his hands on his hips. 'The rules concerning punctuality are very clear, Inès. What is difficult about following them? Everyone else has managed it.'

One of the blondes looked round and glared at me – I couldn't even tell which it was. The faces staring at me belonged to Liliane, Veronica and Roxane. Poor, sweet Roxane. *Drowning makes for a horrible death.*

'Well?' Christophe said. 'Do you have anything to say for yourself?'

'It won't happen again,' I mumbled.

He sighed wearily and crossed his arms. 'Have you seen Roxane?'

'No.'

'Really?' There was an edge of desperation to Christophe's tone. 'Not at all?'

I wiped my hands on my T-shirt, fearing there might be traces of Roxane on them – a strand of her hair, flakes of her skin, fibres from the velvet jacket she'd been wearing.

'I haven't seen her,' I said. 'Not this morning. Sorry.'

Christophe's mouth tightened and he ran a hand over his chin. 'Who was the last person to see Roxane?'

The atmosphere became frenzied as the blondes began to fret. Hélène's face turned white; Cécile gripped Déborah's wrist. Françoise muttered about the ghost, and Élodie threaded her fingers through Maëlle's.

'I don't remember seeing her before bed,' Aurélie said.

'Me neither,' Nathalie said. 'She wasn't with us.'

'I'm sure she was,' Diana said. 'She's just so unremarkable you probably didn't notice her.'

'Why are you always so unkind?' Hélène said.

'I'm only being frank,' Diana said. 'Mr Leriche needs to know the truth. And I'm sure there's a simple explanation for why Roxane isn't here.'

'If you want to provide an *explanation*,' Hélène said, 'then why don't you tell him what you did? You, Déborah and Françoise.'

Françoise's mouth dropped open. 'Why would you blame *me*?'

'Yes, why us?' Déborah said, a hand on her hip.

'Because it's your fault!' The blondes recoiled in shock as Hélène stamped her heel, leaving a black mark on the floorboards. 'Stop making light of it! Roxane is *missing*. We have to look for her. Anything could have happened.'

'Roxane said there is something bad here,' Nathalie said. 'She was right.'

'An evil presence!' Maëlle said.

'If you could only hear yourselves …' Diana said with a shake of her head.

The blondes continued bickering. Lines were being drawn between those who subscribed to the notion of a spectral Grim Reaper stalking the academy and those who believed it but would not allow themselves to admit it.

Christophe made another plea for calm, and I risked a glance at Théo. He looked back at me, his eyebrows raised as if posing a question I had to stop him from verbalising.

'Maybe she went home,' I said.

Everyone turned to look at me.

'Roxane was always saying she hated it here,' I said. 'Perhaps she'd finally had enough and decided to leave.'

'No,' Hélène said. 'She would've told us. She would've at least told *me*.'

'Why?' Diana said. 'Because you enjoyed pretending that you liked her?'

'I *did* like her.'

'Don't talk about her as if she's already in the past,'

Élodie said. 'It gives me the creeps.'

'*You* give me the creeps,' Déborah said.

Christophe stepped between them. 'All right, that's enough. Can anyone remember when they last saw Roxane?'

There was quiet as the blondes racked their brains. It was a while before someone finally spoke up.

'I saw her,' Théo said, his gaze on the piano keys. 'Early this morning.'

I willed him to stop talking, or to at least take it back.

'It looked like she was heading towards Châtelet,' he said.

Christophe sighed. 'Why didn't you say something before?'

Théo shrugged. 'It's hard to get a word in.'

'You're sure it was her?' Christophe said.

Théo looked at me. 'Positive.'

'There!' Christophe said with a relieved smile. 'We have our answer. Roxane has gone for a walk and has probably lost track of time. She will return when she's ready. We should press on.' He nodded at Théo. 'Start from the beginning of the second movement.'

We got into position, and Théo began to play. The blondes concentrated as hard as they could, but their minds were evidently elsewhere, and Christophe grew increasingly irascible as he was forced to correct the same mistakes. After another hour of arduous practice that yielded no tangible results, he gave up.

'Go back to your rooms,' he said. 'Study for the rest of the day. I mean it – no slacking.'

The blondes turned their backs on him to retrieve their bags from the pile and, still divided into two factions, the believers and the deniers, wandered towards the door.

'Not you, Inès,' Christophe said.

I stopped and pivoted slowly. Christophe went to the piano and scribbled something on Théo's music sheets.

'You stay behind,' he said without looking up. 'I need to speak with you.'

Théo's expression conveyed the surprise I was determined not to show in front of the blondes, who whispered and nudged each other. Diana prodded me and mouthed, 'Tell me later!' as she passed me.

Théo slid off the piano stool and traipsed after them.

'Close the door,' Christophe said.

Théo slammed it behind him.

Christophe shook his head. 'I think that boy tries my patience on purpose. But he's the best, and will only get better. I worry he will leave and play for someone else. Someone who can pay him better.'

'Théo is loyal.'

'So you *do* know him well.'

'No better than anyone else.' My heart was pounding. 'Is that what you wanted to talk to me about? Théo?'

As Christophe came over to me, I allowed myself to think that this could be it – this could be the moment he told me loved me, that I was the one. I wondered if it would make me feel better or worse when I was able to confess how I felt about him, or if it would only increase the longing. He put his hands in his pockets and I mirrored the gesture, and when I found my pockets empty I remembered I'd left the knife in my room. If Christophe *was* about to offer me hope, then it would remain just a knife, and I'd toss it into the Seine to join Roxane on the riverbed. But if he wasn't …

'I'm worried,' Christophe said. 'About Roxane.'

My disappointment was so acute I could taste it – salty, like tears.

'You shouldn't be,' I said. 'I think there was an incident with the others yesterday. She probably just needs to hide somewhere and lick her wounds.'

'An incident?' His brow furrowed. 'What sort of incident?'

'I'm not sure.' I glanced down, seeing the scuff Hélène's shoe had left. 'From what I understand, Déborah and Françoise may have found some personal things of hers. Letters, maybe. I think they might have taken them.'

Christophe rolled his eyes. 'What is it with them? Why can't they get along?' He sighed. 'How did this come about?'

'I wasn't there, I'm afraid. I can't tell you exactly what happened. But it will pass, I'm sure. It usually does.'

'You can appreciate why I'm concerned, though,' he said.

'Of course. But I'm certain it's nothing. Roxane is

a sensitive girl, and it has been difficult here recently, what with … everything. Plus, she's done nothing but pine for home since she arrived.' An idea popped into my head. 'If it makes you feel better, why don't you telephone her mother?'

Christophe rubbed his chin with the heel of his palm. 'And say what?'

I took a step towards him. 'Pretend it's a courtesy call or something.' The words were coming to me like someone was feeding them into my ear. 'Roxane speaks to her every day. If she's planning to go home, her mother will know, and you can find out without having to alarm her.'

He pressed his finger to his lips for a beat or two while he considered it, then broke into a smile. 'I don't know what I'd do without you.'

And he'd never have to find out.

Christophe picked up the music sheets and shuffled them. 'You don't need to study this afternoon. Go, enjoy the rest of the day.'

'Thank you,' I said, although I'd rather have stayed with him. 'What will you do?'

'I have some errands to run,' he said. 'People to see, work to plan, and the script needs another polish. There is always so much to do.'

'Yes,' I said, thinking of the knife, 'there is. See you in the morning, then?'

I let the sentence hang hopefully in the air, but Christophe was immersed in the music again, and I was forgotten. But surely not for much longer.

Théo was keen to make the most of the free afternoon, and without the threat of being seen by the blondes, the city felt boundless.

We strolled through the Tuileries gardens, our hands linked. We walked beneath the arches on the Rue de Rivoli, pausing to gaze into shop windows and imagining the things we would buy, the mindless objects we'd accumulate, if we inhabited another world, another life. At the Place des Vosges, we watched, our arms around each other, as a woman fed a flock of pigeons. We sat on a bench and Théo did his impression of Christophe, and although I tried to muster outrage, I couldn't. Instead, I laughed. I laughed until my sides hurt, until I was sliding off the seat and he was pulling me upright, laughing too as he said, 'Inès, Inès.'

It seemed like it was only us. Like it had only ever been us. I pushed my fingers into his coal-black curls, and he let me sit and stare at him.

'I want this,' he said. 'I want this, always.'

He pressed a hand to my chest, and of its own accord, my heart skipped beneath his palm – betraying me, betraying Christophe.

We took another leisurely loop around the city, and stopped at a café on Rue Saint-Honoré. We took a table on the terrace, enjoying the sun on our skin as people passed by – fashionable people, with bags from designer boutiques swinging from their shoulders and shiny phones pressed to their ears. People we could never be. People who would never accept us. But still it couldn't stop me from wondering, *What would life be like if they did?*

'What shall we do next?' I said. 'We could go to the Louvre. Or the Rodin – your favourite.'

Théo picked up his cup and curled his hands around it. 'You know, I heard them talking after the thing with the plaque. Christophe and Justine. She said she felt "something bad" in the academy.'

I stirred my tea and spoke without thinking. 'That's what Roxane said.'

Théo dabbed a blob of froth from his lip. 'I wonder where Roxane is?'

'You were the one who said you saw her this morning. Why did you say that?'

'For you. I said that for you.' Théo drained his cup and pushed it away from him. 'I hope he's worth it. For your sake, and for mine. I really hope he is.'

My tea was cold, and too bitter, too strong, but I could get used to anything. In time, I could normalise even the most unpleasant thing. It was simply a question of adjustment.

Théo didn't want to go to the Louvre, or the Rodin. After our conversation about Roxane, clouds rolled across the sky, hinting at a storm and echoing the shift in Théo's mood. I tried to draw him out of it, to lure him from wherever he had retreated, but I could not reach him.

I suggested we take a walk up to the Canal Saint-

Martin, knowing it wouldn't be lost on him that it was where we had our first kiss. But he showed no interest in reconstructing our past, in standing on the cast-iron bridge where we had realised we were two lost but kindred souls.

'How about another coffee?' I said. 'My treat.'

Théo rose from the chair and fished some change from his pocket. 'I need some space.'

'Space for what?'

He counted out the coins cupped in his palm and dropped them onto the table. 'To think.'

'About what?' I said. 'Think about what, Théo?'

He didn't answer. He had already turned away, and I thought about going after him, but what would I tell him? What reason would I give to make him stay? Théo craved honesty, but what was the truth?

# 27

I lay on my bed, the scant breeze providing little respite from the humidity, and none at all from the angst that Théo's abrupt departure had wrought. The sky threatened an intemperate downpour, and I willed the deluge to come and sweep everything away, make the streets – make me – clean.

As the first drops of rain spattered the window, I leant over and reached under the mattress for the knife.

*There will be a lot of blood. Even more than you imagine. But this is the path you have chosen ...*
*You're almost there.*
Almost there.

A tap on the door silenced the gargoyle's gravelly voice, and my spirits lifted in relief. *Théo*, I thought. *It has to be Théo*, although a glance at the clock told me it was much too early in the evening to be him. I stashed the knife back in its hiding place and rushed to the door, preparing to tell him I was sorry. Sorry for this afternoon, sorry for the lies, sorry for who I was. Sorry for everything I'd done.

I tugged the door open and froze. It wasn't Théo standing in the hallway, but Christophe.

He wore a white shirt under a close-fitting black

sweater, the sleeves rolled up over his wrists. Instead of his usual smart trousers he was wearing dark jeans that hung off his hips. It was the first time I'd seen him so casually dressed. And the first time he'd come to my door.

I must have seemed surprised, or perhaps even shocked, as his smile faded when he saw my expression.

'You were expecting someone else?' he said.

'No, no,' I said, swiping a hand over my hair and cringing at the tangles. 'I was just …' I dabbed a bead of sweat from my brow. 'Busy, that's all.'

'Ah.' He put his hands into his pockets. 'With the new script, yes? The others have got themselves into a lather about it.' His smile returned, playing teasingly on his lips. 'But not you. You look like you've just woken up.'

'Well, I …'

'You don't have to explain anything to me, Inès.' He looked at me for a long beat. 'May I come in.'

It was not a question, and there was no doubt as to what my answer would be. I stepped aside, holding my breath as he entered.

How long had I dreamt of him being in my room? How many hours had I spent longing for it to be just him and me in this tiny space? And now, here he was: so divine, so regal. So mysterious, but so familiar.

As he ran his gaze over the dog-eared books on the bedside table, the shabby dress hanging off the wardrobe door and the lipsticks scattered on the dresser, I became acutely aware of how pitiful my possessions were. The sight of my shoes strewn in opposite corners of the room embarrassed me, and I could see traces of Théo on every surface.

Christophe went to the window and squinted at the view. 'It was a gamble giving you the largest room,' he said. 'I knew the other girls would resent it. And they did, you know. Françoise still reminds me of it now. But instinct told me that you should have the best accommodation I could offer.' He turned to face me. 'And I do *everything* by instinct, Inès. Everything.'

I didn't know what to do with myself, whether to sit or stand, or how to arrange my arms and legs. I was positive he was about to tell me he knew about Théo, and I would have to explain that he was just a distraction, that it was a mutually beneficial arrangement, and profess that it was him I loved. That he was the only one I would ever love.

'You seem nervous,' Christophe said.

I wrapped my arms around my waist to quell the churning in my stomach. 'Tired. It's been a long day.'

He nodded. 'The days are always long now, and seem to be getting longer. I thought time was supposed to pass more quickly as you age.'

'You're still far too young for those kinds of thoughts.'

'If only that were true,' he said. He sat on the bed, linking his hands together and resting them on his lap. 'What did you do with your free afternoon?'

'Nothing, really. I just went for a walk.'

'Alone?'

'Yes. Very much alone.'

'I suppose it must get stifling – the other girls always crowding you, competing for your attention. The way Liliane used to talk about you …' He ran his palm along the bedspread, smoothing out the creases. 'Sometimes I wondered if she was in love with you.'

He glanced up as I laughed.

'What?' he said. 'It never occurred to you?'

'The other girls *despise* me.'

'What? You're good for them. And you're good for me. You're the glue that keeps everything together. You keep *me* together.'

Christophe patted the bed. 'Sit. Please. You're making me nervous too.'

The white dots flickered in my peripheral vision. Slowly, I sat down beside him, leaving as big a gap between us as I could bear.

'I was so worried, Inès,' he said. 'This morning, when Roxane didn't turn up for class … I was terrified. But I followed your advice. I spoke to Roxane's mother.'

'And?' I said, my pulse quickening.

'*And* …' He grinned. 'And Roxane telephoned her this morning to say she was going to stay with some friends in Lyon for a while. She must have been on her way to catch her train when Théo saw her.'

The mattress seemed to ripple beneath me, like the surface of the river.

'I see,' I said, though what Christophe was saying was

impossible. Roxane was languishing in the depths of the Seine: she had no voice with which to call home.

Christophe crossed one leg over the other and folded his arms. 'Her mother promised that she will be back in a few days. She said that Roxane has always been delicate, and takes everything to heart. Which is what makes her so talented. It is a precious gift to feel things so deeply.'

*It was*, I thought.

'I am so grateful to you,' Christophe said. 'For your confidence, for your discretion. You give me such good guidance. I can't describe the relief after I spoke to Roxane's mother. If something had happened to her ...' He took a deep breath and released it slowly. 'If something had happened to Roxane, I would not have been able to live with myself. It would've destroyed the academy. It would've destroyed *me*. If this place goes down, it will take me with it. It is my life, Inès. Without it, I am nothing.'

'You could never be nothing. You're a star. A true star.'

'And you are my talisman. My inspiration. We will do great things together, you and I. Great things.'

Christophe turned his body towards mine and brought his hand to my cheek. He put his mouth to my ear, and I closed my eyes, my lips parting in anticipation. In hope.

'Thank you,' he whispered. 'Thank you.'

*How much blood would you spill for him, Inès?*

All of it. Every last drop.

When I opened my eyes, the room was empty. I touched the space on the bed beside me. It was cold, as if he had never been there. As if the whole scene were entirely my own invention.

The official announcement came later that evening: Roxane, Christophe informed us, had taken a leave of absence.

'From what?' Françoise said.

'From you and your rancid breath,' Cécile said.

'From us,' Élodie said. '*All* of us.'

'From the ghost,' Hélène said. 'The evil presence.'

Diana put a finger to her lips. 'Be quiet!' She spun round to face Christophe. 'Will she be coming back?'

'Certainly,' he replied, glancing at me as he rocked back on his heels. 'Roxane will return when she is ready. And classes will resume tomorrow, two hours earlier than usual. We need to make up for the time we've lost.'

There were the obligatory groans of dismay, but now that the mystery of Roxane's whereabouts had been solved, the blondes were clearly relieved. Only Hélène remained unconvinced.

That evening, she locked herself in her room and refused to come out. Although the others were largely indifferent to Hélène's unease, Diana was determined not to indulge it.

'Hélène!' Diana rapped on her door. 'Hélène, stop being so childish. Come and sit with us!'

As was now their habit, the blondes were in the corridor, where they seemed to spend most of their time. I hated sitting out there with them – the cold floor made my bones ache and their conversations were evermore tiresome – but thought it prudent to keep an eye on them, and an ear to their gossip. I set my book aside as Diana knocked on Hélène's door again.

'Hélène, come *on*!' she said, with even greater impatience.

Françoise was slouched on a pile of cushions she had brought up from the disused communal area. 'Leave her,' she said, flicking the page of the magazine on her lap. 'She's such a pain. Just the sight of her makes me depressed.'

'Depression is very fashionable now,' Cécile said, her feet resting in Déborah's lap.

'Since when?' Maëlle asked.

'Since Veronica,' Aurélie said.

'Veronica might have made depression *un*fashionable,' Élodie said.

'Veronica made *fashion* unfashionable,' Déborah said. She reached for the bottle of nail polish beside her and began painting Cécile's toes a lurid shade of orange.

Diana moved away from the door. 'That doesn't make any sense.'

'Nor does you being so desperate for Hélène to join us,' Nathalie said, shifting closer to Déborah and wiggling her toes, as though hinting that she wanted her nails to be painted next.

'We should be together,' Diana said. 'We must be united. We're a team.'

Françoise laughed. 'You're an idiot if you believe that.'

'She doesn't,' Nathalie said. 'She only wants to make Hélène feel worse so she'll leave and there'll be less competition for the lead.'

'The lead is the *last* thing on my mind,' Diana said with an indignant pout.

Maëlle gave her a long look. 'That's what Veronica used to say. And look what happened to her!'

'It gives me the creeps,' Aurélie said.

'Will everyone please stop talking about the creeps?' Diana said. 'There are no "creeps" here.'

'Except you,' Déborah muttered.

'I really don't …' Diana's voice trailed off and she did a double take as she spotted me getting to my feet. 'Inès, wait …' She skipped over Françoise's cushions and hurried towards me.

I ignored her. I'd had enough of their blathering for one night.

'Inès.' Diana grinned obsequiously at me. 'You've been awfully quiet tonight. Are you all right?'

I hurried to open my door, needing to get away from her as quickly as possible. 'In what universe do I share my business with you?'

Diana appeared startled by this statement of the obvious. 'This one, I thought,' she said. 'I have to talk to you. *Urgently.*'

The blondes watched us with little more than idle curiosity, as if there was nothing unusual about the sight of Diana and me conferring.

'Talk to me about what?' I said.

'Okay, well, you see, the thing is …' Diana lowered her tone to a whisper. 'You said we could practise together again. You said you'd help me.'

I chided myself for being so stupid. Of *course* Diana wanted to talk about herself. The blondes only ever wanted to talk about themselves.

'Is it still okay?' Diana said. 'I *really* need your help.'

The knife flashed into my mind, and it was an effort to banish it. It was still just a knife, but it could become so much more. *So* much more.

'I'd be happy to help you,' I said.

At once, she relaxed. 'Really? Fantastic! How about tomorrow evening? The others are going to see a play. We could sneak into the theatre! It would be perfect.'

'Yes.' I matched her broad smile. 'Perfect indeed.'

I turned to go into my room, but Diana snatched at my sleeve, yanking me back.

'No one can know,' she said. 'The others … You mustn't tell them you're helping me. They'll be so envious, and they loathe me enough as it is. Promise it will stay between us, Inès. Promise me.'

I could promise her, because I knew what she was plotting. She wanted to trick me, to get the better of me. She wanted to eliminate the competition.

But not as much as I did.

'Don't worry, Diana,' I told her. 'Your secret is safe with me.'

I selected a long dress in just the right shade of black and held it up.

'What about this one?' I said.

Théo gave the dress a cursory glance. 'I can't say without knowing the occasion. Are you going to tell me?'

'No. In fact, I remember asking you several times to leave. But as you're still here …' I put the dress back in the wardrobe and took out another – red, this time – and showed it to Théo. 'This?'

His eyes stayed on me. 'Not until you tell me.'

The blondes' chatter drifted through the walls. Théo settled into the chair and picked up his book. His being here this early in the evening was a risk, particularly with the blondes roving between each other's rooms as they got ready for their night out, but Théo had insisted, and I was feeling too ebullient to exercise my usual caution.

'I'm surprised you're not going to see the play with them,' he said. 'You usually do.'

I shimmied out of my jeans and stepped into the red dress. 'Stop it.'

'Stop what? I saw you've made up with Diana again. Maybe you're going out with her tonight. She's staying behind. She says she's "ill".'

'What are you talking about? Did they put you up to

this?' I said. 'Are you in on the joke now? Because if you are …'

From nowhere, tears pricked at the corners of my eyes. I covered my face with my hands and Théo got up and held my shoulders.

'Inès? Inès, what did I say? I'm sorry.' He put his arms around me. 'I'm sorry.'

I let him hold me, nuzzling my face against his neck. His hair was soft on my cheek, his skin so smooth. Had I noticed those things about him before?

Gently, he said, 'You really don't know, do you?' Théo coiled his arms tighter around my waist, binding me to him. 'Poor Inès. My poor darling Inès.'

'What?' I said. 'Tell me.'

He sighed deeply, as though he was about to reveal something he'd rather not.

'People fall in and out of favour with you,' he said. 'You go from obsession to contempt in the blink of an eye. It should make people despise you, but instead, it's seductive. It gives you power. Being the centre of your attention for a month, or a week, or a day, or ten minutes, is hypnotic, and worth the pain that comes when your affections sour. And they do, Inès. They always do.'

I pulled away so I could look at him. 'Why would you say that to me?'

'Because it seems you need to know,' he said. 'And because I'm no different from the "blondes". I compete for a place in your heart, just like they do. And I know I'll fall out of favour with you too – soon, probably. Actually, I'm surprised you haven't tired of me already.' He linked his fingers through mine. 'Sometimes I imagine what it would be like to tire of you first. If I were the one to leave.'

'Then why don't you?'

'I need a reason,' he said. 'I couldn't just walk away.'

'I could give you a reason.'

'No, you couldn't.'

We listened to the blondes laughing as they clattered down the staircase to begin their big night out.

'What will you do tonight?' I said.

Théo stared at my hands, at the fingers that would soon grasp the knife.

'What I always do,' he said. 'Wait for you.'

'How long would you wait?'

'As long as it takes.' His thumb traced my collarbone. 'If I asked you not to go out tonight, what would you say?'

'I would say that it will be over soon. The end is coming.'

'And then what? What will be left? The other day, after Roxane ...' He tensed and took a sharp inhale, and then breathed out slowly. 'After Roxane, I wanted to walk away. From you, from this shitty place. From all of it. I almost did, Inès. I packed a bag and went to the train station. Bought a ticket to Frankfurt.'

'Frankfurt?'

He looked at me. 'My cousin lives there.'

'You have a cousin?'

He nodded. 'There are so many things you don't know about me. So much you *could* know. If you wanted to.'

'Why didn't you go?'

He gave me a doleful smile. 'For the same reason you won't stay here with me tonight. Because love won't allow me to do what's best for me.'

Théo went back to his room. He said it was better that way. I didn't argue with him, but I did wonder. I wondered if he knew about the knife and didn't want to see me tucking it into my pocket before I left.

I wondered if he knew everything.

# 28

Diana gave an agonised cry and dropped to the ground. The theatre felt vast with only the two of us in it, and the deathly silence roared in my ears as she lay motionless on the stage.

Slowly, her head began to lift.

'How was it?' she said, sitting up and putting a hand across her eyes to block the glare of the spotlight. 'Was it okay?'

And by 'it', she meant 'I'. The blondes' sense of self was irrepressible.

Diana squinted into the rows of empty seats. 'Inès, are you there? I can't see you.'

From my place in the stalls, I could've taken aim and shot Diana in the heart and she would never have seen it coming. Instead, I'd chosen a more intimate method for ending her life, one which required an elaborate set-up.

I rose from my seat. 'Magnificent!' I said, clapping with as much enthusiasm as I could summon. This was my performance too – my own final act.

'Do you think so?' Diana watched as I made my way down the aisle towards her. 'Do you really think so?'

'It's the best thing I've seen you do.'

'Really?' she said, as thirsty for validation as ever. 'You really mean it?'

'Oh yes. However ...' I hunched forward, my elbows propped up on the stage. 'I think there's still some room for improvement.'

Her face fell. 'Ah. All right. Yes, of course.' She pulled her knees up to her chest, inadvertently flashing her underwear as she did so. 'Tell me how.'

Naïvely, Diana had allowed me to pick which scene she should work on. To her dismay, I'd chosen the death scene, but she'd set aside her reservations and gamely accepted the challenge. And so there we were, practising as she'd requested. Thus far, Diana had died three times — three preludes to her own death.

'Your performance is good,' I said.

'Good?'

'*Wonderful.*'

She nodded, eager for me to continue praising her.

'But ...' I pretended to consider it. 'But I wonder if we could make it more convincing. Is there a way you can go deeper? Make the emotion more visceral?'

She hugged her calves, like she wanted to fold in on herself, and suddenly she appeared very young, her mannerisms almost childlike — a scared little girl desperate to be somebody so no one would discover that, really, she was nobody.

'I ... I don't know how,' she said.

'Of course you do. Something is stopping you from

giving more. Something is holding you back. What is it?'

Diana fiddled with the strap on her shoe. 'It frightens me,' she mumbled.

'What does?'

She opened her mouth to reply, then closed it again and laid her head on her knees.

'Diana?' I climbed up onto the stage and sat beside her. 'What is it? You can tell me.'

She sniffed loudly and wiped her nose on the back of her hand. 'It's just, well, there's been so much death around these past weeks. It feels like I'm tempting fate.'

'You sound like Roxane,' I said.

'Who had to leave because she couldn't stand it here.'

'It was the pressure Roxane couldn't stand. Talent is only half the battle. A performer has to be robust, has to have physical and mental fortitude. And, as Christophe always says, "Every experience is a gift." Use those emotions. Don't let fear get the better of you.'

'I'm not,' she said. 'But Roxane was *convinced* there was something bad here, and Hélène is absolutely certain of it too. How could they be so sure without it being real?'

I sighed. 'Do you believe in God?'

'I go to Mass every Sunday,' she said, tilting her jaw defiantly.

I shook my head. 'That's not what I asked. You go to Mass because Christophe makes us. I want to know if you *believe*.'

'Well, um'—she tugged up her socks—'it's not really

how I was raised. My father thinks religion is an opiate.'

'There you are, then. You don't believe in God but you stand in a church full of other people who presumably do. And their faith doesn't make you question your disbelief.'

Diana gave me a puzzled look. 'But this is different. I can *feel* the bad thing. I feel it in the dormitory … I feel it in the studio. In my room at night.'

I held her hands in mine. 'Can you feel it now?'

She scanned my face. 'No. Not when I'm with you.' She let her head rest on my shoulder. 'It's not just what's been happening lately that's bothering me, Inès. It's death itself. It *terrifies* me.'

'Ah,' I said. 'That explains it.' I got up and brushed the dust from my dress. 'I am glad we had this little chat. Now I understand.'

She crossed her legs, her head inclined as she gazed up at me. 'What is it?'

'The scene isn't right because I can see *you* in it,' I said. 'You shouldn't be visible, Diana. When you stand on this stage, *you* are not present, only your character.' I crouched in front of her and cupped her chin. Her skin was warm, and the heat from the spotlight had brought out pearls of sweat along her hairline.

'For this scene,' I said, 'you must be oblivious. You don't know death is coming. And that is a luxury. A blessing. You should rejoice in life, ignorant of the fact that death is near.'

'I can't,' she said. 'It's all over me, like tar or something.

I have a dreadful feeling in my tummy.'

'Banish it! Cast it from your mind. You are blissful, you are unaware. The idea of death is buried so deep in your consciousness you believe it will never happen to you. Think of yourself as invincible. Immortal.'

I jumped from the stage and settled into the front row – the best seat in the house for this particular performance.

'Now,' I said. 'Start again.'

'Again?'

I exhaled, my frustration not solely for show. 'Do you want to be excellent, or would you rather settle for mediocrity? Do you want to be the lead, or are you content to wither in the background? I'm sure Françoise wouldn't shy away from practising this scene until she perfected it.'

In an instant, Diana was on her feet. 'What have you heard? Does Christophe have Françoise in mind for the lead?'

'He could have *anyone* in mind. But if you master this scene, he will never be able to overlook you. I guarantee it.'

Diana ran through the scene from the beginning. When she'd finished, I made her do it again, and then once more. Each repetition brought a perceptible improvement; she went from adequate to competent. I could've told her this – what would it have cost me? But my plan made no allowances for charity, and I needed her to keep going. Diana's performance, so to speak, had to be over by the time the blondes returned from their outing. The final curtain had to come down soon, and I had to be certain she was ready, and that the timing – hers and mine – was impeccable.

When Diana 'died' for the seventh time and her legs jerked in her most convincing depiction of death so far, I gave her what I knew would be the last round of applause she would ever receive.

'Superb, Diana. Superb.'

'You truly think so?' Her cheeks were flushed from her exertions. 'It certainly *felt* better to me, but as an actor you never can tell. You really think it was good?'

'I do,' I said, climbing back onto the stage. 'I almost believed you were really dead.'

'Almost? Not totally?'

I took her hands and pulled her upright. 'Don't look so discouraged. You must never let a scene defeat you. You must never let *anything* defeat you.'

'But what more can I do?' she whined. 'I have nothing more to give.'

'You always have more, and you can always reach higher. And I know *how* you can do it. Are you willing to try?'

Her nod came at once. 'Show me.'

'All right …'

I delved into my pocket and took out the knife. Diana's eyes bulged.

'What … How … Is that *real*?' she said.

I held it up to give her a better look at the blade. She seemed mesmerised – *awed* – by it.

'There are some instances,' I said, 'where props will not suffice.'

'Where did you get it?'

'You needn't concern yourself with that. But know that I got it for you. *Especially* for you.'

'For me? Whatever for?'

'To help you,' I said.

I moved closer to her and put the knife to her throat.

'Inès …' Diana leant back, trying to limbo out of range. 'Inès, what are you—'

'Shush.' I took her hand and placed her palm on her chest. 'There. You feel how fast your heart is beating? Now you're nearly there.'

'Nearly where? Inès, I don't know what—'

She gasped as I grazed the tip of the blade along her jaw.

'Ah,' I said. 'Feel how your heart rate has quickened. What else can you feel?'

'I … I'm not sure I understand.'

'You never have, Diana, and you never will. But I can *make* you understand.'

I pressed the knife to her jugular. She quailed and tottered backwards, but fear slowed her reactions and I was faster. Stronger. When it came to it, I would always be stronger than the blondes. They hadn't seen the things I had; they hadn't been hungry, cold, poor. Unwanted.

They hadn't been locked in that damp underground room that felt like a tomb. They hadn't heard the rosary beads clicking, or the voice that probed the darkness.

*For your soul, Inès.*

Yes, for my soul.

Diana spun round and attempted to run, but I caught her sleeve. She shrieked as I yanked her back.

'Inès, I don't like this ... I really *am* scared now.'

'You are,' I said, holding the knife under her chin. 'You are *terrified*. And it's perfect ... *You* are perfect. This will be your best performance ever.'

She wriggled like a maggot on a hook, trying to escape. 'Let *go* of me.' Hot, fat tears rolled down her cheeks. 'Inès, no! You don't have to—'

But I did. Because *this* was who I was.

I plunged the knife deep into Diana's neck. There was no resistance; it sliced into her effortlessly, as though her skin were made of jelly. She made a gurgling sound, her arms flailing in a futile attempt to fight me off. I lunged forward and thrust the knife into her again. Her legs concertinaed and she collapsed onto the stage. Blood spurted from the gashes I had opened, the wounds I had carved, spraying my arms, my face, my lips. It pooled around her, staining the wood – perhaps, I thought, permanently. Diana would leave a mark on the world after all.

She spluttered and reached a hand out to me. A bubble of blood formed between her lips and then popped, spattering her cheeks with red.

I knelt over her body and stared down at her.

'What have you done, Inès? What have you *done!*'

I recoiled so abruptly I toppled over, skidding in the blood. How could she talk? How could she speak?

But Diana's lips hadn't moved, and the voice wasn't hers. It was the one from a long time ago, the one that came from a place deep below the ground – the one that had promised me eternity. The one that, now, had come again.

As the light ebbed from Diana's eyes, I turned to face my audience and let the knife slip from my grasp.

# 29

It was as if I'd left my body and floated out of myself. Everything was tinted with a red haze, and there was something on my tongue – grit, or gravel. As I stumbled off the stage and out of the theatre, I could feel them behind me, their breath on my neck: Liliane, Veronica, Roxane, and now Diana. Following me. They would always be following me.

*What have you done, Inès? What have you done?*

At the dormitory staircase, I sank to my knees. *Just leave me here*, Veronica had said. *I can't go on.*

I can't go on.

I thought of remaining there and letting them find me with blood dripping from my skin, my clothes, the ends of my hair. But the dead blondes were gaining on me, whispering as they advanced. *Don't fall, Inès. Whatever happens, don't fall. It's a long way down … a very long way down.*

I crawled up the stairs, only vaguely aware of the stone scraping my shins. I couldn't see. There was red everywhere – so much red – but when I reached the top my vision cleared, and I saw him. Finally, I saw him.

He was standing outside my room, as if he'd been waiting for me – not just all evening but for much longer than that.

He did not move as I staggered towards him. He simply watched me, like he'd always done.

I could think of nothing to say other than the blindingly obvious, and blind was what I had been. But not any more.

'It's you,' I said. 'Isn't it?'

He regarded me for a moment before he spoke, and I saw the sadness in his eyes. I was the cause of so much of his torment, and the deep well of sorrow within him.

'It's always been me, Inès,' he said. 'You just couldn't see it until now.'

That voice. The one that had come to me when there was no one else. The one that was eternal.

He would redeem me. He would save me.

I traced his features, my palms leaving bloody smudges on his skin. Even though he knew the sins I had committed, the terrible things I had done – and that had been done to me – I was forgiven. He had seen me for what I truly was, just as I was now seeing him, and the kindness of his gaze absolved me.

'I see you,' I said. 'I see you now.'

He brought his fingers to my lips and kissed each one. 'He is not worthy of you, Inès. But I'll protect you. No one will suspect you.'

'You'd do that for me?'

He put his hand on the small of my back and pulled me into him. 'I'd do anything for you.'

He unlocked my door and pushed it wide open. I no longer cared if anyone saw us together, if our secret was discovered. I wanted more. I wanted to be closer to him than I'd ever been before.

He came to me and peeled off my clothes. I turned to go into the bathroom so I could wash away the blood first, but he took my wrist.

'There's no time,' he said. 'We should make the most of what remains.'

'What does that mean?' I said. 'Can't you stay? Like before?'

'Before is gone,' he said. 'It's all history now, Inès.'

We lay on the sheets. The sensation of his flesh on mine was electric, but did not feel strange. I knew the planes of his hips, the distances between the moles on his back, where the whorls of thick, dark hair were. Our bodies fitted together effortlessly – I understood that now. We were the same. We were one.

I opened my eyes to look at him. There was a bloody handprint on his cheek. It wasn't the only mark I had left on him.

'It was you,' I said. 'It was you all along.'

We curled into each other, as we had so many times before. He kissed my lips, softly, sweetly, and sat up to reach for his clothes.

'Stay,' I said, winding my arms around him. 'Please.'

He put his hands over mine, and when he let go I felt empty. Hollow.

Théo got off the bed and stepped into his jeans. 'I can't. Not any more.'

I followed him to the door.

'Wait, Théo …'

He turned.

'What about your dreams?' I said. 'How will you sleep without me?'

His smile was mournful, and distant.

'They were your dreams, Inès,' he said. '*You* were the one who couldn't sleep. You look at life through a mirror – everything you see is the wrong way round.'

And then he left me and, coward that I was, I didn't stop him.

I should have gone after him. I should have seen how it would end.

# 30

The wail of sirens came early the next morning.

Police officers swarmed the dormitory, stringing yellow tape across doorways and sealing items into evidence bags. A few of the blondes flitted around in a panic; others were stunned into immobility. Aurélie stood in the middle of the corridor, staring at the wall as though she were in a trance. Déborah was sitting at the top of the stairs, a foil blanket around her shoulders. One of the officers handed her a drink in a paper cup.

'For the shock,' he told her.

Suitcases were propped against the walls outside some of the rooms. Françoise was yelling about her green sweater, demanding to know where it was and who had borrowed it. When no one answered, she kept on until Cécile slapped her cheek and told her she'd never had a green sweater.

'It was Diana, you stupid cow!' she said. 'Diana had the green sweater!'

And then they both began to cry.

In the midst of the chaos was Christophe. His face was ashen, and there was a noticeable tremor to the hand he held over his mouth. He nodded as one of the officers interrogated him, but uttered only a few words in response. I thought someone ought to offer him a drink in a paper cup too, 'for the shock', but no one did.

Élodie rushed past carrying her overnight bag. I snatched at her arm. She reeled and gawked at me incredulously.

'Where have you *been?*' she said. 'We've been looking for you for hours.'

I felt a throbbing pain at the base of my skull.

'What's going on?' I asked, knowing the answer but still hoping there would be another explanation for the mayhem. One that meant that the knife, and the blood, had been nothing more than props in a terrible dream.

Élodie didn't seem to notice the bag fall from her hand and drop to the floor. 'You don't know? Oh God, you don't know …'

She started weeping, and Nathalie came over and curled an arm around her. 'It's okay,' she said. 'It's okay. We'll be gone from here soon. Very soon.' Her gaze lifted and found mine. 'Diana's been killed.'

'Murdered!' Élodie bawled. 'She was *murdered.*'

She put her head on Nathalie's shoulder, her body racked with sobs. Nathalie held her and made cooing noises, but the solace she offered was perfunctory and stilted.

'Diana's dead,' Nathalie said in a robotic tone.

'She was killed on the stage,' Maëlle called from behind one of the doors. 'Don't forget that … She was killed *on the stage*!'

At that, there was a scream, but Nathalie did not pause to see from whom it had come. 'Hélène found her,' she continued. 'In the theatre. She was …'

She hesitated before describing, in somewhat technical detail, the wounds I had inflicted.

'Her head was almost severed,' she said. 'Her neck sliced nearly to the spinal cord.'

Élodie screeched and snatched at Nathalie's collar. Françoise shot out of her room, surveyed the scene, and slumped onto the floor.

'Hélène has been taken to hospital,' Cécile said. 'She's in a bad way. She refuses to speak.'

'It's awful,' Élodie said. 'It's all so *awful*. I hate this place.'

'Don't worry,' Nathalie said. 'We're leaving. It's over. It's all over.' She looked at me. 'The police have arrested someone, Inès. They've caught the killer. They've found the ghost.'

*No one will suspect you.*

'Who is it?' I asked, folding my arms so they wouldn't see my hands shaking.

'The piano boy,' Nathalie said. 'He confessed to the whole thing. The police took him away. The nightmare is over.'

I whirled in a circle, not knowing what to do. I took several paces forward, then more back, and then stopped still. Christophe caught my eye and held a finger aloft for me to wait. I ignored him and dashed into my room.

I sank onto the chair and stared at my hands. My treacherous, guilty hands. I had scrubbed them until the skin cracked, but they would always be stained with blood. I was a monster. *That* was who I was. Who I would always be.

Christophe appeared in the doorway. 'Inès?'

I did not answer, but he came inside anyway and dropped to his knees before me. 'Inès, Inès …' He threw his arms around my calves and laid his head on my lap.

'I need you,' he said. 'I need you so much …'

I put my hand on the top of his head and stroked his hair. The hair I had longed to touch.

Christophe glanced up at me. His face was wet, streaked with his grief. 'Don't leave me,' he said. 'Please, don't leave me. You're all I have now.'

He was here, the man I had dreamt of being with. He clung to me tightly, as if he were holding on to life itself. There was no distance between us now. He was as close as could be, but I felt no sense of victory, no relief, no joy, and no pleasure, just a dull, nagging ache. And the dread of what was yet to come.

# 31

The academy lost its lustre. The roof leaked, the stonework crumbled, the windows cracked. It was sad how rapidly the decline occurred, how the place descended into disrepair almost instantly, as though it no longer had the will to continue existing.

The staff who had once pledged their loyalty to Christophe now refused to work for him. The bank sent him demands; an avalanche of bills arrived every other day. The press turned on him. They criticised his methods and motivations; they questioned his talent and smeared his reputation. He'd been untouchable for so many years, but suddenly people were asking whether it had all been a con – if they had been duped into believing that Christophe Leriche was the best when, really, he was merely average. The public forgot how he had once enthralled them, and, overnight, their adoration became contempt and loathing.

On the morning that Théo's photograph first appeared on the news, Justine Deschamps telephoned. Hers was the only call Christophe could bring himself to take.

'It's her,' he said when he saw her name on the display. 'It's her!' He laughed deliriously, his relief undisguised –

he no longer maintained an air of mystery – and smiled into the phone as he answered.

It was excruciating to witness his excitement dissipate and his shoulders sag, and to hear his pitch plunge.

He paced the room, offering her assurances I knew he didn't mean, such as 'Yes, I see', 'Of course, that makes sense' and, most disingenuous of all, 'I understand'.

Christophe did not understand. He did not understand anything. He was a maelstrom of confusion, forever asking, 'Why, Inès, why? Why did this happen to me?' He spoke of himself as a victim – his role in the play of his life was now entirely passive.

I sat in the chair I had positioned by the window. I'd rearranged the furniture several times, only to find it had no impact on my mood. What I wanted to change was not the scenery but the characters.

The call ended and Christophe stared at the phone as though he expected Justine to emerge from it like a genie from a lamp.

When the silence became unbearable I asked, 'What did she want?'

Christophe raked his fingers through his hair, which was long and unkempt, and rapidly turning white. The bags under his eyes gave him the appearance of a man twice his age, and the wrinkles around his mouth made him look as if he were perpetually on the verge of tears. Which he nearly always was.

'She's pulling out, Inès,' he said, still gripping the

phone. 'She's taking it all.'

Justine Deschamps had withdrawn every penny of the money she had invested in the academy. By way of an apology, she sent him a bouquet of flowers, an echo of the condolences she had once offered for tragedies of a different kind. She said that while she understood that Christophe was not to blame for what had occurred, her name, and that of her family, could no longer be associated with the Leriche Academy and the terrible things that had transpired inside it. But in truth, what she could not be associated with was the stink of ruin that clung to Christophe. Failure is almost as tough a stain to remove as blood.

The blondes had long since left the academy. Before, disaster had anchored them to the place, but Diana's death was too much for them: as soon as her corpse was taken away, they started to leave. Only Aurélie, in her daze, had begged to stay, claiming that she could not bear to abandon her 'sisters'. However, her loyalty had evaporated when the others did not share her sentiment.

The whole city was in shock, but no one more so than me, although I did not scream and sob like the blondes did as they departed; nor did I echo their token promises to keep in touch – we all knew they never would. I stood at Christophe's side and watched them decamp to the waiting cars of their loved ones. If I said goodbye, it would be meaningless. I would never leave there. Never.

Aside from Aurélie and her histrionics – for which she would eventually be hospitalised, but unlike Hélène, her stay would not be indefinite – the blondes couldn't wait to escape the academy. Once, they had been the lucky few – the 'elite'. Now, they were the key players in a morbid drama, and they cried for their unrealised dreams and their broken hearts.

'Pathetic,' Diana's voice whispered in my ear. 'Utterly *pathetic*.'

Most pathetic of all was Christophe.

He knew he was defeated. Destroyed. His slide from celebrity to infamy haunted the academy with the spectres of the dead blondes, and like the ghost they had once feared, he dared not reinvoke it directly. Occasionally he would turn to me and say, 'It will be all right, won't it? I can start again ... I can build something from nothing. Can't I?' And then he would cling to me and bury his head in my hair.

'Tell me you believe in me, Inès,' he'd say. 'If you tell me I can do it, that I am capable, then I'll know it's true.'

On his better days I'd find him sitting at his desk, making plans. He'd dig out the script he'd written what felt like years ago and reread his notes.

'I know how we can improve it,' he said. 'How we can grab people's attention.'

It was always 'we', never 'I'. He had ceased to be a singular person. We were not two individuals but an extension of each other.

'I think you already have people's attention,' I said.

When I told him truths, when I was cruel, Christophe would break down and beg me to tell him I loved him. I could do that; they were just words, and it was simply a question of saying them in the right order, in the right way. They didn't mean what they had before, and what I had imagined they would. The illusions I'd so carefully curated had been shattered all at once.

Christophe had come to me the morning Diana's body was found and had never left. Everywhere I went, he followed. The more I tried to shake him off, the more he cleaved to me. Eventually, I told him my room was too small for both of us, and he agreed – he agreed with everything I said – and we moved into his. But even a room without walls would not have relieved my claustrophobia, and all the air in Paris would not have eased my suffocation. Christophe was totally dependent on me. And I, in turn, was totally indifferent to him.

I had once been consumed with my desire for him, but now he was obsessed with me: touching me, watching me, kissing me, loving me. It should have been wonderful, it should have been magical, but instead it was tedious. Christophe rolled onto me night after night and whispered, 'I love you. You are everything to me. Everything. I love you. Only you, only you …'

I had fantasised about being close to him, but now I couldn't bring myself to return his ardent affections.

My mind was always elsewhere. My heart was always elsewhere. Always – always – with Théo.

The reports about Théo were unavoidable: even a cursory glance at the news bore at least one mention of him. They described him as sadistic and depraved; they said he was an evil that had made Paris weep. What I was, Théo had become.

In order to keep up with events, Christophe had relented and bought a television. Previously, he'd maintained that television was the very incarnation of indolence, but things had changed: Théo was a murderer and television was now necessary. And so, where Christophe had once turned to books and art for knowledge, he became reliant on the oversized screen in the middle of the room for information.

He called out to me, 'Inès ... Inès, you must see this.'

I was taking a long bath. The door was ajar – I had learnt from my short time in confinement with Christophe that a locked door was more trouble than it was worth. I closed my eyes at the sound of his voice and hoped it would stop. I hoped it would all stop: the news, the arrest, the police investigation ... My fantasies now were of waking up and finding that things had gone back to the way they were before.

The bathroom door opened wider, and Christophe's head poked round it. 'Inès, hurry. They're talking about *him*.'

He found it hard to speak his name. Most days, so did I. Other days, it was the only word on my lips.

'Come *quickly*, Inès.'

He gestured for me to get out of the bath, eager for me not to miss it, though Christophe's television seemed to show little else. One could wake from a coma and believe that the only thing that had happened in the world was the murder of 'those poor girls' from a dilapidated theatre school in the centre of Paris.

I put on my robe and sat on the edge of the chair. Christophe's arm snaked around my waist, and we watched the latest report as if it were a play where the plot thickened with each performance.

And I knew who was stirring it.

The judge assigned to the case announced that new information had come to light, and Jacques Robineau was exonerated and freed. He stood on the steps of the Palais de Justice in the same grey suit and reminded the public of his earlier protestations of innocence, but there was scant interest in the miscarriage of justice, and sympathy was hard to come by. The public had moved on. All eyes were on Théo.

The press unearthed the details of Théo's past – his traumatic childhood, his turbulent adolescence. His secrets were so similar to mine, and it made my heart ache to think of how he would've hated everyone knowing them. 'Sources' informed journalists that Théo seemed uninterested in his fate, or, indeed, in the question of his guilt. Not that there appeared to be any doubt about that: the 'evidence' was startling.

The receptionists at the hotel claimed to have seen Théo strolling casually through the lobby shortly after Liliane was killed. There was footage of him descending the staircase; the timestamp coincided with the time of Liliane's death. A maid saw him sneaking out of the suite, and the forensic teams, deployed to rake over everything once more, found Théo's hairs on the carpet.

In exchange for immunity, Ruslan – which turned out to be his real name after all – testified that Théo had approached him and bought the same kind of pills that had killed Veronica. A waiter in the café told police he'd seen Théo and Veronica together. He said he'd served them hot chocolate, which Veronica had accepted only at Théo's insistence. He thought he'd seen Théo drop something into her glass but did not report it as it was 'so brazen' that he'd assumed he was mistaken.

The day after Théo was arrested, Roxane's distended body washed up on the banks of the Seine. Although her corpse had been ravaged by the water, they found traces of Théo on it that the police said were both definitive and 'miraculous'.

Olivier denied selling Théo the knife, but admitted he'd heard that Théo had purchased the weapon from an 'acquaintance' of his. The judge deemed that the provenance of the knife was not important: Théo's prints were all over it.

But even the most damning pieces of evidence were overshadowed by Théo's confession.

He gave detailed explanations of things he couldn't possibly have done and addresses of places he couldn't possibly have been. I waited for someone to point out that none of it was plausible, but there was no dissent. They accepted everything Théo said.

When asked for his motive, he answered without hesitation.

'Love,' Théo said. 'I did it for love.'

That was the headline the next day, printed above his extensive account of how the blondes had been killed.

'It's impossible … Why can't they see that it's impossible?'

I wasn't aware I'd said it aloud until I felt Christophe's arm coil tighter around me.

He pulled me into him – he liked to think he could comfort me; he liked to think he could still teach me something.

'I can't believe it either,' Christophe said. 'But he has admitted everything.'

That was all anyone cared about. I could not fathom how it was enough.

I thought constantly about turning myself in. I went to the police station half a dozen times but aborted each attempt to confess as my resolve waned, and I turned back without even going inside, my hands in my pockets, my head bowed.

There was a different path, a different way, but I could not find it by myself.

Another week passed. I couldn't take it any longer. I had to find out how it ended.

# 32

The streets were empty. The only sound was the river lapping against the bank. Notre-Dame was cloaked in a dense, soupy fog that was strange for the time of year, but the bizarre rhythms of the cathedral no longer surprised me.

The gates were wide open. When I stepped through them, they closed behind me with a slam louder than ever before, and there was something final about the snap of the lock.

In the souvenir shop, the man with the hooded eyes grinned at me from his spot behind the counter.

'Welcome home,' he said. 'Such a pleasure to have you join us.' He raised an arm and waved me through. 'You know the way up. And you know the way down.'

His laughter followed me as I began to climb the staircase. Inside the tower, it was pitch black, the steps barely visible, but now I could feel my way through the darkness. I knew every stone.

When I reached the top, the gargoyle was staring across the city, its horns extending and contracting like two stumpy aerials. I had the sudden urge to push it over the edge to see if it would take flight or if it would hit the ground and smash into hundreds of pieces.

'Try it,' the gargoyle said without glancing round. 'Try it and see. The question is not whether I can fly but whether *you* can. It's a long way down, Inès. A very long way down.'

It twisted slowly and appraised me with those eyeless voids that somehow saw everything.

'You held out for a long time before coming to me,' it said. 'I'm impressed.'

'I am not interested in impressing you.'

'You were once though, weren't you? And still you lie. But only to yourself. Only ever to yourself.'

'I wish I'd never spoken to you!' I said, boiling with fury at the gargoyle, and at my own folly.

'But you did. And I answered you, and now …' The gargoyle hopped from foot to foot, its glee grotesque. 'Now you have got yourself into a terrible bind.'

'This is what you enjoy,' I said. 'Destroying people.'

The wind changed, and the gargoyle's features scrunched into an angry glare. 'Your destruction is of your own foolish making.'

'Why?' I said. 'Why did you do all this?'

'I did nothing.' It jabbed a finger at me. '*You* did it. You did it all.'

'I would never have done it without you. You put ideas into my head.'

'Those ideas were already there. I am merely a mirror, reflecting your own image back at you. In the end, we all reveal who we are. We all show our true faces. And this'—it pointed to itself—'this, Inès, is yours.'

'I … I don't understand.' My fury turned to dread as the gargoyle stalked towards me.

'Yes, you do,' it said. 'You knew my face all along. You see it every time you look at yourself. And now …' It flashed a smile of pure malevolence. 'Well, think about it. Think about the *blondes*, think about Christophe. About Théo. Innocent, lovelorn Théo. Think about it all. What do you know that's true? How can you trust your own version of events? *You* are the one with the delusions.'

Daggers poked the ridges of my spine. 'But the evidence … That was you, too. You did it.'

'I did what you asked. You wanted my protection, and I gave it to you. I told you no one would suspect you.'

'But now they suspect Théo!'

'They more than suspect him.' The gargoyle chortled, its razor-sharp teeth glinting. 'What is it to you, anyway? You told me you didn't care for him. It is you who's confused, Inès. *You.*'

I whirled around, intending to bolt for the staircase, but the ground was moving, the stone rippling under my feet. The cityscape eddied and swirled, the rooftops flipped upside down, and I could not tell which way was out. I tried to move, but it was as though I were on a treadmill, my legs pumping madly on the same spot.

'Look at your hands,' the gargoyle said. 'Can't you see?'

I held out my palms. They were stained red – red that dripped from my arms and ran along my wrists. Red rained onto my face, staining the ground so far below. As I frantically wiped at my cheeks, the gargoyle cackled with laughter.

'You have to do something,' I said. 'You have to help Théo.'

'Why? You assured me it was Christophe you loved. You said you wanted him more than anything. But now you've seen *his* true face. How does it feel to finally get what you want?'

'Please,' I said. 'Make it stop. Please, help Théo. I know you can do anything.'

The gargoyle extended its wings. A chill radiated from its body that reminded me of a cold, dark place that smelled of earth: a place with a metal door and a dampness that turned my bones to ice.

'Tell me *why* I should help Théo,' it said. 'I want to hear you say it.'

'Because … because I love him.'

'Again,' the gargoyle said.

My hands became fists. 'I love him.'

The two red orbs glowed in the gargoyle's eye sockets.

'There,' it said. 'That wasn't so hard, was it? Think of all the heartache you would've saved yourself if you'd admitted it earlier. All the heartache you would've saved Théo.'

I stared at the thing standing opposite me – the

gargoyle, the creature. The monster.

'You won't help, will you?' I said.

It prodded its chin. 'I didn't say that.'

'I'll go to the police, tell them it was me. I'll confess everything.'

'Go ahead. It would be interesting.'

'Théo can't suffer for this,' I said. 'It's not fair.'

'Was it fair on those girls? The "blondes", as you called them, even though you are the blondest of them all.' The gargoyle reached out a spindly arm and combed a finger through the ends of my hair. 'Ah, like golden silk.'

It chuckled as I shrank away from it.

'Oh, Inès. Poor, confused Inès. *Someone* has to suffer for what you've done. I believe they call it justice.'

'There is no justice when the accused is innocent.'

'It never bothered you before. You never came here begging me to help Jacques Robineau.'

The stone became sticky, as if it had turned to tar. Colours and shapes flashed in front of my eyes.

'There must always be consequences, Inès,' the gargoyle said, its frigid breath on my face. 'You have your fate to endure – your miserable life with Christophe. That won't go well, by the way. You'll be his love, you'll be his obsession as he was once yours, but your heart will be elsewhere. Irreparably broken. Some might call *that* justice.'

I feared the answer, but had to ask. 'And Théo?'

The gargoyle's horns moved back and forth, as

though they were picking up some kind of signal. 'I'm afraid Théo will kill himself in prison. And he'll leave a note saying that everything he did was for love.'

A tear ran down my cheek. I tried to wipe it away but the gargoyle was too quick. It caught the teardrop on its fingertip and licked it clean, savouring the taste of my grief.

'Don't you have a heart?' I said.

'I am just a gargoyle. If I had a heart, it would be made of stone. As you once thought yours was. But now you've discovered otherwise. The heart knows its own bitterness, Inès. It *knows*. Will you weep for those girls? Will you weep for them as you weep for Théo? He would do anything for you. What would you do for him?'

The gargoyle dropped into a crouch, and in one deft motion, sprang up onto the parapet. It sat on the ledge, dangling its legs over the side and kicking its webbed feet, wriggling its long toes. The twinkling vista was now still and tranquil, and the gargoyle's head cocked as its gaze swept across the City of Light.

'It's a beautiful night, don't you think?' it said.

The Eiffel Tower glittered and the Sacré-Coeur glowed. Paris sparkled, promising so much, but not to everyone. Not to me.

I took it all in, everything the gargoyle saw, and drew the city deep into me.

'I would do anything for him,' I said. 'Anything.'

'I hoped you'd say that,' the gargoyle said. 'I hoped

you'd show courage. Because there is a way, Inès. There is a way you can save him. There is one more path. Your final one.'

The gargoyle patted the space beside it. 'Come. Come to me. I will show you.'

A bell chimed. Voices rang inside my head: a cacophony of blondes, laughing, singing, chanting, screaming. The nuns at the orphanage, telling me what I was, and what I would never be. Rosary beads clicked, the metal door slammed closed. The cold, the dark, and that voice, the one that had promised me everything. And now, I had the chance to claim what it offered.

I took the hand the gargoyle held out to me and suddenly there was silence. The sadness inside me dissolved, and my tears evaporated. I got up onto the ledge. My legs shook, but my head was calm, and clear. At last, I could see. I could see everything. I had a perfect view of Paris, of its stories, its characters, and how it truly appeared.

I let go of the gargoyle's hand. It nodded at me and I closed my eyes and lifted my arms.

*For your soul, Inès. For your soul.*

# 33

It is a long way down. A very long way down.

I hurtle towards the ground. They wait for me with their arms outstretched – the blondes, as I called them, although none are as blonde as me. Liliane, Veronica, Roxane and Diana.

I am the lead. I am the star. I am the one.

The air rushes against my face.

I fall.

The release, the impact that would send me into the peace of oblivion, will never come.

I am falling, falling …

I fall.

Always.

Forever.

I am eternal.

# 34

Christophe Leriche stood at the graveside, watching the rain splash onto the coffin. He never imagined he'd experience so much loss, let alone in such a short time span, and the frequent exposure to death had not inured him to it, or lessened its sting. Each passing had been more of an ordeal than the last, but the final one was by far the most painful. With the others, there'd been crowds – families and relatives gathered to pay tribute. For this one, there were no mourners, no condolences, no plaques and no wreaths. Even he could offer only a single red rose in her memory, which he hoped she would have appreciated, but he could never be certain about her tastes. In the end, he had decided that if she was displeased, she would let him know. How he hoped she would let him know.

He stared down at the coffin, thinking of her inside it, and cried until his head ached and his eyes felt raw.

His legs gave way, his knees sinking into the mud. He thought about jumping into the grave and begging to be buried with her – he would have, had he been sure they would be together again. But there were no certainties any more, only the pall of the unknowable.

Christophe craned his neck and looked up to the sky.

The thought came, as it often did, that there was something watching over him. It was possible. On occasion, he had felt it.

He called her name again. He wanted her to hear him but, more than that, he wanted her to answer. He *needed* her to answer. He needed her to come back to him. But, so far, she hadn't, and in his bleakest moments he thought that maybe she didn't want to. Or, perhaps, she couldn't. They'd told him that every one of her bones had been broken in the fall, her beautiful face smashed to a pulp, so maybe she had to heal first – maybe it would take time until she was able to return to him. He refused to think her silence was because once her heart had stopped she'd ceased to exist. Since she'd gone – and that was how he regarded it, as simply an absence – he'd begun to turn his mind to other ideas and notions, beliefs he'd previously scoffed at. He read about angels and saints and cosmic energy, and wilfully surrendered to esoteric theories, no matter how far-fetched. He would rather put his faith in something ridiculous than allow himself to consider that it was the notion of the abyss, the expanse of *nothing*, that was the most plausible explanation.

He sought her out in the books she had kept in her room, scouring the pages for notes etched in the margins to give him clues, but there were none, only the faint smell of cigarettes. He recited the lines he'd written for her, trying to imitate her voice and cadence. Once, he'd even put on one of her dresses, and had wept at the sound of the seams ripping as he tugged it down his body. He knew he'd lost his mind when he considered slicing off parts of himself in order to make her clothes fit him, and that realisation calmed him. If he was insane it would make the sorrow easier to reconcile: being mad meant there was a place for him. It might set him free.

However, the doctors with whom he consulted diagnosed only bereavement and severe depression, and he knew it was more than that. The books and the clothes were not enough. He had to get closer to her. There had to be a way.

He thought again about the coffin. He imagined himself opening it and climbing inside. But still he had the vague sense that she would not be there. If he wanted to find her, below ground was not where he should search.

The days and nights passed slowly, devoid of meaning. He spent hours in front of the television in an attempt to numb his brain, and sometimes he'd see one of his former students in an advert, or a drama show. He'd put his face close to the screen and stare into their eyes to see if there were any remnants of him there, but he knew in his heart there were none. He had been a means to an end for them. They had consigned him to history – an onerous history – and his legacy was the terror that reached for them in the dark, the screams that wrenched them from slumber.

Teaching had once been his purpose, and now he gave himself a new one – a task that came to dominate his existence.

He searched for her. He searched for her everywhere.

After a few more weeks of scalding grief, the answer came to him.

No one recognised him now as he roamed the streets. The depths to which he had sunk and the catastrophes that had struck him had interested people for a while, but not any more. Christophe blamed his obscurity on the insipid suburban neighbourhood to which his financial circumstances had forced him to move, but he could never persuade himself for long. He understood how unforgiving the world was, but that did not make his fall from grace easier to bear, and failed to blunt his yearning for mercy and compassion.

Christophe took two trains to reach the centre of the city and walked the rest of the way. He thought about taking the circuitous route so as to avoid passing what had once been his academy, but a sadistic curiosity led him right to it.

Scaffolding cocooned the building. Christophe had heard that the new owners were refurbishing the entire place in order to reopen it as a hotel, though in his mind it was not a renovation they were undertaking but an exorcism. When the doors opened again, they wanted no vestige of disaster or misfortune left inside.

He lingered outside, gazing up at what was once her window. He was grateful that hers had been the largest and the grandest room, and that she had always been his favourite student. The perks he had given her were a comfort to him now.

If he'd believed she was in there, it would've upset him to see the place being dismantled, but she was not inside what had become known as 'the old academy on Hell Street'. She was elsewhere. Close.

He walked down Rue Massillon with his hands wedged in his pockets and wondered why it had taken him so long to think of it. She had loved Notre-Dame. If she was to be found anywhere at all, it had to be there.

He slipped inside the cathedral, the scent of incense stirring so many memories, but his heart sank as he felt the trail go cold. He sat down in one of the pews, despondent and desolate, and looked up.

Up.

Christophe got to his feet and sprinted for the exit. The sunlight dazed him as he rushed through the doors, and he lost his bearings. His mind emptied, and he had no idea how to get up there. He had to ask one of the attendants.

The woman, so frail, so old, gave him a toothless smile and showed him the way.

There was no queue. He went to the counter to buy a ticket, but the man behind it, who had hooded eyes that were so dark they were almost black, told him there was no charge.

'Not today,' he said. 'Not for you. You'll like it up there. The conditions are perfect.'

The man grinned and pointed to the staircase leading up to the towers. There were more steps than Christophe had envisaged, and he was tired when he reached the top, for he no longer danced and was not as fit as he'd once been. But it was worth the exertion. As soon as he emerged into the light, he could feel her presence.

Christophe looked out over Paris, trying to see what she'd seen, picking out things he thought might have caught her attention. Tears came to his eyes, and as they fell, he was filled with a sense of peace. Those tears would be his last, he was sure. Up there, he could be with her. Forever.

He stepped closer to the parapet and became aware of someone, some*thing*, beside him.

'Where are you?' he whispered. 'I need you ... Where *are* you?'

And then he heard a voice.

'Right here.'

The voice was familiar, and Christophe was perplexed. He glanced around, expecting to see her. But next to him was one of the gargoyles.

The gargoyle had moved from its usual pose, one that, up until then, Christophe had only ever seen on postcards and in books. It had spindly legs – *Is it supposed to have legs?* – and webbed feet. Its horns appeared to twitch as it lifted its chin from its palm and smiled at him.

'Magnificent view, isn't it?' the gargoyle said.

Christophe knew he ought to be shocked – scared,

even – but found he was not. It could simply have been that he was too exhausted to feel anything else, or that his mind had completely gone, but it felt natural to open his mouth and answer the gargoyle's question.

'Yes,' he said. 'The view is perfect.'

The gargoyle's eye sockets seemed to glow. 'You can see everything from up here. I see you, for instance.'

'Me?'

The gargoyle nodded. Its gestures were familiar too, as though the two of them had met before.

'I see your anguish,' it said. 'I see your pain. Your shame, your guilt. Your despair at how much you've lost. Which is the worst of those burdens?'

The stark honesty of the question stunned Christophe. No one was candid with him any more. No one cared about his sorrow, his pain. No one *saw* him. But the gargoyle did. Somehow, he knew it did.

'I don't know,' he replied. 'I cannot separate one from another.'

'I understand,' the gargoyle said.

Christophe wondered how that inanimate thing, that stone sculpture, could possibly understand anything, let alone the trauma he'd been through. And yet, he was certain it understood better than anyone, and the gargoyle's empathy, as bizarre and impossible as it was, flooded him with relief.

'I can make it better for you,' the gargoyle said. 'I can make your sadness disappear.'

'How?'

'There are many paths to choose. I could show you the right one.'

Christophe tried desperately to place that voice, his head beginning to pound. 'Who are you?'

The gargoyle smiled at him.

*I* smiled at him.

'I am no one,' I said. 'I am just a gargoyle. Just a gargoyle.'

Christophe stared into my sightless eyes that see everything. He wanted to believe so badly. He wanted to believe in the gargoyle.

He wanted to believe in *me*.

I laid my stone hand on his arm and felt the life in him, the warm blood flowing through his veins. He looked at me in wonder, and I thought of how I had once loved him, and how that love had set me on this path.

And, now, his love for me would do the same for him.

Dark clouds rolled across the sky. I flapped my wings, knowing now that I *could* fly. That I could do anything.

'Shall I tell you how it ends?' I said.

'Yes,' he said, and nodded eagerly.

They always did.

Printed in Great Britain
by Amazon